A Cowboy for

Meggan

A Cowboy for Meggan

Willow Wood Brides: Book 6

by

Teresa Slack

Copyright © 2021 by Teresa Slack

Published by: Grace Arbor Press
ISBN: 9781732786264

Other Titles

Willow Wood Brides

A Promise for Josie: A Willow Wood Prequel
A Lawman for Lisette: Book 1
A Love Letter for Jessa: Book 2
A Dream for Harper: Book 3
A Wedding for Felicity: Book 4
A Hero for Ellie: Book 5
A Cowboy for Meggan: Book 6

Nine Brides for Cowboy Creek

Rennie
Eliza
Carrie
Bridget
Katie
Marianne
Scarlett
Rachael
Amelia
Candace

Jenna's Creek Serie:

Streams of Mercy
Redemption's Song
Evidence of Grace
A Jenna's Creek Wedding-
(A Christmas Novella)

Legacy of Faith

Tender Blessings Series

Love Begins
A Little Goodbye

Sterling Family Tree

Cheater, Cheater
The Money Tree
Carla Comes Around

The Ultimate Guide to Darcy Carter
Runaway Heart
Joy Redefined

What Readers are Saying about the Willow Wood Brides Series

"**From stagecoaches and sheriffs to outlaws and saloons,** your cowboy loving heart will be satisfied. Add a new lady doctor in town (when lady docs weren't exactly the norm --that's an understatement) and a romance, and you've got a great cozy read to hunker down with." –Linore Rose Burkard, award winning romance author, *Forever Lately*

"**Teresa Slack hits one out of the ballpark again.**" Reader review

"**Mystery. Romance. Intrigue. Suspense...** All this and more are wrapped in a cloak of Christian fiction..." Leone Bihl, *Daily Reporter, Greenfield Times*

"**What's not to love about a whip smart heroine** who knows her way around a horse whip and a Derringer, and frequently saves the frustrated hero, a federal marshal?" Connie Kuykendall, *Award Winning Author of Love Ain't No Soap Opera*

"**Teresa Slack is a one click author for me!!**" –Reader review

"**Great romance & suspense read.** ...will keep you turning the pages and won't let you put the book down. Highly recommended." –Reader review

"Another wonderful read… These kinds of stories keep you intrigued, wondering how the love story is going to pan out." –Reader review

"Rating this book a 5! …Teresa's work never fails to keep me on my toes from beginning to end. I would love to read the next book in the series, or even one of the author's previous series. I am never disappointed with any of her work." –Reader review

"Love this new book! I love the descriptive writing and the fact that it is so different from her other books! I hope she will have more installments of this one." –Reader review

Dedication

In memory of my dear sister in Christ,
Elsie Rankin who loved enough to tell the cold hard
truth, whether we wanted to hear it or not.

Chapter One

July, 1897

“**W**here’d you say you were from, young man?”

Shane Casey tore his gaze away from the young woman sitting across from him on the stagecoach. He’d been trying not to stare since the moment he saw her before they boarded the stage in Smithfield. It wasn’t easy. Her hair was as black and shiny as a raven’s wing and looked as soft. She was tall and slim as a willow branch, only a couple inches less than Shane’s nearly six feet of height. She had smooth porcelain skin and lush red lips that kept drawing his gaze. But what really grabbed his attention were those mesmerizing emerald green eyes. He figured they were even prettier when she smiled. From the firm set of her jaw and proud tilt of her head, he doubted he'd ever know for sure.

Her traveling companion was another matter altogether. The old lady had introduced herself as Gloria Hennessey before they climbed aboard the stage. She was short and round with thinning gray hair combed into a tidy bun. Laughing, faded blue eyes shone out from a face amass with wrinkles. Probably because she smiled so much and never stopped talking.

Back at the station, as Shane took her hand to help her into the stage, she had introduced the younger woman as her granddaughter Meggan Jones. Meggan rewarded him with a ghost of a distracted smile that didn't come close to reaching those green eyes as she rejected his offer of assistance.

Shane had briefly hoped the old lady would doze off once the stage got moving and he could pass the trip home to Willow Wood getting to know Miss Jones. It didn't take two minutes to realize that wasn't going to happen. Mrs. Hennessey showed no signs of drowsiness, and Meggan showed even less interest in getting to know him.

He hoped Mrs. Hennessey hadn't noticed him staring at her granddaughter. Not likely since she hadn't paid Meggan any more mind than Meggan paid Shane.

"I'm from Willow Wood, ma'am," Shane told her.

"Has it been long since you've been home?"

Shane felt like he'd been on the road for a month of Sundays. His boots and britches were caked with dust. His face bore the signs of travel, too, he was sure. He hadn't shaved since he left St. Louis, and his dark hair was mashed flat against his head under his Stetson. As soon as he got home, after hugging his ma and tasting some of her fine cooking, his first order of business was a hot bath and a warm shave.

He wouldn't mind coaxing a smile out of the brunette across from him first.

"Yes, ma'am. Besides a few visits home to see my ma, I've been gone for four years."

"Four years? My, my. What kept you away so long?"

Out of the corner of his eye, Shane saw the brunette stiffen in her seat. She pursed her lips and glanced at her grandmother.

Shane waited half a breath to see if she was about to say something. She hadn't uttered as much as a peep, and he was curious to know what her voice sounded like—or if she even had one. When it became apparent she wasn't going to say anything now either, he turned his attention back to her grandmother.

"I left Willow Wood to study animal husbandry. After I finished school, I worked with a few animal doctors for the experience. The last one was in a little town in Missouri. Too far for coming home for visits."

"Missouri. Did you hear that, Meggan? My, my, that's where we're from. Kansas City."

Shane heard an intake of air as Meggan's green eyes widened. Her jaw clenched tight. Shane was sure she'd speak this time since something had obviously gotten under her skin. But after a visible effort to bring her emotions under control, she turned toward the window, dismissing them both.

Mrs. Hennessey didn't seem to notice Meggan's irritation. "Are you home for good?" she asked Shane without a glance in her granddaughter's direction.

A bubble of enthusiasm spiked in Shane's gut, despite Meggan's lack of interest. He'd worked a long time to see his plans come to fruition, he couldn't believe they were finally within reach.

"Yes, ma'am. I'm going to raise me a strong line of working horses and open my own veterinary clinic."

"My, my, that's quite ambitious for a young man. I expect your parents are very proud of you. And anxious to have you home too."

"Yes, ma'am. It's just my ma, though. Pa passed away when I was little.

Mrs. Hennessey reached across the expanse of seats and patted his hand. "Well, I wish you all the success in your new venture. You sound like a very industrious young man. Doesn't he, Meggan?"

Shane didn't bother looking to see if Meggan had an opinion, one way or the other, since he already knew she wouldn't. He suspected Mrs. Hennessey knew, too, and only included her granddaughter in the conversation out of habit, not because she expected a response.

"I hope so, ma'am," he said.

The old woman tilted her head and gave him a playful smile. "Is there a young woman waiting for you in Willow Wood, Mr. Casey?"

Meggan stiffened, though she didn't look away from the window. Was she curious, too, or simply annoyed her grandmother would ask a question only an old lady could get away with asking?

Heat rose under Shane's skin. "Uh, no, ma'am. My work…keeps me pretty busy."

"I suppose it would. Well, you just never know. Love generally comes when we're not looking for it. Isn't that right, Meggan?"

Mrs. Hennessey finally succeeded in eliciting a reaction from her granddaughter. Meggan gave her a withering look, which the old woman chose to ignore.

"Where are you ladies headed?" Shane asked to steer the conversation in any other direction.

"Seattle. Have you ever been?"

"Granny!" Meggan hissed between clenched white teeth. Her eyes went round in warning. Mrs. Hennessey stared expectantly at Shane—unaware of, or in spite of—Meggan's agitation.

Shane looked back and forth between the women, wondering what he'd missed. Though he'd been too busy the past year or two to pursue a romantic engagement, he would've liked seeing Meggan Jones again and possibly making a better impression on her. That wouldn't happen with her in Seattle.

"No, ma'am, I've never been," he answered Mrs. Hennessey.

"Neither have we. I'm looking forward to it. I love traveling; seeing as much of this magnificent nation as time allows. So does Meggan."

Meggan stared at her grandmother's profile, her full lips pressed together in a hard line. After a few moments of waiting for a reaction that never came, she exhaled and turned back to the window.

Why did she care if Shane knew where they were going? He hadn't kept his own plans a secret. Maybe she feared he was a highwayman bent on following them into the wilderness to rob them—or worse. Or she was tired of her grandmother telling their business to everyone they met on the road.

Whatever the reason, Meggan's ire was lost on the old lady. Mrs. Hennessey smiled at Shane and opened the bulging, well-worn scrapbook on her lap she had shown him nearly the instant the stage got rolling.

When she first removed the scrapbook from her satchel, Shane had groaned inwardly and prepared for a deluge of pictures of children, grandchildren, and newspaper clippings of their accomplishments and deeds. Instead, she had turned the scrapbook around to show him a Wanted poster and gleefully recounted how the man in the rendering had murdered two guards during the robbery of a federal payroll in the Texas Hill Country.

Shane listened with morbid curiosity to more stories of criminals and their villainous acts as she flipped through the pages. It seemed an odd hobby for an old lady who looked more suited to rocking babies than collecting Wanted posters. He had to hand it to her; she sure knew how to spin a good yarn. He imagined she could make a fair living writing dime novels should she take a notion.

She looked up to make sure she still had his attention.

"Here's a good one. This is Harold Watkins. You'd think he was a bank clerk or watchmaker from the looks of him. I suppose that's why he was so good at what he did. Harold lived with his mother in a small apartment in Lawrence, Kansas. Everyone in the neighborhood thought he was a mild-mannered man who sacrificed his future to care for his dear mother."

Mrs. Hennessey's eyes brightened with every word of the story. "Not our Harold. He was a confidence man of the highest caliber. Because of his mild demeanor and ability to lower the defenses of everyone he met, he was able to talk trusting old ladies out of every dime they had. Took advantage of so many. He was so charming and agreeable that even after his crimes were exposed, many of his victims refused to believe he meant them any harm and defended him in court. Isn't that right, Meggan?"

The old woman snickered without giving Meggan a chance to answer. "He's not cheating old ladies anymore, no sirree. Justice finally caught up with him. My, my, thieves and swindlers don't know when to quit. They get away with something once, or even a hundred times, and they think they'll keep getting away with it." She shook her head as she stared at the picture of Harold's bespectacled face.

She was right; he did look like a bank clerk.

"Arrogance. It's the downfall of many an otherwise shrewd individual."

Meggan muttered something under her breath Shane couldn't hear over the creaking of the stage. If he hadn't seen her lips move, he wouldn't have known she had spoken at all.

Mrs. Hennessey turned a few more pages. "Ooh, you'll like this one." Her pale blue eyes shone with excitement.

"This here is Earl McCaffrey. My, my, he was an evil man if ever there was one. He was a lawman, don't you know, who murdered the girl he was courting along with her mother. Earl had a bad reputation—much deserved, by the way—and the girl's parents forbade her from seeing him. Rumor had it that Earl had already gotten away with murdering three people in cold blood.

"He once shot a boy in the back who he said was stealing a pig. For goodness sakes, the boy had already dropped the pig and took off toward home. Earl fired anyway, killing the poor thing right in his tracks. Even the man who owned the pig said the boy's family was hard up, and he wished he had done something sooner to help them before it came to such a desperate act."

Mrs. Hennessey shook her head and managed to look disapproving, but her eyes gleamed in the dusty interior of the coach.

"The girl's parents caught her sneaking out with Earl a time or two. Her pa threatened to kill Earl if he ever came back. Nobody knows if the girl came to her senses or if she was completely bewitched by Earl's charms, but one day he went out to the house when it was just the girl and her mother there. Maybe he tried to get the girl to run off with him. Maybe he argued with her ma."

She shrugged as if it hadn't really mattered, then or now. "Either way, he killed them both. Her pa came home and found them laid out right there in the dooryard, slaughtered like hogs. Earl went on the run for nearly a year. Justice finally caught up with him on a little farm in Missouri near a place called Wilcox. Got his neck stretched, he did. Not by the authorities. The good folks of Wilcox heard about what he'd done and took care of him themselves one day ahead of the law."

She smirked. "You reap what you sow, the Good Book says."

Shane sat back against the wall of the coach. He wasn't sure if he was more distressed by the grisly story or the cavalier way in which the genteel old lady told it.

She sighed and smoothed her hand over the ruthless murderer's face. "If I was a little younger, why I'd think mighty serious about hunting down these animals myself and hauling them in for the reward," she said, pronouncing it re-ward.

She closed the book on her lap and regarded Shane with wide eyes. "Wouldn't that be a hoot? Why they'd never see me coming."

Shane nearly laughed out loud until he realized she was serious.

"Granny, for goodness sake!" Meggan exclaimed. "Why must you say things like that?"

Shane's eyes widened, more surprised by the sound of Meggan's voice—as lovely as he had imagined—than by Mrs. Hennessey's admission.

Indignation stiffened the old lady's spine. "Why not? Sounds a lot more interesting than sitting around embroidering samplers. Don't you think so?" she directed at Shane.

Shane figured just about anything was more interesting than embroidering samplers, especially since he wasn't sure what they were. But he didn't think hunting down outlaws like Earl McCaffrey was a practical occupation for a woman of any age.

Both women stared at him, waiting. He'd been trying to get Meggan's attention for the last two hours. Now that he had it, he wasn't sure what to do with it.

"Well, I…uh…I'm afraid you won't find many bandits hiding from the law in Willow Wood. The biggest crimes you usually hear about are young boys snitching apples off of trees."

Mrs. Hennessey looked disappointed. Meggan turned back to the window.

"Are you staying in town for the evening?" Shane asked, though he already knew the answer. Willow Wood was the end of the line for the stage, and the trains had already pulled out for the day. The ladies wouldn't be continuing to Seattle tonight.

Mrs. Hennessey brightened. "We're staying at the Grand Hotel."

Shane's spirit lifted. Tomorrow morning, he was meeting Lester Cheney at the hotel to inquire about his first acquisition of horses. Maybe he'd arrive a little early and see Meggan—and her grandmother—in the dining room.

Outside the window, he recognized the familiar rise and swell of the landscape. Home. Anticipation stirred in his belly. Though he didn't regret a day of the last four years studying or working with some of the top equine doctors west of the Mississippi, it sure felt good to be back in Willow Wood.

The coach slowed and the driver called out to a man on the ground. Before the dust settled, Shane threw open the door, unfolded his long legs, and climbed out.

He turned quickly before the driver could take the privilege from him and offered his hand to Mrs. Hennessey. "Ladies, may I be the first to welcome you to Willow Wood, Idaho."

The old woman smiled warmly at his gallantry. "Thank you, Mr. Casey. You have made our journey a most pleasant one. Hasn't he, Meggan?"

As soon as the older woman's feet touched the ground, Shane reached back into the coach to help

Meggan. Gazing down at him with those penetrating green eyes, she hesitated a moment before taking it.

She looked like she was about to say something. Something more than thanks. More than an apology for her grandmother's odd conversation.

After she stepped down, she clung to his hand a heartbeat longer than necessary before slipping free. Shane felt like the wind had been knocked out of him. Was it his imagination or wishful thinking? He'd give anything to know what was behind that guarded expression.

"Oh, Meggan, what a lovely town," Mrs. Hennessey crooned, breaking the spell. She groaned in a refreshingly unladylike manner. "Oh my, my tired bones are so happy to be out of that coach. I believe we might rest here a few days."

"Granny," Meggan said, her voice once more fraught with warning.

Or exasperation. Shane couldn't tell which.

He turned to the older woman. "The Grand Hotel is just across the way, ma'am. Do you need an escort? I'd be happy to help you with your bags."

She giggled. Her eyes flitted past him to Meggan, assuming—correctly, he had to admit—the reason behind his eagerness to assist them. "The driver will help with our bags and send someone for our trunk, I'm sure. But thank you for pointing the way, Mr. Casey. As long as the hotel has a dining room, we'll have dinner there tonight. Should you have no other plans, feel free to join us."

Meggan's jaw tightened. Shane considered accepting just to see that light flash in her green eyes.

"I'm afraid I can't, ma'am," he said instead. "My ma is expecting me."

"Yes, of course. I do hope we run into you again, Mr. Casey."

"You just might," Shane said with a glance at Meggan. He tipped his hat and watched them head across the street in a swish of skirts and chattering banter from Mrs. Hennessey to the driver, now turned porter.

Shane picked up his bag from the ground and turned in the direction of the Trego house on the high hill that overlooked Willow Wood. The older sister, Belinda had written in her last letter that he wouldn't need to rent a horse when he got to town. The sisters would supply as many as he needed until he could secure his own and properly begin his practice.

Over his shoulder, he watched the short, rounded figure of Mrs. Hennessey and the tall, willowy Meggan step off the street and into the shade of the hotel awning. Before the driver could set down the bags to open the door, a cowboy jumped forward to do it for him. The cowboy smiled broadly and tipped his hat at Mrs. Hennessey before directing his full attention to Meggan. Across the distance, Mrs. Hennessey's singsong voice called out her thanks and appreciation for all the helpful cowboys in Willow Wood. Meggan glided through the door without sparing the man a glance.

Shane continued on, pleased the cowboy holding the door had made no greater impression on the beautiful, enigmatic Meggan Jones than he had.

Chapter Two

Meggan removed the last pin from her hat and set it on the bureau. She walked through the doorway of the adjoining room and looked at Gloria Hennessey, the woman everyone believed was her grandmother.

Sometimes, even she believed it.

"Must you tell everything about us to every stranger you meet?"

Why did she bother to ask? She already knew the answer.

Gloria looked at her through the reflection of the dressing table mirror. "Whatever do you mean, dear?"

"The cowboy on the stage. You didn't know anything about him. He could've been an undercover agent. Or a thief. You told him our real names, where we're from, and where we're going. You even told him where we're having dinner."

Gloria spun around on the stool in front of the mirror to face her. "Wasn't he the handsomest thing? And such an interesting young man. Has his whole future mapped out. I admire a man who can make a plan and see it through. Not like the worthless bag of bones that turned my young, foolish head. Did I ever tell you about him? Martin Coss, the laziest excuse of a man on God's green earth. Now, that Shane Casey, he'll amount to something, you mark my words. I bet every young woman in this town is excited to have him back." She arched her thinning eyebrows at Meggan.

Meggan stalked across the room to the bureau and began straightening the toiletries Gloria had dumped out of her carpetbag. She didn't want the older woman to see how the comment had stung. She wished Gloria didn't insist on pointing out every handsome, eligible man they met only to remind her another woman would wind up with him.

Meggan focused on what she was doing and not Shane Casey. Yes, he was handsome with his thick dark hair and deep brown eyes. And interesting too. She would've loved to have gotten to know him better. She never got a chance to talk to anyone her own age about anything of substance. Especially a man. But there was no point in getting to know Shane or bemoaning the way things were. After Gloria rested for a day or two, they would continue to Seattle where she'd meet a whole new group of people she'd never see again after Gloria decided it was time to move on.

Shane's intelligence and enthusiasm were evident in the way he talked about raising horses and building an animal husbandry practice. But as usual, Gloria spent the whole time talking about herself and her blasted fascination with killers and thieves. She refused to see how every word out of her mouth could bring justice down on their heads.

Meggan was sick of it all. Sick of Gloria's games, the lies, the Wanted posters, the feigned interest in others to serve her own end.

Meggan glanced at the trunk the bellman had put at the foot of Gloria's bed. All their earthly possessions— their entire life and being—shoved into one battered trunk.

She wasn't a materialistic person, but it didn't seem right. A person should have more to call their own than what could fit into a trunk. She longed to sit in a chair that hadn't hosted a thousand backsides before her. Sleep in a bed molded to her body and not someone else's. She was tired of living like a guest everywhere she went. She wanted to belong. To see a caring face when she looked across the table. Hear an old friend call her name. Most of all, she wanted to stop looking over her shoulder, afraid an enemy from her past had caught up with her.

Her irritation at the situation bubbled over.

"I just don't understand why you need to tell everyone your life story the moment you meet them. You know how dangerous it is. I don't see why you can't be quiet and listen to their stories for once. It's common courtesy. Not to mention, you learn a lot more by listening than talking. Isn't that what you always say? And you wouldn't attract so much attention."

Gloria cocked her head and grinned. "I don't think I'm the one who attracts attention, dearest."

Meggan exhaled in frustration. What was the point in talking to Gloria about anything? She would always do everything exactly the way she wanted, and Meggan couldn't do a thing about it. It had been that way since the day she moved in with the Hennessey sisters when she was ten. After Grandma Elsie died, she didn't have anywhere else to go. Alice and Gloria lived across the hall and had helped take care of Grandma as her health deteriorated. If they hadn't taken her in, she would've been sent to an orphanage.

Sometimes, she wondered if an orphanage would've been better.

There, she may have been adopted. She could've had a normal life. Brothers and sisters. Friends. School. Handsome suitors and dances. Parents to hold her when she cried and teach her more than how to spot an easy mark in a crowd.

"You talk too much," she insisted. "You shouldn't have told Mr. Casey we were from Kansas City. You heard him say he spent time in Missouri. What if he read the papers? What if he knows about the robbery? It's a wonder you didn't tell him what's hidden in your trunk."

Gloria's jaw tightened. Meggan had finally struck a nerve.

"Don't be ridiculous. He was an interesting young man. All I was doing was making conversation to pass the time. You should try it sometime. Our lives would be a lot easier if you tried charming men with the gifts the good Lord gave you instead of acting so stuck up all the time. But no, you leave all the real work to me."

"I have no intention of batting my eyelashes and acting like a simpleton to distract some poor lout while you count the money in his money belt."

Gloria rolled her eyes. She shook the wrinkles out of a pale blue frock and laid it across the bed to change into for dinner. "You've made that abundantly clear. It's a waste if you ask me. I won't be here forever, you know. I don't know how you think you'll make a living without me. You certainly don't know how to talk to people. You have no personality. All you've got is your face and that body. If you don't learn how to use them, you'll starve to death inside of a week."

Meggan turned away. She did have a personality. She had plenty to offer a man besides her appearance. But if the woman who raised her couldn't see it, it wasn't likely anyone else would either.

As usual, Gloria didn't realize she had hurt Meggan's feelings. "It doesn't do any good to take yourself so seriously all the time," she went on. "You should have a little fun when the opportunity presents itself. Like with that Shane Casey fellow. If I was twenty years younger— all right, thirty—you can bet he'd know I was interested."

Meggan pursed her lips, determined not to rise to Gloria's bait. She had been interested in the cowboy, but what good would it do her? Gloria would have her on the train headed to Seattle in a few days, and who knew where to after that. She wanted more than a passing conversation with a man she met in a stagecoach.

She wanted a life.

She pinned an opal brooch to her lapel while she waited for Gloria to change. The brooch was her favorite. She loved how it brought out the light in her green eyes.

Alice had given it to her for her sixteenth birthday. Meggan convinced herself Alice bought the brooch, though more than likely, she had lifted it from the jewelry store after she saw Meggan admiring it. Meggan wouldn't dwell on how the brooch came to be on her lapel. If she did, she wouldn't enjoy any gift the two women had given her over the years.

Downstairs in the hotel restaurant, she surreptitiously watched the other diners. Willow Wood seemed to have its share of wealthy merchants, businessmen, farmers, ranchers, and everyday citizens. Gloria was watching, too—probably deciding who presented the easiest mark with the biggest payday, even though they wouldn't be in town long enough to make use of the knowledge.

"This is a nice restaurant," Meggan said, hoping to distract her. "I'm surprised it's so well appointed for such a small town."

"Not so small." Gloria leaned over the table and kept her voice down. "I noticed some nice homes on our way here. You heard Shane talking about those women who gave him a scholarship. They must be swimming in money. I doubt they're the only ones. There's wealth in this frontier town."

Meggan groaned inwardly. Naturally, Gloria would notice nice houses and successful women and men in well-cut suits—anything that offered an opportunity to enrich herself.

She ignored Gloria's observations. "I noticed a lovely brick church at the bottom of the hill opposite the stage stop. It reminds me of the one I used to attend in Lawrence with Grandma Elsie."

Gloria's lip curled in distaste. "What made you think of Kansas?" She didn't like it when Meggan talked about Grandma Elsie or mentioned the past.

"You did," Meggan reminded her. "You were the one flashing around Harold Watkins' poster on the stage, your very first conquest."

Gloria stabbed a piece of roast beef. Her fork scraped noisily against the plate. "Harold Watkins is a ghost of the past. We needn't speak of him ever again."

"I wasn't speaking of him. You were."

Meggan kept her voice intentionally calm. After two weeks of listening to the older woman's braggadocio stories to everyone they met, she enjoyed annoying her. "All the talk of Kansas reminded me of Grandma Elsie. She would love it here. It's so quiet and peaceful. The type of place where a person can settle down."

"What are you talking about, Meggan?"

"I'm talking about Willow Wood. Going to a real church and making friends. Swapping recipes and talking about husbands and children and flowers and sewing circles. You just said I should learn to interact with a man. To catch a husband."

Gloria nearly choked on her tea. "I never said anything about a husband."

"Well, maybe I want one. I'm twenty-one, Granny. Maybe I don't want to go to Seattle."

Gloria's eyes darkened, reminding Meggan for a moment of Alice. Dread wrapped around her stomach like a tight fist. She wouldn't give in to the memories. She wasn't a child anymore. Alice couldn't hurt her. Neither could Gloria. Not physically anyway.

"You don't have a choice, no matter how old you are," Gloria said, her voice low and menacing. Meggan never stood up to her, never openly defied her, and she didn't like it.

"As soon as I rest a few days, we're going to Seattle to meet our contacts. We didn't come all this way to throw away our hard work in some little drink-water town with nothing to offer."

"Maybe it doesn't have anything to offer you, but I like it. I could get a job," she said hopefully. "I could work as a clerk at the factory Shane told us about. Or a…a seamstress at one of the shops."

Gloria laughed. "Oh, darling, you can barely thread a needle."

She dabbed her mouth with her napkin and slipped back into the matronly persona Meggan knew so well. "Once we conclude our business in Seattle, we'll have enough money to go wherever you want. What do you think about San Francisco? I can introduce you to high society men who can give you the life you deserve."

An image of the dusty cowboy on the stage flitted across Meggan's mind. She didn't want to be kept by a man of high society. She wanted a husband who loved her, one to work with side by side as they built a life together. But she was encouraged Gloria was actually talking about settling down, even if it was in San Francisco.

Meggan had noticed the gray pallor around Gloria's mouth and eyes the last few months. Her age was showing. Since Alice died, she promised each job would be the last. Maybe this time it was true. Maybe she finally realized she was too old for subterfuge and staying up all night and tracking felons across the Midwest.

"Are you feeling all right? You look tired."

Gloria sighed and pushed away the plate she had barely touched. Meggan's concern flared anew. Gloria always had a healthy appetite.

"I am tired," the older woman admitted. "All this travel. A necessary part of our profession, but that stagecoach ride took the strength clean out of me."

As they gathered their things and headed upstairs to their suite, Meggan's gaze strayed out the large windows to the darkened streets of Willow Wood. Could she dare hope her life would ever change? She hated to think it would only happen once Gloria became too infirm to make their decisions. Gloria was the closest thing Meggan had to a family.

But she wanted more. A future. A life of her own. Maybe one with a tall, intelligent, dark-headed cowboy with rich brown eyes, a chiseled jaw, and an easy smile. As she followed Gloria through the dining room and across the hotel lobby, she reminded herself not to get her hopes up. Every time she did it ended in heartache.

Chapter Three

"I rode out to your farm last week," Carl Rayburn told Shane as the family retired to the drawing room in the Trego mansion where Shane had spent most of his life.

Though the two Trego sisters were now married and had different last names, everyone in town still referred to Felicity and Belinda as the Trego sisters and called their huge house on the hill the Trego mansion.

Carl had married Belinda Trego four years ago and moved into the big house. Belinda's adopted daughter Mary still lived in the house when Belinda married Carl. Mary had grown up in Mrs. McClanahan's foundlings' home. She met Belinda after Belinda fell down the front stairs and broke her foot and needed an assistant to come to the house to help her run her business affairs.

At the time, Mary and Shane were good friends and both still in their teens, so the family wondered if the two young people would fall in love. Shane was too busy figuring out how to parlay his love for horses into a career and never gave romance a second thought. Mary thought of Shane as a brother rather than a romantic interest.

Not long after she went to work with Belinda at Trego Leatherworks, she met Michael Milstead, the son of Bob Milstead, a company shareholder. Neither Belinda nor Felicity saw eye to eye with the opinionated senior Milstead, who was also the president of the local bank. But his son Michael soon became a beloved member of the family after he fell in love with Mary. It didn't hurt when the young couple added a daughter to the family and soon after, a son.

"I plan to ride out to the farm in the morning after my meeting with Lester Cheney." Shane told the assembled group. "I'm anxious to see everything. I've been gone so long I can barely remember what the property looks like."

Carl rested an elbow on the mantlepiece. "You've got a fine operation there. It was a smart buy. Two solid barns. The smaller one would work as an examining shed to separate the recovering animals from the boarded ones."

"I'm sure he's thought of all that, Carl," Belinda said. "Shane's always had a good head on his shoulders. If not, we never would've invested in his practice."

Shane's mother Johanna, who had been the Trego's housekeeper since Shane was a tyke, leaned over and laid her hand on his cheek. She hadn't gotten more than three feet away from him since he walked through the door this morning. "I always knew my boy would grow up to do great things."

"Aw, Ma." Shane ducked his head in feigned embarrassment.

Everyone in the house had been making over him all evening. He'd been hugged and kissed and fed within an inch of his life. He had a lot of work ahead of him, but it was nice to put it aside for a night and catch up with the people who always believed in him.

Johanna got up and went to the sideboard for the coffeepot. She circled the room to refill everyone's cups. "I'm just so thankful my boy's finally home and ready to make his dreams come true."

"Sit down, Johanna," Belinda chastened. "This is Shane's reunion. You're not supposed to be working."

Johanna lifted her shoulders. "I barely realize I'm doing it, and I certainly don't mind."

"My dreams still have a long way to go," Shane reminded her as she moved to Felicity, the younger Trego sister. His mother had never been one for sitting still, even when relaxing.

"We made a good investment in Shane," Belinda told the room. "I have no doubt we'll soon see a profit from our partnership."

"Don't forget, we're silent partners," Carl reminded her. Everyone laughed. Belinda wasn't shy about voicing her opinion on any topic. But over the last few years, Carl had helped her learn encouragement went a lot farther than brow beating in achieving a desired outcome.

Johanna put the coffeepot back on the sideboard and resumed her position next to Shane. "Now all he has left to do is find a nice Christian girl and get married and fill my arms with grandchildren."

This time, Shane's embarrassment was genuine. An image of the beautiful brunette on the stage flashed through his mind. He hadn't thought much about women over the last few years. After meeting Meggan Jones, he could think of little else. He doubted she was thinking of him nearly as much as he was thinking of her. It was just as well since she was on her way to Seattle in a day or two. Shane would do well to put her out of his head and focus on his practice.

Felicity leaned back in her seat and rested her hand on her rounded middle. Three years ago while Shane was still immersed in his studies, his mother had written to tell him Felicity's first pregnancy had ended prematurely. Now it was obvious she and her husband Ned Yates would soon have a little one to fill their empty arms. Shane reminded himself to pray tonight for the safe delivery of their baby.

Felicity smiled warmly at him but directed her words to Johanna. "Don't rush the young man. I trust Shane to find a wife the same as I trust him with his business. He'll know when he meets her."

"Be careful there, Shane," Ned Yates said from the other side of the room. "Love has a way of sneaking up behind you and knocking you senseless."

"Senseless, eh?" Felicity said over the sound of laughter. "If I could move a little faster, I'd show you senseless."

Shane let the Yates' teasing take the attention off him as the rest of the room chimed in.

It was good to be home. Even better, to finally begin building his practice. He knew what it would take to become a success in Willow Wood—sweat, hard work, and building trust with townspeople who might see him as a know-it-all kid at first instead of a knowledgeable professional.

As focused as he was on his business, he wanted what the married couples in the room had. Someone who loved and cared for him with whom to share it all. So why did the image of a woman who'd only expressed indifference toward him keep flashing through his mind?

•••

The next morning Shane spent more time getting ready to meet Lester Cheney than he'd spent getting ready for anything in his life. He couldn't fool himself into thinking the extra grooming time was because of Lester, though.

The man ran a horse ranch in Idaho Falls and raised some of the finest herd within a hundred miles. The first time Shane met him was four years ago when Carl Rayburn took him there by train. Shane had been impressed with Lester's operation and vowed he'd own a ranch as good and successful himself one day.

A bachelor who knew horses but little else, Les didn't put much stock in social niceties. He wouldn't bother to shave off six weeks worth of whiskers or slick down his hair to discuss business with Shane. It didn't stop Shane from doing so. If he ran into Gloria Hennessey and her lovely granddaughter, he wanted to look better than he did yesterday on the stage.

As he straightened his tie and settled his Stetson in place, he chastised himself for going to the trouble. Except for that last lingering look as he helped her from the stage, Meggan had given him no indication she even recognized he was alive. He doubted seeing him with a fresh shave and wearing his best shirt would change that perception.

The instant Shane stepped inside the hotel his gaze swept the lobby all the way to the staircase. An elderly couple came down the stairs with their suitcases in their hands, chatting animatedly.

No Meggan or her gregarious grandmother.

He didn't see Lester either, which was just as well since it gave him a reason to hang around and hopefully catch a glimpse of Meggan.

He went to the clerk's counter where a short, round man in a bowler hat was settling his bill. Shane waited his turn and then smiled broadly at the clerk.

Jimmy Hanson's face lit up in recognition. "Shane Casey. I heard you were coming back to town. How you been?"

Shane set his hat on the tall counter and reached across it to pump Jimmy's hand. They had been part of the same group of boys growing up, running the hills and meadows surrounding Willow Wood, teasing each other about their prowess with horses, baseball, and, of course, girls they were generally too shy to approach.

Shane rested his elbow on the counter and angled his body to scan the lobby as he exchanged pleasantries with his friend. "You haven't seen Les Cheney in here this morning, have you?" he asked. "A wiry fellow. Always wears a black leather vest. I'm supposed to meet him about looking at some horses."

"Everybody who ever threw his leg over a horse around these parts knows Les. Or at least knows of him." Jimmy stirred through some papers on the counter. "A courier delivered a message to the night clerk just as I was getting here." He found the message and held it out to Shane. "The name was smudged so I didn't know it was for you. Anyhow, Les ain't coming."

Shane unfolded the paper and read the brief message. "He's been delayed," he told Jimmy. "Don't really say why. Just that he can't make it till the end of the week."

"Sorry to hear it."

Shane swallowed his impatience. "I guess it'll give me more time to investigate my farm. It's not like I don't have plenty to do out there."

"Maybe you can carve out a little time to catch up with a few old friends." Jimmy arched his eyebrows.

Shane smiled in reply. "That don't sound half bad."

Jimmy's gaze drifted past Shane. "I wonder what that's all about."

Shane turned and looked toward the stairwell in time to see Meggan Jones rushing down the stairs. She wore a cream-colored dress printed with little flowers that accentuated her feminine form. Her thick black hair was coiled around the back of her head. Without a hat covering it, Shane saw it was even shinier and more voluminous than he had imagined yesterday. It must reach all the way down her back. That'd be a sight he'd love to see.

The look on her face reined in his imaginings. Her emerald eyes glittered from across the room, wide and red-rimmed. Her face was as pale as a ghost except for two splashes of scarlet on her cheeks. She stumbled when she reached the bottom of the stairs. Shane lunged away from the counter and rushed to her. He caught hold of her elbows as she wobbled dangerously. She searched his face as if trying to place him.

"Miss Jones," he said, "what's the matter?"

"Mr. Casey? Thank God." She clutched his shirt, her knuckles white. "It's Granny. She's—dead. You have to help me."

Her eyes filled with terror for half a breath before she collapsed into his arms.

Chapter Four

Meggan awoke with a start. "Granny?" She started to sit up. A sharp pain at her temple forced her to stay in place.

"Easy there," a masculine voice said. Hands took hers and eased her into a sitting position on the narrow settee. "Don't move too quickly."

She took a few slow, steady breaths and tried not to focus on anything until the pain in her head subsided.

This morning, she had prepared for the day in her room without checking on Gloria. Gloria always slept late, even more so when travelling. Meggan usually went downstairs to order breakfast before awaking the older woman. This morning she suspected Gloria hadn't slept well, so she tapped on the door and stuck her head into Gloria's room to see if she had any requests.

The same hands that helped her sit up pushed a glass of water into hers. As she drank, everything came back in a rush. Granny's swollen face. The rumpled blankets. The pillow on the floor. Granny's fist clutching—no, it couldn't be. She wasn't—dead.

She smoothed stray wisps of hair back from her face. Had she fainted? Fallen? She barely remembered leaving the suite and running downstairs. She looked around the room where she found herself. Small. Tidy. An office of some kind, and two men staring down at her. She recognized the desk clerk who had checked her and Granny into their suite yesterday.

She recognized the other man too. A cowboy with warm brown eyes who made her think of a life completely different from the one she had.

Shane Casey. What was he doing here? Had he discovered her secret? Had he followed her and Gloria all the way from Kansas City and was here to...

She pushed the tumbling thoughts aside. She couldn't worry about that now.

Shane and the clerk stared down at her as if afraid she might fly into a million pieces. Maybe she would.

"Everything will be all right," Shane said. "We sent for the doc and the sheriff."

Meggan's heart lurched. *The sheriff?* He knew! Shane knew! That's why he was here. It was over. She was going to jail, and Granny...

It was all happening too fast.

She put her hand to the side of her head as if it still hurt. In truth, she needed to stall. To think. "Granny doesn't need a doctor. It's too late for that."

"No, for you."

"Oh." She straightened her bodice and moved to stand.

Shane put his hand out to stop her. "You should stay seated until the doc gets here. Just to make sure you're all right."

She stood in defiance and hoped they didn't notice her slight sway. "I don't need to stay seated, and I don't need a doctor. It was just—seeing her that way—" She wrapped her arms around her middle. She looked past Shane to the clerk. "Is it true? Is Granny—"

She stopped talking. Of course, it was true. She wouldn't have made a mistake about such a thing. The proof was all over their suite upstairs.

How had she slept through it? Why had she been spared? She swayed again.

Shane took her arm and guided her back onto the settee. He looked at the clerk and wagged his head toward the door. The clerk went out. "Jimmy'll go upstairs for you. We haven't been to your suite yet, but you said... We brought you in here when you fainted. We didn't know what else to do."

Meggan stared at the floor. "Of course. I'm sorry. It just doesn't seem real. I keep thinking..."

What was she thinking? All she knew was she needed to get up and walk out of here. She needed to go to the station and trade in her ticket to Seattle for—well, it didn't matter where as long as it was far away from what happened upstairs.

She glanced out the window at the quiet street. It was still early. She probably hadn't missed today's train. But where could she go? If Gloria hadn't been safe in an out-of-the-way town like Willow Wood, what chance did Meggan have?

She felt the weight of her derringer in her pocket. She was adept with the little gun, but how much protection could it offer against what had happened to Gloria?

"Why are you here?" she asked Shane, hoping to keep the suspicion out of her voice.

Shane's brown eyes clouded. "Because you fainted."

"No. Why are you at the hotel?" She stopped just short of asking who he worked for and why he was following her.

"I had a meeting this morning. I was going to look into buying some horses."

She remembered now. He mentioned it yesterday when Gloria asked about his animal husbandry business. That didn't make it true. It could all be part of the ruse.

Shane moved to the dry sink and wet a cloth. He folded it in half and handed it to her. He looked as uncomfortable as she felt. "What do you think happened to your grandmother?"

Meggan looked at the closed door. Was she safe in here with this man? Was he laying his trap with those innocent eyes and gentle words?

"I...I'm not sure," she lied. "She was fine last night when we went to bed. Well, not fine, maybe. She's been tired lately. This trip wore her out. You heard her complaining about it on the stage yesterday. But she was in high spirits."

Gloria Hennessey was always in high spirits. Especially now. She was looking forward to getting to Seattle and receiving the biggest payday she'd ever dreamed of.

"Did she have a bad heart?" Shane asked.

Meggan studied him. His sympathy seemed sincere. If he were in on what happened upstairs, he wouldn't have called for the sheriff. Unless the desk clerk went for the sheriff before Shane could stop him. Or he was an undercover agent working with local authorities. She had seen plenty of lawmen in her life. Shane didn't have the look. He didn't act as though he was working to lower her guard before taking her into custody. He truly seemed to care. But what did she know about what true compassion looked like?

He also seemed completely in the dark about what happened to Gloria. She was an old lady. Old ladies died in their sleep all the time, didn't they? Everyone would assume her heart had given out, even the doctor. No one would guess what really happened. Except for Meggan and whoever had...

She narrowed her eyes and watched Shane. "She was as fit as a fiddle, except for being old. But can anyone ever know about a weak heart?" She glanced at the door. "When is the sheriff coming?"

She couldn't let the lawman go through their suite. If he searched the room—if he found what was in the trunk—she was either dead or on her way to prison.

"I need to go upstairs—to be with Granny."

Shane frowned. "I don't know if that's a good idea. Dr. Dutton and the sheriff will be here any minute. We should wait on them. You fainted. You may not be ready to see your grandmother again—like that."

Meggan needed to trust someone, at least until she got upstairs and looked through their things. Could that person be Shane Casey?

She jumped to her feet and grabbed his shirtsleeve. "Please. Can't you go with me? Granny was in her nightclothes. She'll be mortified if the sheriff—I mean, she wouldn't have wanted a strange man to see her in such a state. I know it's silly. I won't dress her or anything; I just want to make sure the bedclothes are in order."

Shane seemed to understand. "If you're sure you're strong enough to see her again."

"It doesn't matter about me. I need to do this for Granny."

He nodded. Despite her determination, Meggan wobbled a little as they left the room. Shane took her arm to steady her. He tucked her hand in the crook of his arm. Fear washed over her as they started across the lobby. She ducked her head and scanned the room through lowered lashes. No one seemed to pay them any mind, but she wasn't sure who she was looking for. If anyone. Maybe she was wrong. Maybe Gloria had died from a heart attack or whatever it was that took tired old people in their sleep.

She tightened her arm on Shane's arm. She wasn't wrong. But she could be wrong to trust Shane. Not that she had a choice at the moment.

Upstairs, she led him to the suite at the end of the hall. Theirs was the only suite in the hotel. Gloria always traveled in style. She loved to say life was too short to deprive oneself of creature comforts when at all possible.

A pang of nostalgia stabbed at Meggan's breast. Gloria was the closest thing to a mother she had known since Grandma Elsie passed away. Without her, Meggan felt strangely adrift as if she were on the deck of a ship, and she didn't know from which direction the next crashing wave would come. She had nowhere to turn, nothing to hang onto. No one in whom to confide.

Was she about to be arrested? Or worse, meet the same fate as Gloria?

She adjusted the knot of hair at the nape of her neck and steeled herself for what was to come. Shane pushed open the door, stepped across the threshold, and ushered Meggan inside. They looked toward the bed. Gloria lay on her back. Her head was flopped to one side. At first glance, it looked like she was sleeping. The blankets at the foot of the bed were disheveled as if she had tried to kick them off. The bed's second pillow still lay on the floor. Meggan knew it hadn't slipped off in the night. It looked more as though it had been tossed aside after serving its purpose.

She advanced to the bed, leaving Shane at the door. She put her hand on Gloria's shoulder and gazed down at her face. Except for a little discoloration around her mouth, she looked like she was sleeping. Had she suffered much? Had she tried to call out for Meggan? Or Alice?

No point in dwelling on that now. It wouldn't change anything. The Hennessey sisters had chosen a dangerous path in life. It shouldn't come as a shock that she had met a violent end.

But it was still a shock. And sad. And a waste. For all Gloria's talk and grandiose storytelling, Meggan realized she didn't know the Hennessey sisters better than anyone else did.

She knew they grew up in Emporia, Kansas in a ramshackle house not meant for so many people. At least that's what she'd been told. There were always too many children and too many down-on-their-luck relatives hanging about with never enough food to feed them all. Alice and Gloria intimated they did what they had to do to survive, as though poverty and desperation excused their illegal activities.

Meggan smoothed Gloria's gray hair back from her face. If she and Alice had made different choices, found different ways to survive, the ends of their lives may have been surrounded by loved ones and grandchildren instead of like this—in a lonely hotel, protecting something that didn't belong to her.

She pulled the covers up around the woman's throat and leaned forward to kiss her cool cheek.

"It's over, Gloria. I pray you finally find peace."

She took the pillow off the floor and put it back where it belonged next to the old woman. She straightened the covers at the foot of the bed. The cowboy had closed the door behind them, but he hadn't come toward the bed. He watched her with a mixture of confusion and sympathy.

"Should you be—moving things around like that before the sheriff gets here?" he asked.

Meggan let her face slip into a mask of grief and resignation. She knew how to play the game as well as Gloria and Alice.

"I wanted to make Granny—comfortable."

He didn't say more, as she knew he wouldn't. No man would question the irrational actions of a grieving woman.

She brushed aside an imaginary tear. "I need to get a few of her things." She took Gloria's leather satchel from the bureau and knelt in front of the steamer trunk at the foot of the bed. Her heart pounded. As expected, the contents of the trunk had been disturbed.

She struggled to keep her desperation from showing as she dug deeper into the trunk. Hopefully, Shane would attribute her trembling fingers to grief. Gloria's killer either found what he was looking for or his search had been interrupted. It was the only explanation for why he didn't come into Meggan's room after he finished in here.

Immediately she noticed the leather pouch containing Gloria's money was missing. Was she wrong, and Gloria had been killed by a common thief looking for an easy score?

The weight of the silver object in her pocket quickly eliminated that theory.

The train ticket to Seattle and letters from Gloria's contact were still in the trunk. Meggan stuffed them into the satchel. She needed the train ticket, and she couldn't let the sheriff find the letters to use as evidence against her later.

Meggan's own train ticket and a small amount of money she carried were still in her bag in the next room—she hoped. At least she wouldn't starve while she figured out what to do next.

She leaned farther over the trunk to block Shane's view and ran her fingers along the lip of the trunk until she found the barely discernible latch that concealed the tiny compartment. She imagined a man's calloused fingers sliding right over the latch without detecting it. Alice had been so proud of her ingenuity when she designed the trunk years ago. For the first time, Meggan was equally grateful for the steps the Hennessey sisters had gone to to maintain their secrets.

She tripped the latch with a fingernail. The compartment clicked open. She exhaled with relief as her greedy fingers closed over the tiny velvet pouch. She palmed it and slid it into the satchel, confident Shane hadn't seen. Her nimble fingers had mastered the sleight of hand. She could practically stuff a squealing pig into her shirtwaist, and no one would see.

She pushed aside a few articles of rumpled clothing and fumbled to open the trunk's false bottom. Inside, the insignificant papers and a few valuables stored there were stirred and soiled. She smiled to herself. Gloria had been right; the false bottom would convince a thief he had found the trunk's secrets while overlooking the tiny door that concealed her true prize.

Unfortunately, it hadn't saved her life.

Meggan jammed most of Gloria's belongings back into the trunk and closed the lid. The scrapbook was on the nightstand. She stuffed it into the satchel.

"This meant the world to Granny," she told Shane. "I want to make sure nothing happens to it with people coming in and out."

In reality, she didn't want the sheriff to see the posters and realize how many enemies Gloria had made.

She heard hurried footsteps on the stairs. She looped the satchel over her shoulder and across her body. She nervously patted her hair into place.

Shane heard the footsteps in the hall as well and opened the door to let them in. A tall, leather-faced man with a badge pinned to his flannel shirt stopped just before entering. He deferred to a slim auburn-haired woman dressed in a green serge skirt and white blouse and carrying a medical bag. Meggan's eyes bulged. Could this be the doctor? Perhaps a midwife was the best the small town could offer.

The woman glanced at the bed before focusing her attention on Meggan. "Miss…"

"Jones," Meggan offered. "Meggan Jones."

"I'm Lisette Dutton, the doctor here in Willow Wood." She took Meggan's elbow and guided her to a straight-backed chair. "I'm so sorry to hear of your loss. The clerk said you fainted in the lobby when you went downstairs to alert the staff about your grandmother."

"Yes, um, I'm better now. I really don't need any attention. It was just…finding Granny." She swallowed, surprised again by a fresh wave of grief. She still couldn't grasp Gloria was gone.

The doctor made the appropriate sounds of commiseration as she lifted Meggan's eyelids and studied her face. She took a stethoscope out of her bag and moved it around Meggan's chest and back. "Do you feel all right now? No dizziness? Nausea?"

"No, no, I'm truly fine. It was…"

"A shock. Yes, I'm sure."

The sheriff had been studying Gloria on the bed while they talked. He glanced at the steamer trunk. "You ladies were traveling?"

What was your first clue? Meggan thought wryly.

There was no point in keeping their destination a secret. She would raise more suspicions by not answering his questions. Gloria had practically shouted their business from the rooftops anyway since the moment they left Kansas City.

"Yes, sir. We were on our way to Seattle."

He removed his hat and took on a sympathetic air. "I'm sorry this has happened, miss. I'm Sheriff Deavers. Did your grandmother have medical complaints?"

"Not really. Nothing more than anyone her age. She was seldom ill."

He nodded. The doctor left Meggan and moved to the bed. Meggan held her breath. Would he notice something she'd missed; a sign that Gloria hadn't died in her sleep?

"Do you have family in Seattle?" Sheriff Deavers asked.

Meggan took a deep breath to calm the pounding in her chest. His words sounded benevolent enough, but she knew how investigators worked. She chose cautious honesty.

"No, sir. We don't have family at all. Granny—she had friends there. I've never met them. She wanted a change of scenery. She was like that. We didn't stay anywhere for long."

He nodded as if mulling the information. "How long were you planning to stay in Willow Wood?"

"I'm not really sure. Two or three days. Granny was tired. She wanted to rest. The travel was wearing on her."

The sheriff and doctor exchanged glances. Dr. Dutton finished her examination, which didn't appear to have raised alarm. "Miss Jones, my office is on Second Street. You can ask anyone where to find me if you feel ill or out of sorts or if you just want to talk. Sometimes it takes a day or two for the shock of losing a loved one to settle in."

She was right about that.

"Thank you, Dr. Dutton."

Sheriff Deavers clasped his hands at his waist. "My men and I will remove the—your grandmother and take her to the undertaker's down the street, if that's agreeable. You may want to leave the room for a little while if you find it unsettling."

"Yes, sir. I appreciate your help."

The doctor and sheriff assured her again they were available anytime should she require their services. The sheriff looked at Shane. "Maybe you could take Miss Jones downstairs for a cup of coffee or some breakfast."

Meggan glanced at Shane. If he were an undercover agent following her and Gloria from Kansas City, Sheriff Deavers wouldn't be so familiar with him. That eased some of her worries. She didn't want to be alone. She couldn't tell the sheriff a killer had been in the suite last night and was probably now watching for her.

As soon as the sheriff learned of the pouch and her and Gloria's plans to sell its contents in Seattle, he would lock her up. The killer could waltz in the jailhouse door with a fake arrest warrant and tell the sheriff he was taking her into custody.

Only one person could help her now; Detective Abner Rollins from Kansas City. He had been like a dog on a trail following the robbery and murder of Mr. Gochberg. Meggan knew he hadn't given up, nor would he until the stolen property was returned to the Gochberg family. She also believed the detective was honest and fair. If she could get word to him that Gloria was dead, he could come and take possession of the velvet pouch. In the meantime, her only chance of survival rested in the hands of the cowboy staring at her.

It wasn't fair to involve Shane Casey in a deadly situation without telling him what he was getting into, but it looked like the decision had been made for her.

Chapter Five

S hane closed the door behind the sheriff and Lisette Dutton and turned his attention to Meggan. She stood in the center of the room, looking from her grandmother to the steamer trunk to nothing at all. Her hands clasped the worn satchel to her chest. Shane could practically see her brain processing everything that had transpired and figuring out what to do next.

She was grief struck, that much was obvious. But she was also—calculating. It was the only word Shane could think of to describe the furtive look in her eyes. He hadn't missed her remove something from the trunk and stuff it into the satchel. He probably wouldn't have noticed if she hadn't gone to so much trouble to hide it from him, which meant the lady was up to something.

Whatever it was meant a lot to her, and she wasn't taking any chances on letting anyone know she had it.

He also couldn't forget her calling her grandmother *Gloria*. Shane's grandparents passed away years ago, but he had never referred to them by their Christian names. He didn't even think of them that way.

Maybe his suspicions were unfounded. Now that he thought about it, she might not have said Gloria. Maybe she had said a prayer over the old woman, urging her departed spirit to Glory. That made more sense than a person disrespecting her grandmother by using her given name.

Meggan hadn't looked at him or acknowledged him since the sheriff and doctor entered the room. Nothing new there. She had treated him with cool indifference on the stage, and it looked like that wasn't about to change.

Even if she asked him to, he couldn't very well walk out the door and leave her in a strange town to deal with the next few hours alone. She might want to be left alone, but the sheriff was right. She shouldn't be here when the deputies came back to collect her grandmother.

It was a good thing Lester Cheney and his horses had been delayed. Shane suddenly had a full week to himself. He couldn't remember the last time that happened. The only item on his agenda was to help the beautiful, mysterious Meggan in whatever way she needed, whether she wanted it or not.

"Would you like to go downstairs for that cup of coffee? Or maybe some breakfast? We should get out of the way for when they—you know." He cut his eyes toward the bed.

She jumped like he'd startled her out of some deep thinking. She went to the bed and laid her hands over Mrs. Hennessey's folded ones. The old lady already looked like she'd been laid out. Sadness washed over Shane. Mrs. Hennessey had been an interesting character. A real spitfire. He would've liked to have known her better.

He tried to think of something comforting to say to Meggan. Words failed him. She sure wasn't as easy to talk to as her grandmother had been. She looked like she'd rather not be disturbed anyway.

She absently straightened the covers. "Will she—be all right?"

"Of course. Stephen Thompson has been the undertaker here in Willow Wood for years. He's a good man. Fair. He'll do right by your grandmother. And you."

Meggan looked from him to the bed. Her eyes were dry. She looked like she was still in shock. Shane figured it would take a few days for the gravity of her grandmother's death and her new situation as an unescorted woman with nowhere to go to fully hit her. She told Sheriff Deavers she didn't know the friends waiting for them in Seattle. With her grandmother gone, she might change her mind about going. Shane sure wouldn't want to go to a strange place to stay with people he'd never met. But he guessed she was already in that position. In a strange town, all alone with the only familiar face belonging to a man she didn't seem to have much use for.

Well, there was nothing either of them could do about it for the time being except get her out of this room.

Meggan looked stable enough, but she could faint again. Or became hysterical. Did women do that in times of extreme grief? Shane had spent the last four years surrounded by battle-hardened men, up to their elbows in blood and animal bodily fluids, and hearing stories of how the weaker sex wasn't up to the jobs men dealt with on a regular basis.

Nearly every woman he knew had the temerity to stare down a mountain lion. He thought of the Trego sisters and nearly smiled. Hysterics weren't in them. Dr. Dutton saw blood and bodily fluids—the human kind— every day, and he had never heard of her fainting or surrendering to hysterics. His own mother had been left alone to raise a boy in the frontier. Shane had every confidence nothing would have scared her away from doing what was best for him.

Maybe everything he'd heard about women and their frailties existed only in the imaginations of men who didn't know any better.

No matter the sex or the constitution of the grieving, Meggan Jones was facing a lot of uncertainty.

"Shall we?" he gently prodded.

Meggan seemed to snap to attention again. "Yes, I suppose I should…" She looked back at her grandmother as if seeking advice. "I need—to get my things," she said.

Shane waited while she went into the adjoining room. He took a small step toward the bed and studied Gloria. He remembered the pillow that had been on the floor when he and Meggan first arrived. Had Gloria put the extra pillow on the floor before going to sleep, or had she knocked it off during the throes of a heart attack? The blankets at the top half of her body weren't overly disturbed, but her lower legs and feet had been exposed.

There was no accounting for how people moved around while sleeping, he supposed, but it struck him as odd.

Meggan came back into the room, tying the ribbon of a big straw hat under her chin. The hat covered much of her face, but Shane couldn't help noticing how the cobalt blue ribbon sparked a light in her emerald eyes and seemed to bring a blush to her smoooth alabaster skin. He gave himself an inward kick for staring.

Meggan avoided looking at the bed. "I need to send a telegram."

Shane offered his arm. "I know just where the office is. I'll walk you over. You look a little unsteady on your feet."

"I—I guess I am."

She placed a trembling hand in the crook of his elbow. When they reached the lobby, her hand tightened on his arm, and her posture stiffened. She glanced around the large room from under the brim of her big hat, paying extra attention to the corners and behind the pillars. Shane followed her gaze. She had done the same thing when he walked her upstairs an hour ago. What was she looking for? Or whom?

On the stage, he attributed her aloofness to disinterest or boredom. Now she looked downright scared. Maybe she was shy and rendered nearly speechless around strange people and situations. Or it could simply be a reaction to what had just happened.

He ushered her through the lobby and out the front door of the hotel. Meggan's anxiety seemed to heighten. The activity on the street was typical for an early summer morning. A few shoppers, the usual small town lay-abouts who never seemed to have anywhere to go, a cowboy on horseback, a farmer driving a creaking buckboard loaded with sawn lumber, and two boys running to get back to wherever they belonged. None of it explained Meggan's near panic or the complete lack of color in her face.

From all her travels, she should be used to more jostling crowds and traffic than she'd encounter in sleepy Willow Wood.

She'd feel better after she sent her telegram to alert whoever was waiting about Mrs. Hennessey's passing. Shane wondered briefly about the telegram's recipient. Meggan said they didn't have family. It didn't sound like they had many friends either. Was she writing to a beau? A beau her grandmother didn't approve of?

Shane tamped down the nugget of jealousy rising in his gut. None of it was his business. Still, something about her behavior nagged at him. It was more than a quiet, timid personality unprepared for change. He knew when a person was hiding something, and Meggan Jones was hiding something big.

•••

Meggan's skin prickled as though a thousand eyes were watching her and Shane cross the street. She could tell from the way his hand hovered over his sidearm as he followed her gaze that her tension had rubbed off on him.

She took a deep breath in an effort to relax. It was no use. She couldn't stop thinking about Gloria's killer. There was no disputing her death had not been a heart attack. The proof was tucked inside Gloria's satchel. Gloria had made plenty of enemies over the years, but only one knew about the contents of the pouch Meggan had tied around her neck and dropped down the front of her dress when she told Shane she needed to go into the adjoining room to get her hat.

No other villain seeking revenge or bent on putting Gloria out of business, would've bothered with finding the trunk's false bottom.

The only man in the world willing to kill for what hung around Meggan's neck was locked away in prison.

Or was he? Had he told someone? Had he taken a partner?

Of course, J.D. Duggar was still in prison. And he wouldn't trust anyone enough to divulge his secrets. Unless he had decided to let a partner do the dirty work and then put a bullet in the man's head once he served his purpose.

That was what awaited her; a bullet in the head. And Shane, too, if J.D. saw them together.

How would she survive until Detective Rollins got here? She'd never spent time in a town this size. She felt so exposed. So vulnerable. No crowds in which to disappear. No stores or alleys to duck into should trouble arise. Just her in the shadow of the mountains too far away to conceal her.

Her only hope for survival was the cowboy beside her who didn't know what he was up against.

Shane couldn't do much to protect her if J.D. suddenly appeared and demanded she hand over the pouch around her neck, but she was grateful she wasn't alone.

"Are you all right?" Shane's deep brown eyes were dark with concern. He had seen her faint once today. He was probably afraid she was about to do so again.

"I'm fine." She gave him a quick smile and picked up her pace. She wasn't being fair to him. Shane deserved to know what had happened to Gloria so he could make an informed decision about if he wanted to help her or not. But how could she blurt it out? How could she explain why she and Gloria were going to Seattle? He would never understand. He would turn her over to the sheriff and be done with her.

Inside the telegraph office, Shane hung back while Meggan approached the counter. Instead of relaying the message to the agent, she asked for a piece of paper and wrote it out. She didn't want Shane to overhear even though he had more of a right than anyone to know what was happening.

Granny dead Stop *Willow Wood Idaho* Stop *I have what you're looking for* Stop *Come right away* Stop *Meggan Jones*

She added the detective's name and Kansas City, Missouri to the top of the paper and slid it across the counter to the agent. She paid the cost and turned to go. When the agent thanked her, she was so nervous her lips wouldn't form a reply.

What if the message didn't reach Detective Rollins? What if he was out of town? Or sick? What if he didn't come?

By the time she reached the door, she was nearly to the point of tears. So much could go wrong, and she would be stuck in Willow Wood. With a killer.

Misreading her agitation, Shane smiled with compassion and opened the door. Meggan stepped onto the board sidewalk and froze.

Across the street, a slim, dark-haired man wearing a black and white buffalo plaid shirt and a black string tie stepped out of the hotel. He combed a strand of thinning black hair out of his eyes and glanced up and down the street. Meggan gasped. Though she knew J.D. Duggar was the only man with a reason to follow her and Gloria from Kansas City, she nearly cried out in alarm at the sight of him.

Shane heard her intake of breath and followed her gaze. "What's the matter? Do you know that man?"

"No. Yes." She grabbed his hand and pulled him in the opposite direction before J.D. looked over and saw them. "If your offer for a cup of coffee still stands, I would appreciate it. Just not at the hotel. I can't go back there with Granny—it's too emotional."

Shane pulled to a stop so quickly Meggan's hat slipped to the back of her head, the ribbon nearly choking her.

"Listen," he said firmly, "I'm willing to help you with whatever you need, but I gotta know who that man is and why you're running away from him."

Meggan's heart sank. She wasn't surprised Shane had recognized something was up; she just wished it hadn't happened so quickly. But she couldn't explain the whole story in less time than it would take for J.D. to see her standing in the middle of street. "I wasn't running away. I just—it's been a stressful morning. I have a terrible headache." Not exactly a lie. "He reminded me of someone I know. I was wrong."

Shane wasn't convinced. "You sure looked like you know him. Maybe I should go back there and ask if he's looking for you."

"No!" She grabbed his arm and squeezed until she felt his skin beneath his shirt. "I don't—feel well. I think it's the heat. I need to get out of the sun."

Over Shane's shoulder she saw J.D. turn in their direction. She didn't think he had noticed her yet, but he would if they didn't get moving.

She couldn't go back to Kansas City. Even if she hadn't sent the telegram to Detective Rollins, she couldn't get on a stagecoach or a train to return the pouch to where it belonged. J.D. could easily board the same train, wait for darkness, slip up behind her, and...

She had no choice but to put her life in Shane's hands.

First, though, she needed to get him on her side.

She began again. "I'm sorry, Shane. I just can't face a lot of people right now. I'm too upset over Granny."

He shook his arm free. "Enough of the damsel-in-distress routine. Tell me who that man is and why you don't want him to see you, or I'll go over there and ask him myself."

"He's not anyone. I've never seen him—"

"Tell me why you called your grandmother by her first name."

Meggan's jaw dropped. "What? I didn't—"

J.D. Duggar stepped off the sidewalk and started in their direction. Meggan remembered the last time she saw him; in the courtroom, in handcuffs and shackles, his face purple with rage as he yelled that he would get even with Gloria—and her.

"Well?" Shane's jaw clenched and unclenched.

She grabbed his hand and dragged him into an alley next to a tiny store. A row of barrels lined the wall of a mercantile. The sound of boots purposefully striking the ground thundered in her ears. She spun Shane around so his back was to the opening between the buildings, concealing her from view. "I hope you'll understand."

"Understand what?"

Meggan threw her arms around his neck and kissed him.

Chapter Six

S hane's hands slid up Meggan's arms to her wrists as if to unlock her hold on him. Meggan tightened her grip and deepened the kiss. After barely a heartbeat's hesitation, he responded and pulled her closer.

Fire stirred in Meggan's belly. Blood pounded in her ears as Shane's mouth moved against hers. She had never kissed a man before. She'd never even been this close to one. Growing up, Alice and Gloria kept too close an eye on her to give her time to think about the male of the species. She never had a friend with whom to discuss matters like kissing. Locked in Shane's arms, she couldn't form a thought except how she didn't want this to end.

Approaching footsteps paused on the boardwalk between the two buildings. Meggan thought she heard a soft chuckle, then receding footsteps as the man moved on. Reluctantly, she loosened her arms around Shane's neck and drew back.

She adjusted the satchel strap around her neck. It hung cockeyed across her body, and her ribs smarted from where Shane had crushed it against her during the kiss.

He stared down at her, confused, flustered, and— interested. Meggan took another step away from him. What had she done? What must he think of her? She was breathless as if she'd just run up a flight of stairs. Her mouth was so dry, she couldn't speak, even if she knew how to explain. Was this what kissing did to a person? No wonder Alice and Gloria made sure she never had time to find out.

Shane's eyes searched hers. His confusion turned to anger. "What was that?"

"I—I'm sorry. I didn't mean…"

She couldn't even answer the question to herself. What had she meant to do? She needed to keep J.D. from seeing her, but surely there had been another way—a way that didn't so blatantly involve Shane. One that didn't endanger him.

His stance softened. He took off his hat and ran his hand through his rich brown hair. He looked as shaken by the kiss as she felt.

"Miss Jones, I can't say I hated what you just did. But I'm not stupid. I know it had nothing to do with me." He replaced his hat. "You owe me an explanation."

"You're absolutely right. I had no right." She stepped out of his shadow and looked around the corner of the building in time to see J.D. Duggar turn the corner at the end of the street.

She exhaled to still her wildly beating heart. For now, at least, it had little to do with J.D. She almost wished she could go back into Shane's arms and focus on nothing but his lips against hers. She feared as soon as she told him what she needed tell him kissing would be the last thing he wanted to do.

"My granny didn't die in her sleep," she said quickly before she lost her nerve. "She was murdered. I think she was smothered with her pillow by the man who just walked past here. Now he's after me." She snagged her bottom lip with her teeth. "And maybe you too."

"Me? What? I don't know what you're talking about."

"I know. I'm sorry." She needed to stop apologizing. She took a deep breath and started over. "He may have seen us together at the hotel. He'll think you know something."

"Know something about what? I don't understand any of this."

"Mr. Casey—Shane—I promise I'll tell you everything. I just can't do it this minute and I can't do it here. We have to get off the street. I need to stay out of sight for a few days, and I don't know how to do that on my own."

"No, what you need to do is go to the sheriff. Why didn't you tell him back at the hotel somebody killed your granny? He'll investigate. He'll protect you."

She shook her head as she began to shiver in the shadow of the building. "He can't."

Shane opened his mouth to refute it.

"He won't believe me," she exclaimed. "That man followed us here from Kansas City. I don't know how. He's supposed to be in prison. He must've..."

Meggan stared out at the street. It wasn't likely J.D. had been released after what he'd done. He must've escaped. She only prayed he hadn't hurt someone else in the process.

Shane took hold of her arms. "Miss Jones, it'll be all right. I'll help you. I don't know who this man is or why he'd want to harm you or your granny, but we'll keep you safe. You have my word on it" He stepped toward the light of the sun shifting the shadows between the buildings. "I'll take you to the sheriff and vouch for you. He knows me—"

"No!" She lunged forward and grabbed his arm. Tears blurred her vision. "Shane, please. That man's name is J.D. Duggar. He's a killer. He murdered a man during a jewelry store robbery. He killed my granny because—please, I can't let him know I spotted him. If he sees us going into the sheriff's office—"

Shane looked at her hand on his sleeve but didn't pull away. "I know where the sheriff lives. We'll stay out of sight till after dark. I'll take you to his house—"

"No!"

She yanked his arm, nearly knocking him off balance. He must think she was crazy, but she couldn't help it. She had to make him understand. "We can't go to the law. I know for a fact they won't believe me."

No lawman in the country would believe her once they found the velvet pouch around her neck.

"Mr. Casey—Shane, I don't know what else to do."

She squeezed his arm one last time and dropped her hand. This wasn't Shane's problem. It wasn't fair of her to make it so. If J.D. hadn't recognized her, Shane wasn't yet in any danger. She should thank him for his help thus far and walk away. She needed to face this predicament alone.

Maybe he would lend her a horse. She couldn't afford to buy one. But even with a horse, where would she go? How long could she stay hidden in the mountains alone while she waited for Detective Rollins? How would she know when the detective arrived?

In the courtroom, while Gloria played the part of curious neighbor and befuddled grandmother, Meggan had watched Mrs. Gochberg, the wife of J.D.'s victim. Every day she sat flanked by her two stoic-faced sons while the prosecution recounted how her husband had been shot by the defendant when he walked in on the robbery.

Each evening, the neighbors who attended the trial would gather in their building's common room and rehash the day's proceedings. They would speculate on J.D.'s chances and how they thought both sides presented their cases. Everyone lied and said they knew J.D. Duggar was a criminal from the moment he moved into the neighborhood.

Only Gloria knew from the beginning, but for once, she kept her mouth shut.

No one seemed to spare a thought for Mrs. Gochberg. Meggan could think of nothing else. The woman had lost everything to J.D. Duggar. Her family had been destroyed. Meggan could've helped. She could've come forward and told what she knew. But she didn't. Now Gloria was dead, and she was J.D.'s next target.

She couldn't give Mrs. Gochberg her husband back, but she could make sure her property was returned to the family. It would never happen if she fled to Seattle or if J.D. tracked her into the mountains, took back what he believed was his, and left her bones for the buzzards.

Despite her intentions not to involve Shane, she knew she wouldn't survive without him.

Shane was staring at her, his face filled with questions. After a long moment, his stance relaxed. "What do you need from me?"

Meggan nearly burst into tears of relief.

"I need to stay out of sight until help arrives."

"What help?"

Meggan looked into his dark brown eyes, nearly the color of a walnut shell. He had been nothing but patient and compassionate so far. Even after the kiss. Her brazen behavior would've given most men the license to do whatever they wanted with her. Shane Casey obviously wasn't like most men. She could trust him.

Now she had to convince him to trust *her*.

"The telegram. I sent it to a detective in Kansas City. He was the lead investigator in the case against Mr. Duggar. He knows the whole story. He'll come as soon as he can, but it will take a few days. I can't leave the area, but I can't let J.D. see me either."

Shane stared over her shoulder as he worked out a plan. "I'll hide you somewhere, like the livery, and go back to get your things. He knows you're staying at the hotel. That's where he'll focus his efforts looking for you."

"I can't move my things. I don't want him to know I spotted him. He needs to think I haven't realized yet what happened to Granny."

He studied her closely. Meggan held her breath, willing him to see she was right. He took her hand and peered out from between the buildings. He quickly led her two doors down and stepped inside a store. A bell jangled over their heads. To Meggan, it sounded like a gong announcing her location to the entire town.

A counter, crowded with pails of all manner of nails, wood files, and ax heads, lined one wall, allowing barely three feet of space between it and the opposite rows of shelves. Meggan had to stand nearly against Shane to keep from colliding with barrels of brooms, ax handles, and scythes.

The proprietor looked up from an ink blotted ledger. "Well, hullo there, stranger," he called out merrily to Shane. "Your mama told everyone at church yesterday you were coming back to town. It sure is good to have you back. You an animal doctor yet?"

"I got all my credentials," Shane said after an equally warm greeting. "I'm anxious to start as soon as I take care of a few chores out at the farm and buy me a starter herd of horses."

"Well, I'm glad to hear it. Your mama sure is proud of you."

The hardware store owner craned his neck to look around Shane. Meggan angled her body away to keep him from getting a good look at her face. She figured she needn't bother. Within the next hour, everyone in Willow Wood would know she was the granddaughter of the woman who died at the hotel this morning and she had been here with Shane.

Social constructs dictated that Shane make introductions. Instead, he stepped closer to the counter, concealing Meggan behind him.

"How's Willow Wood, Mr. Paquette? Looks like the railroad and mining company is booming under Ellie Lundy's leadership."

The old gentleman nodded emphatically. "You can say that again, though she isn't Ellie Lundy anymore. After she married that Walsh fella from Luz-iana, the two of them made all kinds of changes. They got some contracts from the government for the railroad. Brought in all kinds of work to the area. Went and spent the money on safety improvements at the mines and increased wages."

He chuckled. "You know ol' Hershel List who owns half the company? He wasn't none too happy in the beginning, but he's come around. Miners from all over the country have come here for work. Instead of a bunch of rowdy miners running roughshod through town on the weekends, folks are moving in with their families. It's been good for all of us. Why, I'm busier than a one-armed paper hanger. Even had to hire a clerk to come in and help out on Fridays and Saturdays."

Shane rested his elbow on the counter. "That sure is good to hear. More people mean more animals so that'll be good for my business too."

The men began to chat about the advances in animal husbandry and Shane's concerns over the size of his barns. Meggan knew what he was doing. The window provided a clear view of the front of the hotel and

Endicott's General Store on the adjacent corner. If J.D. went that way, they would see him before he saw them.

Meggan edged toward the window to look at the storefronts on her side of the street. As if he knew she was looking for him, J.D. stepped out of a shop a few doors down. He opened the door of the next shop and went inside.

He was going from shop to shop. He wouldn't stop until he went through each one. Meggan turned as casually as she could to avoid attracting the hardware store owner's attention and arched her eyebrows at Shane. She cut her eyes toward the window. Shane dipped his head in understanding.

"Mr. Paquette, there are a few items I need to look for while I'm here." Without a word he wove his way down the narrow aisle toward the back of the store. Meggan followed as close behind as she could without stepping on his boot heels.

"You take all the time you need, young man. Holler if you need any help finding something. You too, young lady."

Neither Shane nor Meggan answered. The bell jangled over the door. Shane and Meggan ducked into an aisle, cluttered with barrels and dusty washtubs. Loud voices and laughter filled the store. Mr. Paquette called out a greeting.

Two men in grimy overalls strode to the cluttered counter. The door jangled again. Meggan peered between cans of lye and paint to the front of the store. This time it was J.D. Shane jerked his chin toward a small door at the back of the store she hadn't noticed before.

Mindful not to kick a washtub or knock over a display of rakes, Meggan followed him to the door. The step to the ground was a lopsided rock. She clutched the heavy satchel against her body and stepped as nimbly as she could to the ground. Shane grabbed her hand, and they ran between the two buildings.

"My horse is at the hotel livery," Shane said breathlessly as they stepped around the corner. "We'll have to get another one for you. Can you ride?"

"I haven't done it a lot, but I can handle myself."

"You'll have to."

He cut across a field to the next street. Meggan mentally calculated the cost of a horse as she hurried to keep up. She would have to cash in both train tickets to Seattle. It wasn't like she needed them anymore. That would give her enough money to survive the next few days.

She didn't know what would happen after that. When Detective Rollins took her back to Kansas City, she would need a lawyer. Or would she? She was guilty. Lawyers were for people who needed to defend themselves. There was no defense for what she'd done.

Shane barely looked at her as he pulled her along alleyways and backstreets until they reached a hill and began to climb. Meggan didn't have time to notice the homes around her, but it was obvious they were traveling through an affluent neighborhood.

Halfway up, Shane pointed to a small space between a stone wall and a large elm. "Wait here while I get you a horse."

He walked through a wide gate and disappeared between two outbuildings. Through the trees, Meggan

74

saw a manicured lawn and the back of a beautiful stone and wood house. She figured this was the Trego mansion where Shane worked with his ma. She hoped he wouldn't run into her or a stable hand with a lot of questions to which he didn't have answers.

Weariness tugged at her. She slumped to the ground and leaned against the stone wall. Gloria was gone. Alice was gone. She would never have to tell another lie. Never pick another pocket or lift another hair comb from under a salesclerk's nose.

She was free! But for how long?

Birds flitted in the branches over her head. From the bottom of the hill came the voices of townspeople. Wagons rattled along the street. She heard the distant rumble of men working in the railyard. Meggan wondered what it was like to belong to a community where people asked about your ma and missed you when you were gone. Where good men cherished their wives, and sons chose to build their lives close to home.

It wasn't long before Shane returned with a saddled horse. Meggan removed Gloria's satchel, which had been digging painfully into her neck and shoulders, and slid it into one of the saddlebags. With Shane leading the horse, they headed back down the hill to retrieve his horse from the hotel livery.

"I'll pay you for the horse as soon as I can turn in my tickets to Seattle," she told him as they mounted up.

"You don't owe for the horse. The family is allowing me to use as many as I need until I get my own herd." They rode in silence a few moments. "You shouldn't turn in your ticket anyway. I'm sure your friends in Seattle are expecting you."

"They were Granny's friends, not mine. I don't have friends. I didn't have anyone but Granny."

"I'm sorry you lost her, Meggan."

She couldn't remember the last time anyone had called her Meggan besides Alice and Gloria. She liked the sound of it on Shane's lips.

"Thank you, Shane. For everything."

He edged his horse closer to hers. "I don't need your thanks. Just the truth."

She opened her mouth to tell him she planned to answer every question he had as soon as they were in a safer place.

Shane looked past her. His eyes widened. "Looks like we've got company."

Meggan turned in her saddle. She groaned aloud. A horse was coming up on them. When the rider realized he'd been spotted, he urged his horse into a gallop. Despite the distance, Meggan knew right away who he was.

"This way," Shane shouted. Meggan leaned low over her saddle and spurred her horse forward. It jumped under her and took off after Shane.

Chapter Seven

Meggan clung to the saddle for dear life. The only time she ever spent on a horse was for recreation in parks or on well-tended trails. Never over rough, uneven terrain at breakneck speed.

She could barely see through the dust and grit churned into the air by Shane's mount. She didn't really need to see; she couldn't have controlled the horse if she wanted to. In less than a hundred yards, Shane turned his horse off the road. Meggan's horse fell in line after it with no direction from her. She settled into the rhythm of the horse, trusting Shane and the animal under her. She couldn't hear the rider behind them over the pounding hooves, but she knew J.D. had not given up and was very likely gaining on them. She dared not risk throwing herself off balance by looking over her shoulder to check.

Suddenly, the slope of the ground angled downward and the horses ran down a steep ravine. It was all Meggan could do to keep her grip on the reins and the horse's mane as it jarred and pounded into the gulley, the impact clacking her teeth together. Mercifully, the ground leveled off. She stole a glance over her shoulder toward the top of the ravine. J.D. appeared at the crest. He hesitated only a moment before starting down, though not as fast as they had.

Shane found her gaze and jerked his chin to the right. Meggan started after him, her mount picking its way through loose gravel and scrub growth. She looked around her as they went to get her bearings. The gulley led into a bottleneck canyon with a stream running through the opening. Trees grew thick along the creekbank and blocked out the sunlight.

Past the trees, huge rock cliffs loomed on either side, hemming them in. As they drew nearer, dread stirred in Meggan's chest. She prayed Shane knew what he was doing. Was there a way out of the canyon? Would they be trapped inside with no way to defend themselves.

An image of Grandma Elsie's kind face and understanding smile came to mind. Even though Grandma had been gone since Meggan was ten years old, she could still hear Grandma's sweet voice and gentle counsel urging her to pray and put her trust in God.

Advice Meggan hadn't taken much lately.

Shane slowed as the horses crossed the stream. Meggan brushed the hair and grit out of her face and thanked the Lord for getting them this far.

Ahead, she saw daylight. The horses spotted it, too, and picked up their pace. They burst out of the bottleneck and into the sunshine. A narrow meadow lay before them strewn with large boulders and natural alleyways of rock and scrubby trees. Shane turned to the right. The trail led to the end of the meadow and a short climb out of the canyon. Meggan assumed it went back to the road they'd come off. J.D. would find his way out just as easily and they'd have to escape him all over again. She needed to lose him in this canyon.

"Show me the way, Lord," she whispered.

Straight ahead, a circuitous route led into a labyrinth of boulders. Shane urged his mount into a gallop, assuming Meggan was behind him. Instead, she spurred her horse into the boulders.

She thought of Grandma Elsie's advice anytime she faced a tough spot; *"Use your head, Meggie Doodle. Don't get yourself pushed up against a wall."*

"I don't plan to, Grandma," she said aloud as she leaned over the saddle. Behind her, a horse splashed through the stream. She resisted the urge to look back.

She allowed the horse to pick its way through the rocky undergrowth at its own speed. She wanted J.D. to see her and follow her instead of going after Shane. Her only hope of escape was losing him among the boulders. He was too good a horseman and too tenacious for her to leave him behind in the open.

Several natural passages fanned out before her. She chose the narrowest. If she could get through, J.D. would, too, but she hoped it would slow him down enough until she figured out a way of losing him.

His horse was moving faster. He wasn't taking precautions for his mount's safety. She urged her horse as fast as she dared through several narrow twists and turns.

The rock walls amplified the sound. Meggan imagined J.D. right behind her though she couldn't see for sure.

She had nearly passed a narrow dogleg passage concealed by growth and overhang when she spotted it out of the corner of her eye. She ducked under decades-old branches and brambles and slipped into it. The horse's shoulders barely squeezed through. Prickly brambles clawed at Meggan's skirt. She ignored a limb that lashed at her face and knocked her hat loose. She urged the horse through. There was no room to turn back even if she wanted to; she only hoped she and the horse didn't become stuck.

The passage took a sharp right before opening into the meadow Shane had crossed moments before. She sat up in the saddle and looked behind her. The growth closed back over the opening, concealing it again for another decade unless one knew exactly where to look.

She heard J.D.'s horse pounding up the mountain face, but it sounded farther away. He must've missed the dogleg. In the distance she saw Shane. She spurred her horse forward and caught up with him just as he reached the crest above the meadow.

They stopped and looked down into the canyon. "Smart move," he said. "How did you even see that passageway?"

"I almost didn't. I hope it will take J.D. a while to realize he lost me."

"It'll take the rest of the day," Shane assured her. "Those passages keep getting narrower and narrower as they go up, and there's no place to turn around. He'll have to follow the trail all the way to the top over there."

Meggan's gaze followed his pointing finger to a densely forested ridge.

"He can't see us from up there, and he'll have no idea which way you went." Shane stared at her for a long moment. "You took quite a chance leading him into that maze. A hundred things could've gone wrong."

She nodded solemnly. "I knew I'd find a way out. I'm pretty good at losing myself in a crowd."

She knew her response raised more questions than it answered, but she couldn't explain now. He would be better off if she never did.

Ignoring his stare, she turned her horse down the mountain toward the road. Once they reached it, they slowed the horses to an easy trot for the next mile before turning off the road again.

After another twenty minutes of riding, they rode into a deserted barnyard. Shadows lengthened. The heat of the day had passed. The horses snorted and lifted their heads, ready for a break. A huge timber and stone barn loomed ahead. A smaller barn sat to the left. A large two-story house was on the right, nearly hidden in the shadows of a wall of ponderosa pines. Several outbuildings were scattered around the property. Fences had been bleached from the sun and wind but looked sturdy.

The place looked like the owner had stepped away and never came back.

"Is this your farm?"

Shane seemed to expand in the saddle. He looked around as if seeing the place for the first time the same as her. "This is it. I've only seen it a few times since I bought it two years ago while I was home from school. I have a lot of exploring to do before I set up my practice. We're actually not far from Willow Wood even though it took half the day to get here."

He pointed out the multiple paddocks and holding pens. "This place is perfect for what I have in mind. The previous owner raised thoroughbred horses for folks back East."

Meggan nodded in appreciation as she looked around. "You couldn't have found a better place to begin your practice."

Shane fixed his steady gaze on her for a long moment as if looking for sincerity. Meggan braced for another round of questions. Instead, he turned his horse toward the larger barn where they dismounted and led the horses into a stall.

"Could you get them some hay while I get the water from the well?" he asked.

Meggan took a pitchfork from along the wall and went to a fresh pile of hay in the center of the barn. She'd never handled a pitchfork before. By the time she reached the manger, two-thirds of each forkful lay scattered on the barn floor.

Shane came inside and dumped two pails of water in the trough. He motioned to a wheelbarrow farther down the wall. "Feel free to use that and save yourself the trips back and forth."

Meggan sniffed. "That would make things easier."

Shane grinned. His brown eyes warmed with flecks of gold. Heat rushed to her cheeks as she remembered his kiss, his soft lips on hers.

She spun around and hurried to the wheelbarrow. She had no right thinking about that. He'd only kissed her because she forced herself on him. She had used him to shield herself from J.D. Duggar. She didn't know much about men, but she figured they didn't appreciate being used, even if it did involve kissing.

After filling the wheelbarrow once, the horses had plenty to eat. She dried her hands on her skirt. "This place looks deserted. How is there fresh hay and a primed pump?" she asked when Shane came inside with the last load of water.

"My mother and the Tregos knew I was coming home this week. Belinda's husband Carl came out the other day to stock the place for me. We can't stay here long. It's not difficult to track two fast-moving horses through these woods if you know what you're doing. I expect your friend knows what he's doing."

"He's not my friend," Meggan declared.

Shane's brown eyes flashed. "Then who is he and why did he kill your granny?"

The moment had come; time to tell him exactly what he faced by helping her. She prayed he wouldn't walk away once he found out. "Is there any food in the house?"

Shane looked taken aback for a moment. "I'm sure there is."

"Good." She headed out of the barn, giving him no choice but to follow. "I'll fix us something to eat and tell you everything I can."

Chapter Eight

As Shane followed Meggan out of the barn and across the yard, he tamped down his impatience. He wanted to tell her she was going to have to do a lot better than telling him what she could. He wasn't taking a step off this property until she told him *everything*.

Inside the house, Meggan went straight to the kitchen and began sorting through the jars of food Carl had left in the larder. There were enough staples to last Shane about a week of ordinary living. However, nothing about this situation was ordinary.

He moved from window to window with his gun at the ready, watching every possible approach while Meggan prepared a simple meal. Though he was confident they had lost their pursuer in the mountains, he couldn't count on more than a few hours respite. Satisfied they were safe for a while, he holstered his gun and went to the table.

Meggan looked up at him as she finished pouring peaches from a jar onto a plate. "We should eat everything cold, so no one will smell our woodsmoke."

He nodded in agreement. This woman didn't cease to amaze him. She was more than a pretty face; he just wasn't sure what.

It was apparent she was afraid of the man on the chestnut horse. Despite her fear, she had proven her ingenuity by drawing him into the passageway where he had no choice but follow it to the end. Shane knew the canyon nearly as well as the back of his hand, and he hadn't remembered the dogleg passage that allowed Meggan to escape.

She set the plates on the long table where she had set out other jars of food. "I've never seen a table or stove this big outside of a school or hospital. Everything about this house is big."

Shane pulled out a chair in front of one of the plates and poured a healthy serving of cooked meat that had probably been prepared by his mother. "The family that built it had twelve children."

"Twelve! I can't imagine."

"It's pretty common in this part of the country. Everywhere, I expect."

Her smile faded as her thoughts turned inward. Shane was tired and frazzled with a lot of work still ahead of him if he was going to keep them safe during the night. He didn't have time to soothe her fear and grief, especially when she hadn't exactly been forthright thus far. He offered a quick blessing over the food, adding a prayer for safety, and went to the window where he could watch the trail they'd rode in on.

Meggan stayed at the gargantuan table that must've served thousands of meals to a dozen hungry children through the years. Strands of ebony hair hung loose around her face. Her straw hat with the pretty blue ribbon that brightened her cheeks was gone. She must've lost it while running through the narrow passage. A bloody scratch and smudge of dirt marred her chin. Scratches from branches and brambles were scattered across her forearms and the backs of her hands. She frowned as she focused on her plate. Shane considered saying something to encourage her, words of assurance that everything would be all right. He would do whatever it took to protect her against whoever was after her.

Instead, he perched on the windowsill and began to eat. He wouldn't be distracted, no matter how needy or despondent she looked.

"Tell me about this Duggar. How did you and your grandmother get mixed up with him?"

Meggan swallowed a bite of peaches with difficulty. "It's a long story."

He narrowed his eyes. "I got time."

She stirred some cooked carrots into the meat on her plate. "Granny didn't show you, but J.D.'s Wanted poster was in her scrapbook too. He was wanted everywhere from Tennessee to Missouri to Arizona. There was a big price on his head. Until Granny and Alice turned him in for the reward."

Shane nearly fell out of the windowsill. "Reward? How did they—? What did you—? Who's Alice?"

Meggan looked amused by his stammering questions. "Alice was Granny's—I mean, Gloria's sister. I lived with both of them until Alice passed away last year."

He waved aside the answer. "Okay, let's get back to Duggar. How did they turn in somebody like him for a reward?"

It took a moment for her to formulate her answer. "They are—they were bounty hunters."

"Bounty hunters?" He shook his head in disbelief. "Is that why Gloria carried the scrapbook? Were all those men her captures?"

"Oh, no. I guess you could say it was her wish journal. Every time she and Alice found a new Wanted poster, they imagined tracking down the culprit, even those in Canada or Mexico. They didn't particularly care about justice. They loved the excitement and spoils of the capture. Even after Alice died, Gloria kept dreaming. I don't think she ever would've given it up."

Shane still couldn't imagine the sweet little grandmotherly lady from the stage hunting down criminals for a living. "She must've known it was dangerous. That she could get herself—" He stopped talking just in time.

Meggan nodded solemnly. "Not all criminals on Wanted posters are like J.D. Duggar. Most were bail jumpers or had been convicted of nonviolent crimes like insurance fraud. That's how she and Alice got started. Even with the lesser crimes, the payouts were much greater than…picking pockets and petty theft."

Shane set his empty plate on the table. "What do you mean, picking pockets?"

"I mean exactly what you think I mean." She lifted her chin. "That was our trade. As you already figured out, Gloria wasn't my granny. My real grandmother died when I was a girl. I didn't have any parents. The Hennessey sisters lived in our building. They took me in after Grandma Elsie died.

"They recognized my—potential and taught me how to take a watch out of a man's pocket without him noticing I was there. I got very good at it." She gave him a challenging look. "No one suspected two old ladies and a little girl of anything. We did very well. Then Gloria and Alice discovered bounty hunting and realized that was where the money was."

"But bounty hunting? It's a wonder they didn't get their skulls smashed in the first day. I'm sorry. I shouldn't have said that. I've just never heard the like."

"It was dangerous. And ill-conceived. They relied on wit and cunning rather than brute strength. You saw for yourself how good Gloria was at gaining a person' s confidence. One sister would lower the guard of their target. She'd bake him a pie or ply him with coffee and listen to his down-on-his-luck story while the other gathered the evidence and went for the constable.

"They didn't usually involve me in those capers. Mostly because they didn't trust me. My involvement was usually as lookout or distraction. Before they met Mr. Duggar, they tracked down a man who had shot his brother-in-law. Even in that case, the man wasn't much of a threat. He swore he only shot the brother-in-law in self-defense. The reward was bigger than anything Alice and Gloria had gotten from insurance scams. It was enough to whet their appetites for bigger game.

"They became obsessed with finding a big payout so they would never have to worry about money again. I knew they would never be satisfied, no matter how much money they got. They were as greedy as the day was long. Then they heard about a jewelry store robbery where the owner had been shot and killed. It was in all the newspapers all over Missouri. A few lucky breaks, and they found the thief. He was arrested, and they got the reward money. But it wasn't enough. It was never enough."

Shane had never heard such a story in his life. He forgot about watching out the window and sat down across from her "If he was arrested, what's he doing here?"

"I guess he broke out of prison. He's done it before."

"What did you mean by the reward money not being enough?"

Meggan studied her plate for a moment. "Before his arrest, Alice and Gloria found the jewels that had been stolen in the robbery. Then Alice caught pneumonia last winter and died, leaving Gloria to find a buyer."

"In Seattle?"

"The connection is in Seattle. The buyer is in Asia. China, I think. I don't really know. I try not to learn many of the details."

"So Duggar broke into your suite to find his jewels?"

"Not his. Mrs. Gochberg's, the jeweler's widow."

"He must not have found them if he's still after you."

"You're right, he didn't." She put her hand to her throat and withdrew a slim leather thong with a velvet pouch attached. His eyes widened.

"The jewels?"

"After I found Granny this morning—Gloria, I knew what the killer was after. I wasn't sure it was J.D. until I saw him on the street. That's why I couldn't tell the sheriff. Gloria and I are in possession of stolen property with the intent of selling it. He'd throw me in jail until someone from Kansas City came to collect me and the jewels. Then I'd be—" A shiver passed through her. "J.D. would break into the jail the first night and murder whoever was guarding me and the jewels. He'd get what he wanted, and Mrs. Gochberg would never get her property back."

Shane stared into her startling green eyes, trying to absorb the gravity of the situation. "If he catches you—us—he'll kill us and take the jewels and that lady still won't have her property."

She nodded gravely. "I know. I'm sorry I got you into this. I wouldn't blame you if you left now and went straight for the sheriff. I'm as guilty as Alice and Gloria. I didn't stop them from taking the jewels and I didn't turn them into Detective Rollins when I had the chance. Now Granny's dead and J.D.'s not about to give up until he gets what he came for."

Shane got up and stalked back to the window. He looked out at the gathering darkness, though he couldn't see much past where the lane met the road. When he turned back to Meggan, she had slipped the pouch of jewels back inside her dress.

"We need to get moving," he said. "Pack as much food as will fit in the saddlebags. I'll go upstairs and gather some bedding."

She jumped to her feet. "Where are we going?"

The pitch in her voice betrayed her fear. He didn't know her at all. Every word out of her mouth could be a lie, though her story explained the man chasing them through the canyon. Or she could be close to breaking down. He imagined most people in her shoes would've done so by now. He didn't know how he'd handle it if she did.

"There are natural cave systems all around and under these parts. It's what created the mining industry. About a mile down the road is an abandoned mine. The entrance is nearly overgrown, and it's pretty much forgotten by everyone but us local boys who used to play in the caves. If we can get inside, we could hide forever."

She shivered. "In a cave?"

"It's not as bad as it sounds. The mines are well dug and stable. Some of them are downright hospitable. The miners created air shafts and separate rooms where they could easily work twelve and twenty-hour shifts. We boys never had a mishap in there except for the time Jimmy Hanson, the clerk at the hotel, got lost for a night. We found him by morning. Our parents never got wind of it, so no real harm was done."

All the color had drained from Meggan's face. "Are you sure there's ample air down there? And light?"

"Well, now, there's no light. It is a mine."

She dropped back into her chair. "A mine. I'd almost rather face—" She shook her head. "No, you're right. We have no choice. What will we do with the horses? Will they go in with us?"

"The openings aren't big enough for that. If they were, Duggar wouldn't have much trouble following us."

"I suppose not." She went to the cupboard and began pulling dishtowels and cleaning rags out of the drawers. Her hands shook as she wrapped a jar in an old feed sack.

Shane wanted to go to her and comfort her. He wanted to take her in his arms and assure her everything would be all right. But he wasn't sure it would be.

Chapter Nine

S hadows lengthened over the horse's head. Meggan followed Shane along a wood-lined trail in the deepening gloom. She tried to focus on the sounds of the night animals coming out to feed and not on where she and Shane were going.

An abandoned mine. A dark, airless hole in the ground.

She shuddered every time she thought about it. What if Shane was wrong? What if he was misremembering? What if he was leading her to the wrong one, and they became trapped with no way out and slowly suffocated as the oxygen was used up?

Resolute, she pushed her fear and dread aside. J.D. was out there. He hadn't given up just because she'd lost him in the canyon. He would never give up. Meggan couldn't either. No matter the risk, she had to get the stolen jewels back to Mr. Gochberg's family. She had to trust Shane's plan and thank God he was willing to help her.

Eventually she heard rushing water. A little further along the trail, she saw the rising moon reflecting off it. She had no idea how far they were from Shane's farm or from Willow Wood. Worse, she had no idea where J.D. was.

Without a word, Shane dismounted and took his horse's reins. Meggan followed suit. They led the animals through the trees down a slope to the water. The slope was steeper than Meggan expected. Several times she had to tighten her grasp on the bridle to keep from falling.

The trees grew close together at the water's edge, blocking out the last light of the summer evening. Shane walked about twenty yards to a large outcropping.

"We'll stake the horses here where they'll have shelter and water."

Meggan looked around as he worked. "Where's the mine entrance?"

"Not here. We'll have to climb up to the road and go on a little ways to reach it. The horses would leave too much of a trail for Duggar to follow"

A gentle breeze blowing across the water provided a nice respite from the day's heat. Meggan shivered and rubbed her arms, though she knew it was more from nerves and not the falling temperatures. "Do you think you'll have any trouble finding it in the dark?"

"I sure hope not."

He cut a few sapling branches and propped them alongside the horses. Meggan figured it was to make them harder to spot if J.D. came this way.

"Why didn't we leave the horses in the barn?" she asked.

Shane didn't look up from his work. "Too far. Better to have them close."

Meggan didn't ask more questions. All she could hope for was staying one step ahead of the man who had killed Gloria until Detective Rollins arrived from Kansas City.

When Shane was satisfied the horses were secured for the night, they filled their canteens, shouldered the saddlebags, and headed back the way they came. Meggan slipped and slid to the top of the bank. She didn't see anything that looked like a mine opening and wondered anew if Shane knew where he was going. It was now nearly full dark. He admitted he hadn't been out here in years. Even in broad daylight, an overgrown, abandoned mine opening would be hard to find.

She shouldn't have to worry about J.D. tonight. Just cave-ins. Lack of oxygen. Going down the wrong tunnel. Starvation.

If something happened to her in the mine, no one would ever know. Or care. There was no one to launch a search. No one to realize she was missing, except maybe the hotel staff when they tried to decide what to do with her things. No one else in the world cared one stitch about her.

Except Shane.

Meggan stared at his back. He cared. Maybe not more than he would any other person in her shoes. But he was here. He had willingly gone to all this trouble. His interest might not have anything to do with her. He seemed like a man of integrity who would want to see justice for Gloria and the Gochberg family. She suspected there was more to it than that. She had seen it in his eyes. She had felt it in the way he returned her kiss.

A flutter stirred in her stomach at the thought of his strong arms around her. Her face warmed in the darkness. She was glad he couldn't see. She sighed at the memory.

Shane looked over his shoulder at her. "You say something?"

"No, I...I think I tripped over something."

He stopped and faced her. She nearly ran into him. He reached for the saddlebag. "Here, let me carry this for you."

She turned her shoulder out of reach. He was already carrying the lion's share of the supplies. "Honestly, I'm fine. Is it much farther?"

"No, we're nearly there." He began walking again. The knot in Meggan's stomach grew, and not only from the memory of Shane's kiss. Did they have enough water? It wouldn't be hard for Shane to get turned around and wander for hours before he realized they were lost. How long would two canteens of water sustain them in the depths of the earth?

"Please, God, help Shane remember," she prayed under her breath. "And help me not panic and cause him more problems."

Shane stopped walking. The half-moon didn't provide much light, especially under the thick trees. Meggan couldn't see anything but skinny saplings and a thick wall of earth. Shane slid his supplies to the ground and removed a hatchet from one of the saddlebags. He chopped at a few small trees. He kicked others aside as he moved along the face of a rock as tall as his hips.

He moved a few feet along the rock face, cutting and hacking as he went. Finally, he stopped and pushed aside a huge rock. He yanked a young tree out of the way to expose a sliver of an opening, just big enough for them to squeak through.

Shane's face shone with accomplishment in the darkness. "I knew it was here," he said in a loud whisper. "The smaller the opening, the easier to stay hidden. You'll see it opens up once we get inside."

Meggan nodded, though he had already looked away to gather the supplies he'd set down. She couldn't speak. Her tongue was glued to the roof of her mouth. She wouldn't endanger him more than she already had by giving in to her mounting fear. She had to trust his plan. And God to keep them safe.

Shane lit the lantern he had brought from the house. He handed her a bundle of dried sticks he had gathered for a fire and shouldered the saddlebags. He tucked a few larger limbs under his arm and entered the mine.

Meggan folded her body nearly in half and turned sideways to fit through the opening with the armload of sticks. She slithered inside. Light flickered off the uneven walls, looking like hands reaching out to grab her. She straightened and took a few deep breaths, praying the whole time. Shane gave her an encouraging smile. Her heart filled at the warmth and strength in his eyes.

Both their hands were full. She managed to uncurl a fingertip from around the bundle of sticks and brush his arm. He lowered the lantern and looked at her. Meggan wanted to thank him. She wanted to tell him she was sorry for putting him in this position. She wanted to ask why he was doing this for her, a complete stranger. Instead, she stared into his brown eyes, hoping her look said it all.

His gaze dropped to her mouth. She could tell right away what he was thinking because she was thinking the same thing. She wanted to drop everything in her arms and rush to him. She wanted to cry for Gloria. Cry that she hadn't taken the time to know the woman better. Cry that she was completely alone and had no idea what she was going to do beyond surviving the night in this cavern. Cry that she didn't have someone like Shane to love and protect her and grow old with her.

Shane seemed to be battling his own inner thoughts. He exhaled loud enough for her to hear and stepped away.

"Put your back against the wall. It'll help you keep your bearings. We have light now, but we can't count on it."

Meggan's heart lurched at the suggestion. It took all her resolve not to run back outside into the open air. She didn't want to think about losing her bearing. Or the light.

Following Shane's instructions, she put her back against the wall. She kept her arm against his. If the kerosene lamp went out, she wasn't about to lose contact with Shane.

"We'll take ten sliding steps along the wall and then a right turn," he said. "Twelve more steps and another right turn. Keep count. Don't forget that if we have to find our way out of here in the dark, we'll be moving in the opposite direction."

Meggan nodded as she slid along the wall. She focused on the number and length of her steps, and not becoming trapped in the pitch black.

Shane kept up his litany of instructions, seemingly unaware of her near panic, or maybe because of it. "When we turn the next corner, you'll feel a draft from the ventilation shaft in the chamber where we'll spend the night. Keep against me and don't move away."

He needn't worry about that.

"Feel the air?" he asked after another turn. "We'll walk directly across this floor to the chamber. Our light will be concealed from the turns we made. Even if Duggar found the opening we came through, he won't see our light. Once we get to the chamber, we'll build a fire so we can save the kerosene in the lantern. The ventilation shaft will make us able to sleep without worrying about the fire using up our oxygen."

She hadn't worried about that until he brought it up.

The flame in the lantern danced, announcing they had reached the chamber with the ventilation shaft. Meggan felt like dancing herself as fresh night air washed over her. She dropped her pile of sticks and brush in the middle of the floor. It, along with Shane's small pile, didn't look like enough fuel to last the night. Perhaps he knew where to find more inside the cavern. If the fire went out and the lantern ran out of kerosene, Meggan didn't know if her faith was strong enough to bear it. She prayed again, imagining Jesus sitting in the mine with them. The Bible said he was a friend who stuck closer than a brother. She would rest in that promise tonight.

As Shane built up the small fire, Meggan looked around the small chamber. Several narrow tunnels snaked into the darkness. The ceiling—the part of the cave that gave her the most concern—was supported with crossbeams that appeared to have been there for years.

99

"Please, God, don't let them fall in on us," she prayed.

Shane finished with the fire and slapped his hands together. "Did you say something?"

"I was wondering if there's another way out if we need it?"

He pointed vaguely to one of the tunnels. "Farther along that way, but I hope we don't have to try to find it. I was in here exploring with a buddy once and we stumbled across it purely by chance."

Meggan grimaced. She refused to think on it. She wouldn't think on anything pertaining to the darkness pressing in on them from every side. In the shadows, she found a wooden stump and wrestled it to the middle of the floor. She set out the jars of food they'd brought to keep them from getting broken in the night should they lose the light.

Shane took a few steps down one of the tunnels looking for more firewood. Meggan fought down the bubble of panic in her throat every time he moved into the shadows, even though she could clearly hear him moving around. Sound moved easily inside the cave. If J.D. found the entrance, he could follow the sound of their voices straight to them. But anyone outside of the cave wouldn't hear her if she screamed at the top of her lungs unless she was directly under the ventilation shaft.

By the time she arranged the bedrolls side by side—inappropriate to be sure, but she wanted Shane within arms' reach at all times—he reentered the chamber with an armload of ashy remnants of wood. "This'll heat up the place nicely."

He dumped the wood next to the fire and sat beside her on a bedroll. She poured half the contents from one of the jars onto a metal plate and handed it to him. She hadn't realized until this moment she was ravenous. She hadn't eaten breakfast this morning, and their meal at the ranch had long been worked off.

She settled next to Shane with her plate. Once she was able to forget her surroundings, it wasn't so bad sitting here. She'd never spent much time with anyone other than Gloria or Alice. They kept her isolated, virtually an observer of life rather than a participant. She wondered how she would learn to live any other way.

"Tell me why you wanted to get into animal husbandry?" she asked as they began to eat.

"Ma and I have been on our own for nearly as long as I can remember," Shane said after thinking on it. "When Pa died, the Trego family promoted her to housekeeper and insisted they needed her to move into the house. Ma knew it was charity on their part since she had a six-year-old boy to raise."

He seemed happy to talk. Meggan wasn't sure if he hoped to distract her from the darkness around them, or if it unnerved him more than he let on.

"Mr. Trego was alive back then. He was a great man. Took me under his wing, I guess you'd say. He let me trail him sometimes around the factory in Willow Wood. What I really loved, though, was when he gave me jobs in the family stables working with the other men. They were harder on me than Mr. Trego. I got under their feet and talked too much. I learned quick enough to shut up and learn by watching rather than peppering them with aggravating questions.

"I ran errands for the family at home and around the factory floor. I came into contact with men who had no patience for kids or animals. I saw a lot of abuse toward both. Men who'd rather beat a thing into submission than take the time to teach it how to follow instruction."

He took a bite and chewed in silence. Meggan waited, absorbed in her own thoughts. She had seen much of the same thing growing up. She had seen children slapped to the ground for not getting out of someone's way fast enough. She'd once seen a man beat a mangy dog to death with a piece of wood for going after a hunk of bread that had fallen off his grocer's cart. She'd had nightmares for a month.

"Many people are completely ignorant of how to treat an animal or train it to reach its potential," Shane went on. "I thought if I could treat a sick or injured animal, I could train the owner at the same time on how best to get what he wanted out of his animal without getting mad and beating it."

Meggan stared down at her hands, fighting back unexpected tears. She had no idea there were men like Shane Casey in the world. Maybe there weren't. Maybe she had just caught Shane on a good day.

He stared into the fire as he ate the last of the food. He shoved his napkin into the empty jar and closed the lid over it. "Eat every bite," he told her. "We don't want to leave a crumb to attract rats."

Meggan nearly jumped off her bedroll. Rats. She had heard scuffling along the walls since they entered, but she had been too consumed by her fear of the darkness to worry about vermin. The rats' presence meant ventilation and ways in and out of the mine shafts. Her skin crawled nonetheless. She quickly finished every bite of food around her dry throat and stuffed the napkin in the other jar.

When she lay back to sleep, she tightened the bedroll like a cocoon around every inch of her body, even her face. Shane's breathing immediately lengthened into sleep. Meggan's eyes remained wide open, staring at the light through the blanket, alternately imagining rats scurrying across her body or the cave roof crashing in on them.

Certain she would never fall asleep, she did anyway. She jerked awake. Her lungs were filled with smoke. She sat up and tore the blanket from her face. She coughed and blinked through the haze of smoke. Shane was kicking free of his blankets beside her.

"Get up," he said in a harsh whisper. "The ventilation hole's been plugged. If we don't get out of here, the smoke'll kill us before Duggar has a chance."

Chapter Ten

Meggan kicked the blankets free and scrambled to her feet, nearly falling into the glowing coals from the fire. Shane kicked the ashes over the dying flames to extinguish most of the light.

Meggan clutched at his arm. "I can't see."

"We don't have a choice. The fire will eat up our oxygen."

In the dim light from the remaining coals, she could barely make out Shane's shape. She clung tighter to his arm "What's happened?"

"Duggar must've smelled our smoke."

"Maybe a tree fell over the opening."

He put a hand over hers. "It's plugged too tight. Could only have been done by a man."

Meggan wanted to cry. Would this never end! She covered her nose and mouth with her sleeve. She wouldn't give it to the fear. "What do we do now?"

"Just because he knows we're in here doesn't mean he's found the opening. We'll have to find another way out. Grab your saddlebag and let's get moving."

"Another way? You said you couldn't remember it."

Shane gripped her elbows and pulled her against him. "We don't have a choice, Meggan. It'll be dawn soon and he'll find where we came in if he hasn't already. Even if he doesn't, we need fresh air. Are you with me?"

Meggan put her head against his chest and nodded. He wrapped his arms around her and held her for a brief instant. She reveled in the warmth of his broad chest. She didn't want to pull away. Not ever.

He released her too soon. She dropped to her knees and fumbled for the saddlebag. She removed the satchel and hung it across her body. She couldn't risk losing it. She put her hand to her chest to make sure the pouch of jewels was still in place.

When she got to her feet, Shane turned toward one of the tunnels. The light from the embers offered enough light for her to know they were on their way out of the chamber. She stiffened her legs. "I can't."

He leaned close to whisper in her ear. His breath was warm and comforting on her cheek. "We have to find the entrance I told you about. It's narrow and much more difficult to navigate, but it's our only way out."

She put her hand over her mouth to muffle a cough. Smoke seared her eyes. She blinked furiously, too scared to cry. "We can't. It's been too long. What if it's not

105

where you think it is? What if you take a wrong turn? I can't do it. I can't get lost in here. Please."

Shane's saddlebag slid back to the floor of the cavern. He grabbed her face between both hands and kissed her. Meggan's breath caught in her throat. Her heart slammed in her chest. For the briefest of moments, she forgot the air clogged with smoke and her terror and the pressing darkness.

Shane broke the kiss but kept his nose against hers and his warm hands on her face. "We can't stay here, Meggan," he whispered, his breath soft on her face. "If we don't get fresh air, you won't have to worry about getting those jewels back to Kansas City."

Fear tightened its death grip around her again, but the need for oxygen was stronger. Shane rested his cheek against hers. She burrowed her nose into the hollow of his neck and breathed as deeply as she could.

"I'll get you out of here," he whispered into her ear. "You have to trust me. All right?"

Peace washed over her, temporarily easing the pain in her throat. She wasn't sure why, but she did trust him. Maybe because God had put him in her life when He knew she would need someone. She had already prayed for Shane to remember the way through the cavern. She needed to have faith God had heard her. She nodded against his throat and pulled away.

He let go of her and stood still in the center of the room concentrating. Meggan tried to still her pounding heart. She couldn't find her way out of the intersecting mineshafts if it had been full light.

Shane looped his saddlebag around his neck to keep one hand free. Meggan followed suit.

"Put your left hand on the wall and your right hand on my belt. Don't let go of either, no matter what. And please, don't speak. I need to count steps. It'd be good if you counted too. I don't want to get turned around in here, but it can happen easily enough."

Meggan did as directed. All she could think to pray was; "Jesus. Jesus. Jesus." as they stepped deeper into the darkness. By the second turn, the light from the fire was completely gone. The lantern didn't do much to illuminate the space around them, but it held the pressing blackness at bay.

How did miners work like this? How did Shane keep moving forward with no belt to hold onto?

She feared she would choke on the panic. Smoke still filled the cavern, though not as bad now that they were a few turns from the fire. She knew the greedy coals would soak up the oxygen no matter how far they went. She thought about screaming just so J.D. could find her and rescue her from this godforsaken place. She couldn't imagine a fate worse than the oppressive darkness and the thought that she would never see the sky or breathe fresh air again.

Shane stopped. Meggan's toes banged against the back of his boots, and she nearly lost her hold on his belt. The number of steps she had counted flew out of her head. Oh, no. Was it one hundred? One hundred and ten? She had no idea. They would never get out of here, and it would be her fault.

Shane put his hand over hers and squeezed gently. She sagged against him and nearly gave in to the sobs waiting to burst out of her sore throat.

"What's happening?" she whispered to the back of his head.

"Move with me."

His hand still covering hers, he squatted. Meggan kept her left hand on the cavern wall as she did the same.

Cool air stirred the wisps of hair brushing against her face and soothed her singed throat. She breathed in a delicious mouthful. Were they nearly free? She wanted to ask if it meant what she thought it did, but she dared not speak and make him lose count of his steps the way she had.

Shane started forward at a squat. Meggan clung to his belt and followed. She stepped on her skirts and heard a loud tearing of fabric. She didn't dare let go of Shane's belt to free the fabric. She kept moving blindly toward fresh air.

Shane stopped in a narrow passageway. Meggan's hand on the wall was now nearly against her shoulder. Without reaching up to investigate, she sensed the ceiling only a few inches above her head.

"We have to put out the light," he said.

"What?" she shrieked, forgetting to check her voice.

"We're going to have to crawl, and I can't do that while holding a lantern. We can't leave it lit either or it'll lead Duggar straight to us."

"Then we'll go back," she said in a harsh whisper. "We'll find another way. This one's too small. We won't fit." Panic laced her voice. She tried to take a calming breath. She tried to pray. All she wanted to do was scream.

"Meggan, can't you feel the air? I don't know of any other way. There might not be another one."

She wanted to reach into the darkness to feel his face. His lips. His eyes. Just to know he was real, and she wasn't alone. She didn't. She was too afraid to let go of the wall or his belt and lose all sense of where she was. "It's too small," she repeated. "What if you're wrong? What if it doesn't lead anywhere? What if—"

"Meggan." The reprimand was sharp. "I told you to trust me. I've been through this passage before. I didn't get stuck, and you won't either."

She wanted to remind him he was a boy then. A boy without a saddlebag around his neck. The passage could've caved in. Trees on the other side could obstruct the opening. What if he got stuck or injured and she had to go back without him?

A noise sounded behind them. It was too loud for a rat or small animal. Her waffling was costing them valuable time. Without Shane, she would probably already be dead, and J.D. Duggar would have made off with Mrs. Gochberg's jewels. She owed it to all of them to get out of this wretched place.

"Do you trust me?" he hissed.

She breathed in the fresh air. "Yes."

His hand touched her face and slid down her cheek. Warm lips brushed hers. Meggan wanted to sink into them. Before she could react, he pulled away. The shadow of his hand wrapped around the dial on the lantern. The light shrank and disappeared. Blackness enveloped them. Fear clogged Meggan's throat. She blinked several times, half expecting the light to be on each time she opened her eyes. It wasn't.

Shane stretched forward and got onto his hands and knees. Meggan lost her grip on his belt. She found the heel of his boot in the blackness and crawled after him.

After a few moments of crawling, Shane dropped to his stomach. Meggan didn't react quickly enough. Her forehead smacked soundly into the ceiling of the tunnel.

"We're almost there," he said ahead of her. "You'll see daylight soon."

Meggan fell to her stomach. The tunnel continued to narrow. She couldn't hear if J.D. was in the depths of the mine behind them over the sounds of her own panting and her body scraping the walls of the tunnel. She had no idea how Shane managed to keep moving forward when she barely fit.

Suddenly, the walls spread out, and she was able to get onto her knees, though she had to keep her head down to avoid the ceiling. Just when she was about to ask again how much farther, light permeated the darkness. She could see the sides of the tunnel and Shane's hips moving in front of her. She let go of his boot and crawled faster toward the gray light.

She got to her feet in a crouched position and watched as Shane hacked with his hatchet at saplings and overgrowth that blocked their exit. He turned his body so his head was facing her and kicked the last of them aside. He crawled out and reached back in to take her hand.

Meggan gulped in the fresh air as she burst out of the hole. She collapsed in a heap on the grass and coughed so hard her ribs ached. Shane pressed a canteen into her hands. She drank greedily until her raw throat was sated. Shane stood over her, his face red from coughing too.

Meggan got to her feet. "I'm sorry." She held out the canteen.

He shook his head at her apology and lifted the other canteen in his hand.

Dawn brightened the sky around them, though a few hours of darkness remained. Meggan didn't hear sounds of horses or a possible partner watching for their escape. If J.D. heard them crashing through the opening, she wondered if he could tell from where the sound had come. She hoped not.

Shane knelt in front of the cave opening and began to cover it back with brush and debris. By the time he finished, Meggan could barely tell where they had broken out. She knew the inside was now as black as pitch again. She almost felt sorry for J.D. trapped in the blackness alone.

Almost.

Chapter Eleven

Shane was never so glad to feel fresh air on his skin. The only things that kept him anchored inside the labyrinth of tunnels were knowing Meggan was about to lose control and God's grace. Had he been alone, he might've panicked himself and not been able to find the tunnel that led out of the mine.

He took a deep breath and swallowed a mouthful of water to avoid another fit of coughing. He hoped Duggar was lost inside the mine and wouldn't hear them, but he couldn't count on it. Now that the ventilation shaft was stopped up, the killer couldn't breathe in there any better than they could. He would be forced to go out the way he went in and wait. Unless he got turned around and never found his way out. Shane figured Duggar was too resourceful for that. If the man were lost in the mine, he wouldn't stay that way for long.

Daylight whispered across the sky by the time they broke out of the trees. Shane lowered his shoulders and led Meggan across a small clearing to another row of trees and the stream in case Duggar was above ground and watching for them. He hadn't realized how far they had traveled through the tunnels until he saw how far they had to backtrack to get to the horses.

The horses dozed under the outcropping without a care. Meggan ran to her mount, threw her arms around its neck, and kissed the horse's long face. Shane laughed, relieved she still had a sense of humor after everything they'd been through.

She faced him with a mock glare. "Don't laugh. I'd kiss the ground if my legs weren't shaking so hard, I don't think I can."

Shane wanted to ask if she had a kiss for him too. Suddenly, he could think of little else. His gaze caressed her face. The curve of her flushed cheeks. The slope of her forehead. The long dark eyelashes framing her shimmering green eyes. And finally, her full red lips that seemed to beckon to him.

Meggan sobered and quickly turned away. Was she thinking the same thing about him? She slung her saddlebag over the horse and went to the edge of the stream. She knelt and began scrubbing her hands and face in the fast-moving water. Shane removed his hat and joined her. The water was bracing in the early morning chill and took his breath, but it never felt better.

She moved a few feet away and turned her back to him. She began removing the pins from her hair. Shane marveled at the rich tumble of ebony waves spilling down her back. He would like nothing more than to sit and

113

watch her comb her wet fingers through her hair and pin it back into place, but even in his limited experience with women, he knew she'd be more comfortable if he didn't.

He set his Stetson on his head and went back to the horses. He drew a jar out of one of the saddlebags. Miraculously, it hadn't broken during his belly-crawl through the tunnel. Meggan was seated on a fallen log securing the last of the pins in her hair. Shane pried the lid off the jar with the tip of his knife, speared a pale pear, and offered it to her.

Her dark eyes lit up.

"Ah, breakfast." She took the slippery fruit off the end of the knife and held it carefully so she wouldn't lose it to the ground.

Shane chuckled and dropped down beside her. He hated to admit it, but his knees were a little wobbly at the memory of the cavern walls pushing in on him. He had been almost thankful for the darkness so Meggan couldn't see his trepidation. The moment he felt the cool air on his face, he nearly shouted out loud. He stabbed another pear half and popped the whole thing in his mouth. "There must've been an earthquake up there," he said after swallowing. "That shaft sure was a lot tighter than the last time I crawled through it."

Meggan motioned for another pear. "Yes, I'm sure that was why you were so cramped this time."

"I have to admit I was nervous there a couple of times. My gun belt kept jabbing me in the side. I half expected to shoot myself in the gut."

Meggan winced. Shane regretted his flippant remark. It wasn't a laughing matter, especially with the fear still evident on her face.

He noticed an angry red knot in the center of her forehead. He leaned a little closer. "You got a right smart goose egg there. Why didn't you say something?"

She gingerly touched it. "There was nothing to say except I should've watched where I was going. A bump on the head was nothing compared to what could've…"

She ate the half of the pear and rinsed her fingers off in the water. When she looked up at him, tears sparkled on the end of her eyelashes. "Thank you, Shane, for—for everything. I don't know what I'd do without you."

He was beginning to wonder what he would do without her. If he hadn't met her and Gloria on the stage, he would be at the Trego mansion right now, eating Ma's fluffy biscuits, smothered with gravy and bits of crispy bacon, preparing to head out to his farm. He wouldn't be eating pears out of a jar after having spent the night in a grimy mine with a beautiful woman.

He had kissed her in the mine to comfort her, to give her courage for what lay ahead. Now he wanted to kiss her all for completely different reasons. When she kissed him in town, it had nothing to do with him. She only threw her arms around his neck so Duggar wouldn't recognize her. Shane wanted it to be about him. He wanted her to see him as a man, not a means to an end.

He stabbed the last pear and held it out to her. She waved it away. Shane stuck it in his mouth. Not much of a breakfast compared to what Ma was surely fixing in the Trego kitchen, but he'd take what the Lord provided and be thankful for it.

He dried the knife blade on his pants leg and stood. He returned it to the sheath and reached for Meggan's hand. "You don't need to thank me for anything. I would've done the same thing for anyone."

Now, why'd he gone and said that? It wasn't a lie, but it wasn't exactly true either. Had someone else come down those hotel stairs yesterday morning, he would've helped as his Christian duty required. He'd have offered them a seat, a drink of water, and a comforting word. Beyond that, he would've walked out the door, leaving them to the doctor, the sheriff, and the desk clerk.

Not so with Meggan. He wanted to do more for her. He wanted to be the one to save her.

Something flitted across her face. Something that looked like disappointment. She stood and shook a cloud of black dust out of her skirt. "We should go if we're going to beat J.D. back to town. Do you think he's still waiting for us at the mine?"

Shane stood and swiped his hands down his shirt. "Hard to tell. He probably stuck his head inside the cavern and realized he couldn't track us with no light, no oxygen, and no knowledge of the tunnels. Don't worry. I know a direct route. We'll get there first."

After they saddled up, they rode along the creek for a few hundred yards until they came to a gentle slope that took them to the meadow. They rode slowly and avoided talking to keep the noise down. Shane figured Duggar would guard the mine entrance for a while, but he wasn't taking any chances.

When the ground leveled off, he reined his horse in close to Meggan's. "While you're at the telegraph office checking for messages from the detective, I'll get more supplies and visit with my ma. If she doesn't see me pretty near every day, she'll think I've been mauled by a grizzly and pester the sheriff into rounding up a posse to come look for me."

Meggan's hands tightened around the pommel. "Where will we go then? We're not coming back here, are we?"

"We couldn't even if you begged me. With that ventilation shaft plugged, there isn't enough fresh air, and of course, Duggar knows where it is."

She glanced around as if expecting the man to come riding out of the brush. "So what will we do?"

"There's an old cabin at an abandoned stone quarry a few miles on the other side of the mine camp. At least the cabin was there when I was a boy. Probably still standing. It's remote. A good way's from town. I thought we could go there and hole up a day or two until that detective has time to get here from Kansas City."

"After I check at the telegraph office, I need to find out what the undertaker's done with Granny, too."

"You realize once Duggar gives up on finding you at the mine, he'll head straight for the hotel."

Her jaw tightened. "Hopefully, I'll be finished with everything by the time he gets there. My suite is paid for until Thursday. I want to make sure the staff doesn't think I've gone to Seattle and clean out my things. When Detective Rollins arrives, he needs to know where to find me."

When they were far enough away from the mine, they spurred the horses faster, though they kept to the tree line. Shane hoped Duggar—if he hadn't got lost in the mine—was as tired as he was.

After twenty minutes of riding, a well-worn road came into view. The sun was just rising above the horizon at their backs. Shane reined his horse to a stop. Meggan stopped beside him.

"That road'll take you straight into Willow Wood. It's not far, and it's well traveled so you shouldn't have any trouble. Just keep your head down."

She nodded wearily. Dark smudges of fatigue circled her eyes. "I will."

"I'll cut across the fields and come into town the back way. I'll stop and see Ma for a few minutes and get us some food. On the street behind the hotel is a bath house and laundry. Go down the alley and wait for me there. I'll meet you as soon as I make sure you're not being followed."

"No, Shane, spend some time with your mother. I don't want to be the reason she worries about you. I'll be fine for an hour or two. Mr. Duggar wants the jewels, but he is an escaped convict. He won't want to be spotted in Willow Wood, Idaho. I'll be fine as long as I stay in plain sight at the hotel or the undertaker's office."

Shane's stomach clenched. She was probably right, but he didn't want to leave her alone that long. He didn't want to leave her at all.

He was mentally and physically exhausted. Now he faced another day—maybe two—of keeping her safe and hidden from a convicted killer. His body wanted nothing more than to go home to his loft apartment above the Trego stables and sleep for a week. That wasn't an option. Meggan depended on him.

He liked the thought even if every muscle in his body ached from crawling through the tunnels and kicking his way out of the narrow opening. More than once inside the mine, he thought he had gotten turned around and led them to a dead end or right into Duggar's arms. When the tunnel narrowed so he could barely squeeze through, he never felt so helpless and scared. Not for himself, but for Meggan. A dark, abandoned mine would unnerve the most stalwart of constitutions. Meggan was no exception, though she was stronger than she gave herself credit for.

"Just stick to the road," he said. "If someone seems to be following you or gives you an odd feeling, you can ride into the nearest yard and pretend you're a long lost relative. Everyone in Willow Wood is friendly; they'll probably invite you to breakfast."

She smiled in appreciation. She had scrubbed her face as best she could at the creek, but black soot still circled her hairline, eyes, and nostrils. Her hair was dulled by a fine layer of silt. Her complexion was ashen from a fatigue and worry. Shane wanted to assure her everything was under control. He wouldn't let a dirty jewel thief near her. But he wasn't convinced he could stay true to his word.

She studied him for a moment before she wheeled her horse and headed toward town. Shane watched until a bend in the road took her out of sight. With one last look in the direction of the mine, he broke across the field. He prayed for strength, wisdom, and cunning. He'd need them more than he ever had before.

Chapter Twelve

When Meggan reached the first residential street, she slowed the horse to a walk. The back of her neck prickled, though she believed J.D. would stay at the mine to insure he didn't miss her and Shane coming out. She fixed her gaze on the end of the street to keep from looking around. The last thing she wanted to do was attract attention to herself.

She had spent her life avoiding detection. It became harder to do as she grew and developed into womanhood. As a child, people stopped her on the street to tell her how pretty she was. Before long, the compliments from women stopped, and they began to look at her as if she had done something wrong. Men often stared at her in a hard, ugly way she didn't want to understand. As far as she could see, the only thing that had changed was the way the world perceived her.

With each movement of the horse, the smell of smoke and soot rose up around her. Despite her efforts to clean up at the creek, her fingernails and the creases in her hands were caked with dust and grime. Cobwebs and dried leaves clung to her hair. She could only imagine what people would think when they saw her.

She tied her horse to a hitching rail behind the hotel and headed around the building. She wanted to go straight to her suite and clean up, but she needed to stop at the desk first to see if there were any messages for her or if anyone had asked about her. She didn't think J.D. would draw attention to himself by talking to a desk clerk, but he could be desperate enough to.

The desk clerk's eyes widened at the sight of her. His gaze traveled quickly up her soiled dress and stopped at the knot in the center of her forehead. Meggan resisted the urge to touch it again as she asked for any messages.

"Only the undertaker, ma'am. He said he can take your grandmother to the cemetery at noon. If you don't have a preacher to speak over her, he'll say a few words for you."

Dread rose in Meggan's chest at the image of a secluded cemetery where J.D. would have a thousand places to hide. But Gloria had to be laid to rest somewhere. There was no avoiding it.

"Noon will be fine."

She looked at the big clock over the registration desk. It was barely eight o'clock in the morning. She had to stay in town but out of sight for the next four hours.

"I'll send a messenger over to tell the undertaker you'll meet him at his office at noon," the clerk said.

Meggan uttered a barely discernible reply and hurried upstairs, her mind awhirl. She wasn't sure of her financial situation. Gloria had paid for three nights in the hotel. She loved to travel in style, especially when there was a big payout waiting at the other end. She also lived beyond her means. Hopefully Meggan would find enough cash to last a few weeks that J.D. had missed, along with any valuables she could sell. She wasn't going to Seattle, but she had to go somewhere, and she needed money to get there.

Guilt pricked at her for using funds stolen from Gloria's victims to get herself out of a bad situation. The story of her life.

She cautiously entered the suite and looked around. She went to the wardrobe and peered inside, under the bed, and behind the curtains, though they were too thin to conceal a full grown man. Finally satisfied she was alone, she locked the door and barricaded it with a chair. She wished she had time for a proper bath. Instead, she took a sponge bath in front of the pitcher and bowl on the bureau. She let her hair down and properly brushed out the silt and cobwebs.

Her poor dress was a disaster. It was one of her favorites. She loved how the blue and pink poppy flowers danced across the fabric and played with the color in her cheeks. Now, the hem hung loose in several places and one of the sleeves was torn from the back. Worst of all was the black grime ground into the skirt from crawling on the ground of the mine. It looked ready for the rag bag. She hoped it could be salvaged. Who knew when she could afford a new dress?

She changed into a dark brown skirt and an old blouse that had once been a crisp white. She wrapped a brown shawl around her shoulders and put one of Gloria's poke bonnets over her raven locks. She looked in the mirror and almost didn't recognize herself. This would do just fine.

A knock sounded at the door. Meggan nearly jumped out of her skin. She put her hand over the derringer in her pocket and considering not answering. J.D. wouldn't likely knock. It was probably the undertaker or desk clerk. She stepped out of the line of the door and leaned over to peep through the keyhole. She saw the hip and dark skirt of a maid. She relaxed but only a little.

"Yes?" she said through the door.

"Housekeeping, miss," said a maid. "I brought hot water for a bath."

Hot water. Better late than never.

Meggan moved the chair and unlocked the door. As the maid came in, Meggan looked past her into the hallway. It was empty. She closed the door and locked it.

The maid looked into the bowl at the blackened water Meggan had used to sponge off with and wrinkled her nose. Meggan turned back to the mirror and removed the bonnet.

The maid poured the hot water into the pitcher and emptied the dirty water into her bucket. "Would you like more water, miss?"

Meggan would like nothing more than an entire tub of steaming water, but J.D. Duggar could burst through the door any moment.

"No, thank you. Could you take my dress downstairs and have it cleaned? Please have the tears repaired as well. As much as possible anyway."

The woman's lip curled slightly as she lifted the filthy dress from the floor and held it out away from her. The acrid smell of smoke was nearly unbearable. Meggan could only imagine what the woman thought she had done in it.

"Anything else, ma'am?"

"I sent telegrams to alert family about Granny's demise. They could arrive at any time. Could you let me know if anyone asks about me or Granny? My uncle was already in route to meet us here and hasn't received word about her passing. If he comes, please don't tell him anything. Just let me know and I'll give him the details."

The lies slipped off her tongue. She wondered what Shane would think at how easily she could spin a story to fit her narrative. She wasn't sure why it mattered what Shane Casey thought. God was her only true judge. Still, she hated to disappoint Shane.

The maid dipped her head in acquiescence and turned toward the door. Meggan planned to wash off another layer of grime as soon as she left and go through Gloria's things to find what money she could find. Movement on the street caught her eye. She gasped aloud. J.D. Duggar was crossing the street. He glanced upward and seemed to look straight at her, though she doubted he could see anything past the glare of the sun on the window.

She snatched the poke bonnet off the bureau and jammed it onto her head. "Oh, dear, I just remembered. I have an errand to run."

She found a coin on the dresser and pressed it into the startled maid's hand. It was a generous tip, but Meggan hoped it would remind the maid of her instructions should anyone ask for her.

The maid glanced back at the pitcher of steaming water she'd just filled. "Will you be needing fresh water later, miss?"

Meggan slipped the satchel over her shoulder and tightened the shawl around it. "No, it won't be necessary. If I change my mind, I'll ask someone. I'm really in a hurry. I'll go down the back staircase with you. I need to speak with the cook."

"I can give her any special instructions."

Meggan grabbed the woman's elbow and ushered her toward the door. "I don't mind." She fumbled with the lock before throwing the door open. Footsteps sounded on the staircase. Her heart hammered nearly as loud. She walked beside the maid toward the back stairs, her pace hurrying the woman along. When they reached the stairwell, she ducked in front of the maid to block her body from view of whoever was coming up the stairs. She nearly ran to the bottom.

On the first floor, Meggan spotted the laundry room to her left and the kitchen straight ahead. Through the laundry room was a narrow door slightly ajar to let out the heat. Daylight shone beyond it. Meggan headed that way.

"If you want to speak to Cook…" the maid called after her. Meggan kept going. She didn't slow down.

Chapter Thirteen

Meggan stepped around some barrels filled with food scraps from the hotel dining room and peered toward the second floor. She half expected to see J.D. Duggar looking down at her. The small window was empty. She didn't know if the jewel thief had been the one coming upstairs. If he went into her room, it wouldn't take him long to realize she'd been there. She wondered if he would take the time to conduct a more thorough search for the jewels or come straight after her. Either way, she wasn't about to wait around and find out.

She crept down the alley to the back street. As Shane said, she faced a laundry and a bathhouse.

It had been less than an hour since she left Shane. She wasn't sure what to do or where to hide until he got back from his ma's. She didn't want to hide too well in case they missed each other, but she couldn't wait in the broad daylight either. Even if J.D. didn't recognize her in her disguise, he would recognize the horse.

At the end of the street, she saw a large barn with the doors open to the morning air. She unhitched the horse and walked him in that direction. Hopefully, the barn was a business, and she could secure the animal in a stall while she waited for Shane.

Behind the barn she saw a secluded paddock. From her vantage point, it looked empty. Even better. If anyone asked what she was doing, she would say the clerk at the hotel told her she could stable her horse there. For all she knew, the barn was for the use of hotel guests.

Halfway around the barn, she heard a horse coming down the street at a fast clip. The rider probably wasn't looking for her, but her pulse pounded nonetheless. Using the horse as a shield to block her from view, she peered around it. The rider drew up to the barn and stopped. A large horse snorted. Her horse whinnied in reply.

"Meggan?"

Her knees buckled in relief. She stepped out from behind the horse. Shane dismounted and walked his horse toward her. His gaze took in her drab outfit and oversized bonnet. "I almost didn't recognize you," he said admiringly.

She laughed in relief. "That was the idea. What are you doing here already? I thought you were going to visit with your ma."

"I did. She's used to me running in and out. She didn't even realize I was gone last night."

Meggan looked at his cleanshaven face and fresh clothes. He looked even better than he had the first time she saw him on the stage. He smelled better too. "I see you had time to clean up a little."

"I couldn't show up at my ma's table looking like I spent the night in an abandoned mine."

Meggan sniffed and tried to look annoyed. "She wouldn't like that very much."

Shane glanced over his shoulder toward the hotel. "Did you learn anything?"

Her stomach tightened. "A little. The undertaker scheduled Granny's burial for noon. Do you know someplace in town where I can hide until then? I saw J.D. going toward the hotel. I ran out the back. He's probably going through my room right now. He'll know I'm back in town."

Shane clenched his fists. "I have half a mind to go over there right now and end this."

Meggan's heart lurched. She grabbed his arm. "No! Please. I couldn't bear it if anything happened to you."

She realized she meant it in more ways than one.

"I couldn't bear it either," he said with a teasing smile.

She took a deep breath to bring her emotions under control. "I mean it, Shane. Anything could go wrong. I want him back in prison, not dead in the street—or standing over you dead in the street. The man is ruthless. He believes the jewels belong to him and he'll stop at nothing to get them. Even if it means…"

She released his arm. Weariness washed over her. Weariness from the last twenty-four hours—outrunning J.D. Duggar on horseback, hiding in the mine, knowing he killed Gloria and wouldn't hesitate to kill her or Shane if he caught up with them.

"We have to stay away from him until Detective Rollins gets here and takes care of the situation legally. Not confront him."

Shane brushed his knuckles down her arm. Her skin shivered in response despite the rising temperatures. "I don't like standing around waiting for a killer to come after you."

"Neither do I." She managed a small smile and was rewarded with one back. "Is there somewhere we can get out of sight?"

Shane nodded. "Of course. I'm sorry. This whole situation has me thrown. I've never felt so..." His gaze bored into hers. "...useless."

She reached for his arm again, missed, and grasped his hand. "You're not useless. Not at all. I..." She wanted to admit she needed him. She'd never needed someone as much.

He turned his hand over in hers and grasped her fingers. "We'll go to the Trego mansion so we can keep the horses hidden too. I'd rather Ma not see you. She'll immediately think all sorts of things—like I'm keeping company with a beautiful lady."

Warmth filled Meggan's cheeks. If only that was all that was going on. "We don't want her to think that."

"Not if it isn't true."

She looked away. When she first saw him at the stagecoach stop in Smithfield, she knew he was interested in her. Her interest has been piqued as well, especially after Granny drew him into conversation. She had wanted to get to know him. But not like this. He deserved better. He deserved an honest woman who could help him with his practice and take care of him, not put his life in danger at every turn. He didn't need a woman who once earned her living from theft and chicanery.

They mounted up and rode the horses slowly down a residential street to avoid attracting attention. It was still early morning. The few people they saw were busy with chores. Many threw up a hand in greeting but paid little mind to the tired cowboy and the young woman in the drab brown dress with her face concealed by a prairie bonnet.

As each street fell behind them, Meggan relaxed more and more. Most likely, J.D. was still at the hotel waiting for her. He probably figured she was having breakfast somewhere. He wouldn't sit around and wait long. A brief respite was all she and Shane could count on to catch their breath and consider their next move.

The horses headed up a narrow street lining the back sides of sprawling properties. This neighborhood must be where Willow Wood's wealthy railroad and mining families lived. And Shane's benefactors. This was the kind of people Shane had grown up with. Hardworking. Honest. Ambitious. People like him. Not her.

They entered a shady yard, dotted with small sheds, and rode straight to the large stable and carriage house. Meggan heard someone working at the far end of the barn but didn't see anyone. They dismounted, and Shane led the horses to a manger. He pointed out a flight of stairs along a back wall. "Go on up and make yourself comfortable while I see to the horses."

"I can help you."

"I'd rather not take the chance that anyone see you. I took some food up while I was here earlier. We can eat while we wait for your appointment with the undertaker."

Meggan was too tired to protest. He was right anyway. The sooner she got out of sight, the better.

The apartment was small and sparsely furnished. There was a small eating and sitting area. On the table were a stack of plates and forks and a few crocks wrapped in towels. Her stomach growled at the sight of them. She was tempted to grab a slice of ham or piece of potato or whatever waited inside. But she'd wait for Shane. It was the least she could do. Through an open doorway, she saw a narrow bed neatly made with an Indian style blanket and one pillow. Though dust coated the floorboards, and cobwebs hung from the corners of the seldom-used room, she saw signs of Shane.

She found a rag in a basket under the sink and attacked the grime on the only window facing the back alley. By the time she heard Shane's feet on the stairs, the window shone, and sunshine threw a square of light onto the worn rug.

"You didn't have to do that," Shane said from behind her.

She could tell he was pleased. "You were downstairs working for me. I couldn't sit up here doing nothing."

He chuckled. "Yeah, but now Ma will know someone else was up here. I haven't washed that window in years."

"It's still dirty on the outside. She'll never notice."

He offered her the only chair at the table and pulled a milk can across the floor for himself. "Food should still be hot enough," he said, unwrapping one of the crocks.

Meggan unwrapped the other two. The aroma of food filled the tiny room. Fresh biscuits in one, fried potatoes and a generous dollop of gravy on top in another, scrambled eggs with several slices of bacon in the last.

131

Shane slapped his thigh. "I forgot the butter."

Meggan chuckled and handed him a plate. "No matter. I'm so hungry I won't even miss it. Everything smells delicious."

"Ma knows this is my favorite breakfast. She always cooks like this when I've been gone for a time."

Meggan folded her hands in her lap as Shane asked the blessing, but she didn't hear the words. She couldn't fathom anyone missing her enough to go to special trouble upon her return.

After the prayer, Shane put a serving fork into the bacon and eggs and motioned for her to go first. "I didn't want Ma to see how much food I was bringing out here, so I waited until she was busy in another room. She'll think I'm plumb starved to death when I go back for more to take with us."

"I hate to make you lie for me." She already did enough of that herself.

"I don't lie. Especially to my ma. She knows there wasn't much food at the ranch, and I'd need plenty over the next few days. I just didn't tell her someone else would help me eat it."

They dug into the food and ate in silence for a few minutes. Everything was warm and comforting and filling, just what Meggan needed.

Shane was the first to break the silence. "Tell me exactly how you ended up with Gloria and Alice. After your grandmother passed away, wasn't there family to take you in?"

The biscuit went dry in Meggan's mouth. "As far as I know, Grandma Elsie was the only family I had. She told me stories about growing up with her brothers and sisters, but she never said what happened to any of them. My mama, well, she was always gone. Grandma told me she was dead. She left when I was a baby. I don't know if she died or if Grandma told me that to explain to a little girl why her mother never came back.

"We lived in a tenement building across the hall from Gloria and Alice in Lawrence, Kansas. Grandma's health was poor, so Gloria and Alice offered to take me off her hands some afternoons. They took me with them to shops and meat markets on the street. I always looked forward to the outings. Grandma and I never had money to go anywhere. Her health wouldn't allow it anyway, and she didn't let me wander the streets alone.

"Gloria and Alice were nice to me, or so I thought. As I grew older, I realized they were using me. One time I fell on the step of a dress shop. I split my lip and banged my knee. Gloria and Alice yelled that the owner didn't have the tile nailed down properly and that's why I fell. It was dangerous and it was a wonder I hadn't broken my leg. They yelled and carried on so much, the poor owner was beside himself. He ended up giving me a pretty yellow dress straight off the rack. I couldn't believe it. I'd never had a new dress in my life. My lip was swollen and sore for weeks. My knee was black and yellow and hurt when I walked. But all I could think was how much Gloria and Alice must've liked me to take up for me the way they had and get me that dress."

She stared thoughtfully at her plate. "That night as I tried to fall asleep with my sore leg and sore lip and dreaming of my pretty yellow dress, I kept thinking of one thing. The sisters had sent me into the store in front of them. I'll never forget the feel of someone's hand on my back just as I stepped over the threshold. One of them *pushed* me."

Her voice cracked. "One of those ladies pushed a little girl so I would fall, and they could yell at Mr. Copas until he gave me a new dress."

Shane gaped at her in disbelief. "Why would they do that?"

"To draw me in."

She dragged her fork through the scrambled eggs, her appetite gone. "Grandma Elsie and I were poor. We didn't have nice things. I didn't mind. I knew she loved me. But a little girl likes to be doted on. She likes pretty things. Alice and Gloria went on and on about how pretty I looked in my new dress. They said I needed new hair ribbons to match. It gave me a sick feeling in the pit of my stomach. I didn't want them to yell at someone else. A few days later we went out again. In a different store, Gloria stood at the counter and chatted with the saleslady about how smart I was and wasn't I a pretty thing. I didn't see where Alice was. Later as we walked through the park, Alice reached in her pocket and pulled out the longest, prettiest hair ribbons I'd ever seen. I hadn't seen her pay for them. I hadn't even seen her talk to the saleslady. But I didn't think about that. All I thought about was how long and soft those ribbons were and how I would never take them off.

"It didn't take long for me to realize what was happening. Most of the time, the sisters used me as a decoy to pilfer things for themselves. They put cuts of meat inside my coat. They told me to cry about something in front of a store clerk. While one of them yelled at the clerk for making me cry, the other would steal things. I felt terrible while it was happening, but afterwards, they gave me little trinkets and told me what a good girl I was and how much they liked having me around. I knew what I was doing was wrong. Grandma Elsie taught me about the Bible. I knew who Jesus was. I knew He would never let a liar or a thief into Heaven. But I wanted Alice and Gloria to like me. They were there, and well, Jesus wasn't. At least not that I could see."

She swallowed the lump in her throat. Remembering a painful past never did a person a bit of good. At least it had never done her any good. She needed to eat more and talk less. It might be a long time before her next meal. She put a piece of potato in her mouth and chewed, despite how cold and greasy. She couldn't bring herself to look at Shane. He was probably disgusted by a little girl who got so good at lying.

He covered her hand with his. "None of it was your fault, Meggan. You must know that. You were a child. They took advantage of you."

She bit her lip. She wasn't a child now. She had known the truth about Alice and Gloria for years, but she never said anything. She never told them to stop. She never told the police or a judge what they had done, though she had chances. The days they attended J.D. Duggar's trial—because Gloria didn't want to miss a moment of the action—she could've stood up at any time and told the judge J.D. was telling the truth. The sweet little old lady who had turned him in for the bounty had also stolen the Gochberg jewels. It was why the authorities couldn't find them.

The authorities believed every word Gloria Hennessey said. J.D. Duggar was a thief and a killer who

TERESA SLACK

had hidden the jewels for safekeeping until he was able to break out of prison. No one believed for a minute the white-haired grandmother in the courtroom, holding tight to her granddaughter's hand, was guilty of any crime beyond befriending the wrong man. They certainly didn't think of looking for the missing jewels under the loose floorboard in Gloria's closet. Meggan almost believed the story herself.

Chapter Fourteen

Shane's heart ached for the little girl inside Meggan who still blamed herself for giving in to the desire for pretty things—and worse, the need for acceptance by the two women who used her to con others.

Meggan pulled her hand out from under his and stood. Shane couldn't tell if she wanted his comfort or she'd rather he left her alone. She was a hard woman to read. Every time she opened up and started to give him something of herself, she pulled away as if afraid she said too much. She hadn't spoken a word to him or anyone else on the stage. At the time he figured she didn't get much chance to talk with her grandmother chatting the whole time. Now he saw she had good reason to keep quiet. To avoid scrutiny. She had told him more in the last five minutes about her true self than she'd said since he met her. Still, she was holding plenty back.

He watched her go to the window and seemed to stare out at nothing.

"Why don't you stay here and take a nap while I go scout out the cemetery?" he asked. "I want to find a spot where I can watch the service without anyone seeing me. I also want to see if Duggar has the same plan."

She looked too tired to argue. "All right. Just please don't confront him if you can avoid it."

"I won't. Get some sleep and I'll come back in a couple hours to wake you."

She continued to stare out the window. His fingers itched to reach out and touch her face to ease the worry and fatigue. He wrapped the nearly empty crocks with the towels and set them back in the box he'd used to bring them upstairs. He left the plates and forks where they were. He'd wash them out later. He didn't want Ma asking about the breakfast guest who used the second plate.

He tucked the box under his arm and went to the door. "Lock the door behind me, though nobody knows you're here."

Despite assuring her of her safety, after returning the box of dishes to the kitchen and avoiding his ma, Shane circled the stable twice to make sure no one was lurking in the corners before he headed down the hill. He didn't bother saddling one of the horses. The cemetery was only a few blocks from the Trego house, even less if he cut through yards and backlots. It'd be difficult to hide on horseback.

As expected, the cemetery was empty except for two fellows digging a hole in a rear corner. The spot wasn't conveniently located on a pathway or close to any family plots. It must be for Gloria—a stranger who would likely never have a visitor after Meggan left town.

And she would leave. She had no reason to stay in Willow Wood. She certainly wouldn't stay for him.

He pushed the self-pity aside. This situation wasn't about him. It was about keeping a woman safe from a killer. He would do it for anyone. He'd already told Meggan that. But he doubted he'd go to this much trouble. Deep down, he relished the idea of spending time with her and protecting her.

He knew more about Meggan than he had but not nearly as much as he'd like. He didn't know what she planned to do after the detective came and took Duggar into custody. Without the jewels, there was no reason to go on to Seattle unless a beau waited for her there. Which was unlikely since she said she was all alone now.

There was certainly no reason to stay in Willow Wood, Idaho where she knew no one except him, and she'd given no indication she thought more of him than someone who'd helped her out of a tight spot.

He made a wide circle around the perimeter of the cemetery, keeping out of sight among the trees and headstones in case someone else was doing the same. From his vantage point, he could see nearly the whole town. Below him, Willow Wood spread out in a loose grid in all directions. The hotel took up one of the corners of the town square directly below him. He watched the hotel for a few minutes to see if anyone came out. His gaze drifted to the window of the suite that faced the street. Since the hotel only had one suite, he knew which windows belonged to it. He wished he could see through the walls to see if Duggar was inside. He doubted it. The bandit wouldn't linger, knowing he'd attract the attention of the hotel staff, who'd most likely call the sheriff.

He stepped into an overgrown thicket of trees at the edge of the cemetery. It was still within the cemetery's boundary, but there were no graves here since an abundance of tree roots made digging difficult. It also provided plenty of coverage for him to hide.

It grated on Shane that he couldn't walk down the hill and ferret Duggar out of whatever hole he was hiding and end this whole mess. He wasn't the kind to let someone else fight his battles. In this, however, Meggan was right. Duggar was a killer, thief, and escaped convict who had crossed state lines. That made him guilty of all sorts of charges with not a lot to lose.

Duggar had murdered a man in cold blood who had only wanted to protect his property and family. He had killed an old lady and was now trying to murder Meggan. Heat flooded through Shane's limbs again. He'd let the authorities have Duggar, but if the man went near her again, they may not have more to collect than his bones.

Shane took hold of a low branch and swung into an oak tree in full leaf. He moved around on the branches until he found a limb that provided a clear view of the men digging the hole. The spot also gave him a vantage point where he could see the road leading up the hill. He could watch Meggan and the undertaker arrive. He couldn't see every possible approach from where he crouched in the tree, but it was the best he could do.

A new thought occurred to him. Would the bandit be bold enough to walk right up to the graveside and bow his head as if sharing in Meggan's grief? Shane clenched his teeth. He needed to do more to protect Meggan than hide in a tree two hundred feet away. He dropped out of the tree and headed down the hill, hoping inspiration would strike as he walked.

•••

Shane secured Meggan's horse in a stand of trees at the bottom of the hill on the backside of the cemetery so they'd be ready to ride out after Gloria's memorial service. While Meggan had napped in his apartment above the stable, he loaded the saddlebags with more food and ammunition than he hoped they would need for the night at the quarry cabin.

Meggan walked to the undertaker's office while Shane followed on horseback a half a block behind. He didn't want to be seen with her more than necessary, and he wanted to watch for anyone following her.

The next few hours would be the most dangerous of the day. Shane would be within shouting distance if she needed him at the cemetery but too far away to react immediately if Duggar stepped out from behind a tree right next to her.

The worst part for Shane was the waiting, and that's all he was doing—waiting for something bad to happen.

From the end of the street, he watched Meggan enter the undertaker's office. As soon as the door closed behind her, he turned and rode to the street behind the hotel. He knew every alley and back corner of Willow Wood. He'd take a look around and see if he could find where Duggar was hiding out.

He pulled his hat low on his face and kept his head down as his eyes darted back and forth to either side of the street. He sure didn't want to get jumped if the killer saw him first.

At the end of the street, he turned right. Typical weekday activity sounded from every direction. He heard the ringing of a hammer on an anvil from the direction of the smithy. From an open window came the sound of a baby crying while a mother worked to soothe it. Two boys chased each other out of an alley. They barely glanced in his direction as they crossed the street in front of him. They disappeared between two houses. Shane nearly smiled to himself. He remembered those carefree days, learning every hidey hole and dead alley in Willow Wood.

Which reminded him…

A little farther down the street he came to a narrow alley that provided a clear view of the back of the hotel. A ramshackle woodshed butted up to the alley and didn't get much use this time of year. It would provide a place for a fellow to stay out of sight and close to his prey as long as he was quiet and careful.

Shane didn't expect to find Duggar waiting in the shed with a welcoming cup of coffee, but he hoped there'd be evidence if the man had been there or not. If Duggar used the shed once, he'd come back.

Shane was nearly abreast of the shed when he heard the shuffle of a horse's hooves on the packed earth. He slid off his horse and looped the reins through a hitching ring on the side of the shed. His pulse quickened. He palmed his six-shooter. He didn't hear movement other than the horse, but a horse meant a man had to be close by. He circled the building and saw a chestnut horse, fully saddled.

Shane crouched low, pulled back the hammer of the gun, and glanced in every direction. Quiet. He advanced on the horse, careful not to spook it. He knew his way around a horse and could soothe one without making a sound. The horse lifted its head to look at him. Shane reached for the halter and stroked the animal's neck.

"There you go, fella. What're you doing here by yourself?" he whispered. He glanced out onto the street. There wasn't much business going on. Much of the activity was too far away to explain a saddled horse waiting alone.

Shane ran his hand down the horse's neck. He was sure it was the same one that had chased him and Meggan yesterday through the canyon.

He grasped the animal's leg and lifted its hoof off the ground. Sure enough, the shoes were scraped from rocks and debris from running up the mountainside among the boulders. He lifted the other foot and found the same damage.

"You had a rough time of it yesterday, didn't you?" As he straightened, he heard the scrape of a boot. He started to turn but wasn't quick enough. The butt of a gun slammed down and hit him behind the ear. He dropped to the ground.

Chapter Fifteen

I t took all Meggan's resolve not to turn around and look for Shane in the trees. He told her he'd be sitting in a large oak over her left shoulder about two hundred feet from the freshly dug grave. Over the undertaker's droning voice, she tensed for the sound of approaching footsteps, a shout, or even gunfire.

The grave was far from the trees, and the July sun beat down on her head despite the poke bonnet. The gravediggers waited in the shade with their hats in their hands, though they appeared to be half dozing.

Mr. Thompson the undertaker reminded Meggan of a crow. He was thin and slight, a couple inches shorter than Meggan. He had thin black hair, a long, hooked nose too big for his face, and thin hands that looked like talons wrapped around his well-used Bible. But his gray eyes were warm and kind, and his firm yet gentle voice had immediately put her at ease.

But the little man didn't look strong enough to scare a rabbit away, should one hop onto the casket, let alone protect her from J.D. Duggar. She was thankful Shane was close by and watching.

She doubted J.D. would walk up to her with Mr. Thompson right next to her and the gravediggers close by. But she didn't doubt for a minute he was watching, and he would catch up with her as soon as the service broke up.

She dropped her hand to the pocket of her skirt to feel for her derringer and shifted a little closer to the undertaker.

She brought her gaze to the pine box the undertaker and the two gravediggers had pulled it out of the wagon and set in the dirt.

Unexpected tears welled in her eyes. Mr. Thompson was reading from the twenty-third Psalm, a burial staple it seemed. She should tell him he needn't bother. As far as Meggan knew, Gloria didn't believe in God. She never went to church. When someone in the neighborhood invited her, she launched into a laundry list of illnesses and aches and pains that prevented her from entering a church. The same aches and maladies never stopped her from going to the park or attending crowded street events that provided plenty of pockets to pick and harried vendors who wouldn't notice a sweet old lady pilfering their wares.

Last November, Meggan stood next to Gloria in front of an open grave as another undertaker spoke similar words over Alice's casket. Life improved for Meggan after Alice's death. Gloria became kinder and gentler. Her changed attitude may have had nothing to do with any tenderness toward Meggan, but because of the jewels hidden in the closet, and knowing she was one step closer to facilitating their sale in Seattle.

Gloria and Alice left this world no better off for having been a part of it. Meggan wanted more. She didn't want to be planted on a lonely hillside with no one to grieve her passing. She wanted her small existence to leave a mark on someone. To make a difference in that person's life. She couldn't undo the damage she'd done since she moved in with the Hennessey sisters, but she could try her best to get Mrs. Gochberg's property back to her.

Then God would see and maybe He'd forgive her.

The undertaker had stopped talking, drawing her out of her thoughts. On the other side of Gloria's pine box, the gravediggers had replaced their hats.

The service was over. Meggan had paid the burial fee at the undertaker's office. Mr. Thompson was finished with her. The gravediggers were waiting for her to step away so they could finish their job and get home before the sun got any hotter.

She smiled demurely. "Thank you for everything," she told the undertaker. "Granny—would've been pleased."

He replaced his hat over his shiny, black hair. "Can I give you a ride back to the hotel?"

"No, thank you. I believe I'd prefer to walk."

"If there's anything else you need…" he said as he headed to the hearse. She imagined he was anxious to get out of the heat.

Meggan turned toward the backside of the cemetery and forced her feet to move slowly. She didn't want to look like she was running from something. The hearse rattled down the hill. Meggan scanned the grounds ahead of her. Where was Shane?

Where was J.D.?

The path turned, and the ground sloped gently downward. The sounds of the gravediggers' shovels faded away. A shiver worked its way down Meggan's spine. She picked up her pace. Shane told her he'd be waiting in an oak tree. She wished he'd been more specific. There were at least fifty oak trees up here. Why hadn't he come to meet her yet?

She sensed more than heard someone behind her. She put her hand over the derringer in her pocket and whirled around.

It wasn't Shane.

J.D. Duggar lunged forward and grabbed her arm. "You're a lot harder to nail down than the old lady."

At the thought of the coffin lid closed over Gloria, Meggan's indignation overrode her fear. "Get your filthy hands off me. Who do you think you are?"

J.D. barked out a humorless laugh. His piercing black eyes narrowed into angry slits. He tightened his grip on her arm. "Any other time I'd like me a girl with some vinegar. But that's not what I'm here for today. All I care about right now is what you got that's mine. Hand it over, and I may not kill you."

Meggan jerked against his hand on her arm, still too mad to be scared. "No one has any of *your* property. Now, kindly unhand me. One scream and those two men back there will be all over you."

Before she could blink, a gun appeared in J.D.'s hand. He jerked her toward him and shoved the steel into her side. His face was practically against hers, his hot breath scalding her cheek. Spittle collected in the corners of his mouth. Belatedly, fear washed over her. Could Shane see them? Why didn't he come and help? Had J.D. already found him where he was hiding and taken care of him first?

"I don't particularly care how this goes, missy," J.D. said. "You may be able to sweet talk your way out of trouble with every other fool who crosses your path but not me. I saw past your pretty face the first time I ever laid eyes on you."

Cold sweat began to trickle between her shoulder blades. "I—I don't know what you're talking about."

"Save it! Let's get this over with. Are you handing them over or am I going to take them?"

He shoved the gun deeper into her side. "If you even think about screaming, I'll fill you with lead before you make the first peep and I'll take what I want anyway."

Meggan's stomach filled with dread. Shane! Where was he?

She sucked in her breath to relieve the pressure from the gun against her ribs. She needed to bluff. Stall.

"I don't have them…"

J.D. shoved the gun painfully into her side. "I'm losing my patience with you, girlie. We can do this hard or easy. But I'm not going to stand here and be polite much longer."

Meggan's entire body trembled. She thought of the gun in her dress pocket. It wasn't doing her any good with J.D. hanging on her arm. She didn't want to die on this secluded path. She needed Shane. She wanted him to help her, but at the same time, she knew if he appeared, J.D. would kill them both and still take the jewels.

"I don't have them on me. I—"

J.D. yanked painfully on her arm. "Save it. I've searched your rooms from top to bottom. They're not there. Either hand them over or take me to where they are. I'm not playing games with you another minute."

Meggan's legs shook. "I—I'm not playing. I can't do anything with you jerking on me."

She hoped he wouldn't notice the leather thong around her neck. Where was Shane? If she left the cemetery with J.D., he might never find them.

If he was still alive.

"Make up your mind, girlie. How's this gonna happen?"

"Let go of me and I'll take you to them. But I need a horse. And I need to know what you did to my friend."

He laughed. "So now you're making demands, are you?" But he loosened his grip on her arm.

Meggan pulled her arm free and rubbed the spot where he'd grabbed her. "Where's Shane?"

"Do you mean the cowboy I saw with you yesterday? You don't need to worry about him. He ain't here. I am." He pushed the gun back into her side. "Now get going."

He spun her around and shoved her down the path. "You'll never get away with this," she said as she stumbled in front of him. "The whole state of Missouri is looking for you. I already notified Detective Rollins, the man who was in charge of your case. He knows you're here."

That part wasn't exactly true, but the detective would figure it out soon enough, though, once he tripped over her remains in this cemetery.

J.D.'s black eyes narrowed. His lips pulled back from yellowed teeth. "Thanks for the head's up, girlie. I may just hang around a while so I can put a bullet through his head, too. I'll throw his body over the same hill as yours. Now hurry up, and let's get this over with."

Meggan slipped her hand into the pocket of her dress. Before her fingers closed over the derringer, J.D. put his hand in the middle of her back and shoved hard. Her foot slipped in the loose gravel. She pretended to stumble. J.D. lowered the gun and grabbed her with his free hand. Meggan whirled around and threw her weight into the arm holding the gun. It flew out of his hands and landed in some overgrown weeds on the other side of the path. He pinwheeled his arms to regain his balance. He wasn't successful and fell backward. Before he even hit the ground, Meggan was off and running in the direction where she hoped to find Shane waiting.

Chapter Sixteen

S hane staggered from the blow of a rifle butt and dropped to his knees on the hardpacked earth in front of the horse he had been examining. His vision blurred. He struggled to remain conscious. He stared at a worn pair of boots. He gulped air and blinked away the blackness.

The owner of the boots leaned forward and hissed in his ear. "Never could abide a horse thief. I should put a bullet in your head right now. Ain't a man around who'd fault me none."

Shane bit back the nausea. His head and right ear roared. He could barely hear, but he understood enough to know he needed to proceed cautiously if he hoped to get back to his feet. He sat back on his knees and lifted his hands into the air. "Easy there, mister. I'm no horse thief. As you can see, my horse is tied on the other side of this shed. What do I need with yours?"

This seemed to bring the man pause. Was it possible Duggar hadn't yet recognized him? Shane had only seen the bandit from a distance and wasn't sure he could identify him as easily as he'd identified his horse.

He kept his eyes on the boots and braced for a kick in case Duggar knew who he was. "I'm a veterinarian. I saw the horse tied here, but I didn't see a rider. I came over to see if everything was all right."

The man snorted. "Don't you know messing with a man's horse is the fastest way to a bullet in your head."

"I do now." Shane pulled in a leg to stand. One of the boots landed firmly against his side and shoved him to the ground.

Shane landed with a grunt. He rolled onto his back. The sun was directly over the man's head. He couldn't make out any features. He raised his forearm to shield his face.

"I wasn't stealing your horse, mister. I just wanted to see if it was all right."

The man wasn't talking back. Shane slowly lowered his arm. When the man didn't try to stop him, he cautiously sat up. With the sun out of his eyes, he was able to make out details. His eyes traveled up the man's body. The jeans over the boots were frayed and faded but clean. A worn belt strained against a rounded belly, unlike what he'd seen of the trim Duggar yesterday. A gray beard lay over a plaid shirt faded to a dull red.

Recognition flooded through Shane, but he remained cautious. He could still easily have his head blown off for getting mistaken for a horse thief. He raised his hands higher. "Mr. Harrison, don't you know me? It's me, Shane Casey."

Wes Harrison farmed a small plot of land outside of town and ran a tool shop where he sharpened sawblades, plows, and the like for locals. At the Trego mansion the other night, Felicity told Shane Mr. and Mrs. Harrison had adopted Ronan and Grant Pollard from the foundlings' home a few years back. The Harrisons had seen their share of trials. After losing their only son to a tragic accident, they became embittered and nearly divorced. After reuniting, about the same time Felicity married Ned Yates, they realized they still had plenty of love to offer and adopted the brothers.

"We know each other, Mr. Harrison. I used to work for the Trego sisters in their stables. You and me have done business together."

The older man lowered the rifle and squinted down at him. Shane got to his feet, moving slow in case Mr. Harrison's trigger finger still believed he was dealing with a horse thief.

"Why, it is you, Shane. I thought you left town a while back."

"I did, but I'm home. Home for good. I'm opening my animal husbandry clinic soon."

Wes took a step back, but he kept hold of the rifle. Suspicion clouded his eyes. "I've been looking everywhere for this horse since yesterday morning when he disappeared from my paddock."

He looked closer at the saddle. "This here ain't my saddle. Else the hombre who stole him brung his own saddle or stole this 'un off somebody else. What was you doing looking so close at his feet?"

Shane decided a little honesty couldn't hurt at this point, and Wes might know more than he realized.

"A fella on this horse chased me through a canyon yesterday. If the horse is here, I figured the man on it was close by."

Wes looked around as if expecting the horse thief to step out of the shadows. "I reckon the two of us better head over to the jail. I'm taking my horse, a' course. I sure am happy to get him back." He looked at Shane's head and winced. "I'm sorry about knocking you upside the head. I just thought, well, when I saw you there, I was sure I had my thief."

Shane gingerly touched the knot behind his ear. There was no blood, but his head thrummed like a marching band. "I probably would've done the same thing, Mr. Harrison. You should go straight over to the sheriff and tell him about the horse. But I suggest you don't take the law into your own hands if you see another fellow looking at you funny."

He would hate to see Wes Harrison in a faceoff with the likes of Duggar.

"Ain't you coming?" Wes asked. "We both need to tell the sheriff what we know if there's a horse thief in town."

Shane started around the shed. "I got something else right urgent I need to see to first." He swung into the saddle of his horse and headed onto the street at a fast clip.

•••

Meggan wished she had picked up J.D.'s gun, but that would've taken too long.

Behind her, she heard him getting to his feet, cursing her and his own clumsiness. She glanced over her shoulder. He was kneeling in the weeds with his back to her, grappling for the gun. Maybe he'd get bitten by a poisonous spider.

She turned off the path and let the slope of the hill propel her into the overgrowth. Hopefully, J.D. wasn't as agile on his feet. She wouldn't count on it. She ran faster.

He called out for her from the top of the hill. She made another sharp right, continuing downhill toward town as she put as many turns and trees between them as possible. Would he attack her on a busy street? Shoot her in the back and take the pouch of jewels off her dead body as a crowd gathered?

She already knew the answers to her tumbling questions. Unless stopped, the outlaw would do whatever it took to get the Gochberg jewels back in his hands, even if it meant shooting a few townspeople while he was at it.

Above her, J.D. reached the overgrowth. He continued to yell and curse, apparently confident no one else was within earshot. Meggan made another sharp turn into the thickest brush she saw. She'd been disappearing from pursuers, constables, and angry shopkeepers all her life. She needed those skills now if she hoped to reach the bottom of the hill alive.

She zigzagged a few more strides and burst into a small clearing. On the far side was a crumbling, ramshackle house. It's bleached siding blended in with the trees. She prayed J.D. would run right past without noticing the clearing the way he missed the cut in the boulders yesterday.

She nearly reached the house's small front step when she noticed a door cut out of the hillside a few steps away. A smokehouse or cellar.

She changed direction and lunged for the door. Its hinges squealed in protest as she jerked a few times to get it open. A few of the boards were splintered and cracked. She had to lower her head to look inside. Two steps had been cut out of the hillside leading down into the musty, cramped interior. The back wall had fallen in, leaving only a few square feet of space.

And nowhere to hide.

It was just as well. After last night at the mine with no air and no light, Meggan couldn't force herself to drop down into what remained of the cellar.

Running footsteps crashed through the trees behind her. She waited a split second and ducked out of the doorway, letting the door slam shut behind her. She jumped behind the corner of the shack just before J.D. ran into the clearing.

As she hoped he would, he barely glanced at the house, and instead ran straight for the cellar door, still gently swaying in her wake.

He stuck his head and shoulders inside. Meggan rushed out of her hiding place and rammed into his backside as hard as she could. He lost his footing and fell down the steps and onto the earthen floor. She slammed the door shut behind him. On the ground, a long metal nail the previous owners probably used to keep the door closed glinted in the sunlight. With trembling fingers, she slid the nail into the hasp just as J.D. banged against it from his inside.

The door shook. Meggan yelped and jumped away. She doubted J.D. could break through using only his brute strength since there was no room for a running start, but a gun and belt full of ammunition would obliterate the door in no time.

She glanced around and spotted a large rock that had once been part of the house's foundation. She set it in front of the cellar door. It would take a lot more rocks to keep J.D. inside. As she grabbed another rock, she thought about forgetting the whole thing and running. But J.D. would blast his way out and be after her inside of thirty seconds.

She dropped a second rock into place. So far, no gunfire. Was it possible J.D. didn't have a gun? Most likely he was thinking. Plotting. Imagining how to tear her limb from limb the moment he freed himself.

Over her heavy breathing and pounding heart, Meggan heard someone coming down the hill. She glanced over her shoulder as she knelt for a huge cornerstone. The rock was too big. She couldn't lift it. She grabbed another. Shane appeared through the break in the trees.

"Help me," she said, too exhausted and relieved at seeing him to ask where he'd been. "J.D.'s in there."

As if to prove her point, gunfire blasted a fist-sized hole through the door. Meggan shrieked and leaped away from the door. A splinter of wood banged into her chest.

She dropped to the ground. Shane ran up and dropped to his stomach beside her.

"I'm trying to barricade him in," she whispered breathlessly.

Shane looked at the rocks she had set in front of the door. He got to his hands and knees and crawled toward the shack's foundation. Keeping his head and shoulders low, he grabbed the cornerstone that had been too heavy for Meggan to lift.

Meggan joined him and grabbed the largest stone she could manage. Just as Shane set the cornerstone in place the gun clicked. Meggan opened her mouth to cry out but realized the only sound was a click of the hammer hitting an empty chamber.

She and Shane exchanged glances. Both hurriedly grabbed more rocks. Another click sounded inside the cellar. J.D. cursed and went silent. Meggan and Shane kept wrestling stones away from the shack's foundation and placing against the door.

"Go for the sheriff," Shane whispered in her ear as they bent for the same stone.

Meggan grabbed the stone. "It'll take too long," she hissed back. "We need to take care of this ourselves." She braced for more gunfire as she set the rock in place. J.D. could be pretending to misfire in order to get her or Shane in front of the door.

"You can't keep me in here, little girl," J.D. yelled from inside the hole. "You're not as smart as your granny." He stuck his fingers through the hole his bullets had made in the door and began to pry at the wood.

Meggan stared at J.D.'s long fingers. The splintered wood was no match for his indignation and determination to escape. She grabbed an apple-sized rock and rapped his knuckles with it.

"Ahh," he screamed as the fingers withdrew. After a string of curses that brought color to Meggan's cheeks, he railed, "You'll be sorry for that, girlie. I'll rip your fingers off one by one when I get out of here."

Meggan's heart lurched. She had no doubt the man would do exactly what he said if given the chance. She piled faster.

She and Shane ignored his curses and threats as they piled the largest foundation stones they could lift against the door. Inside the cellar, J.D. stopped pounding and cursing. The stillness was worse than his shouted threats. Meggan knew he had not accepted his fate. He was reassessing the situation.

"Hey. Cowboy," he called out, "do you know what that girl stole from me? A wealth of jewels, that's what. More money than either of us will earn in a dozen lifetimes. You and me can do this together, you know? She's probably already showed you where she's hiding them. You take them and I guarantee we won't hurt her. We'll lock her in here. Once we get out of this jerkwater town, we'll send a telegram to the sheriff to come let her out. She'll be safe and you and me'll be rich men the rest of our lives."

Meggan couldn't believe her ears. Did he really think he could convince Shane to help him?

Could he?

Shane straightened and worked a kink out of his back. "You'd fill me with lead as soon as you got your hands on the jewels."

J.D.'s eye appeared in the crack he'd made in the door, but he kept back in case Meggan planned to whack him again.

"You don't have to trust me. You know I don't have a gun. Mine's jammed and it's too dark in here to fix it.

Just take them from her now. Or make her take you to wherever she hid them. Leave me half of them in the grass and get rid of these rocks so I can finish busting through. We need never lay eyes on each other again."

Shane set another rock in place at hip height. "The jewels don't belong to any of us. I'm no thief and I'd never tangle myself up with one to take something that doesn't belong to me."

J.D. burst out laughing. "That's rich. What do you think you've been doing all along? How do you think that pretty little thing out there with you got her hands on those jewels? She sure didn't find them coming out of choir practice."

The blood drained from Meggan's face. Shane had probably been asking himself the same questions since he met her. He only had her word that she sent a telegram to the detective in Kansas City. For all he knew, she'd sent the telegram to an accomplice. She may have even killed Gloria herself so she wouldn't have to share the booty.

Shane took off his hat and combed his fingers through his damp hair. Sweat had plastered his shirt against his broad back. A smear of gray dust streaked his cheek. She wanted to tell him no; she wasn't a thief. Not like he thought. She had done terrible things, but she was going through all this to make them right.

"You may have a point," he said to J.D. as he replaced his hat. "She probably isn't as guileless as she looks."

Meggan's heart sank lower.

A corner of Shane's mouth quirked upward, and he winked at her. "But I'll still take my chances with her instead of a sidewinder like you."

She exhaled in relief. He was only trying to keep J.D. talking as they could finish barricading the door. If she wasn't so tired, she'd touch his arm in gratitude.

"You're a fool," J.D. shouted. "You're not the first, you know. This is how she makes her living. Tricking idiots like you into doing her dirty work."

Meggan shook her head, but Shane had turned away. He went after another stone. They continued to stack them until the barricade was chest high. Meggan's arms trembled with fatigue.

Shane mopped his brow with the back of his arm. "You'll be fine in there a day or two without water," he called to J.D. "If the detective doesn't get here soon from Kansas City, we'll tell the sheriff where to find you and you'll be his problem."

"Don't think this'll hold me," J.D. growled, the diplomacy gone from his voice. "Even with a busted hand. I won't forget what you done to me, girlie. Both 'a you are gonna pay."

Meggan gazed anxiously at the door. "Are you sure it will hold him?" she said under her breath.

Shane shook his head. "Not at all. But it'll have to until we get far away from here."

He took her hand, and they ran across the clearing to the trail.

Chapter Seventeen

"**H**ow far is it?" Meggan asked.

After only thirty minutes of riding at an easy canter, her back ached and her thighs chafed against the saddle. She'd never ridden for more than recreation, and usually she rode sidesaddle. Her blistered hands stung against the reins. Yesterday's flight through the canyon had every muscle in her body screaming. It didn't help that the afternoon sun beat down relentlessly. As least the oversized poke bonnet cast a shadow over her face and halfway up the horse's neck.

"It's a fair piece to the quarry," Shane replied. "We're taking the long way since I don't want to ride within sight of the mines. The less people who see us, the better. We'll go past my farm on our way to see if anyone followed us out there last night."

"How long do you think J.D. will be stuck in that root cellar?"

"A long time, I'd guess. Especially after you banged his fingers the way you did with that rock." He chuckled, admiringly.

Meggan winced. "I don't like hurting people, even J.D. But when I saw him stick his fingers through that hole, I had to do something to keep him from picking his way out."

"It had to be done, and it'll slow him down considerably. Once he gets out, though, which he will, he won't know where to begin to look for us. Especially after he learns he doesn't have a horse and saddle."

"How do you know that?"

Shane gingerly touched a spot behind his right ear. "Let's just say I met the owner of the horse Duggar stole when he got to town. Every man around here will now be watching for a horse thief. It'll be a little more difficult for him to procure his next mount. Unless he wants to go the honorable way and pay for one."

She sniffed. "Not likely."

He chuckled. "I don't think so either."

Some of the tension slid out of Meggan's shoulders. She had gotten a few hours of sleep at Shane's apartment while he scouted out a spot to watch the funeral—a spot he never used—but she was still weary and gritty-eyed. While she slept, she had a nightmare of getting trapped in the complete blackness of the mine. She still tasted the smoke and soot in her mouth.

It wasn't long before she recognized the countryside surrounding Shane's property. In the shade of the tree line she loosened the poke bonnet and let it hang down her back. Even under the trees, the air was hot and sticky. The only sound over the creaking of the saddles was flies buzzing around the horses and occasionally taking a nibble out of her.

Shane turned his horse off the trail and down a rocky slope to the creek. The horses would've walked right into the water if Shane and Meggan hadn't held them back so they could dismount on dry ground.

Meggan wished she could take off her shoes and go into the water after the horses. She loved to wade through the fountains in the parks when she was a child. She seldom got far enough away from Alice and Gloria to talk and laugh and splash with the other children before they noticed she was missing and called her back. But she could still feel the cold water under her feet and hear the other children's squeals and laughter.

"What are you thinking?" Shane asked.

Meggan turned toward him. He was squatted at the edge of the water, splashing water on his face and neck.

"Excuse me?"

"You were smiling. I haven't seen you smile since I met you and your granny in Smithfield."

The comment caused a knot to form in her throat. She couldn't remember the last time she smiled a sincere smile either. A grin or a belly-laugh had been even longer.

She knelt beside Shane and cupped her hands in the water. She raised her arms and let the cold water run into her shirtsleeves.

"I was thinking of the trips to the park Alice and Gloria took me on when I was a kid."

She didn't tell him what they did there, or how they singled out people who had their guard down and made for easy pickings, especially for a little girl. "It was the closest I ever got to acting like a regular kid."

She filled the canteen with fresh water and drank deeply, then handed it to Shane. He didn't take his eyes off her as he drank. Warmth filled Meggan's cheeks under his caressing gaze.

She stood and stepped back from the water. "It made me awkward around new people. Like you."

Shane laughed and stood next to her. "Me?"

Meggan's blush deepened at the admission. "I wanted to talk to you on the stage. I wanted to ask about your animal husbandry practice. I wanted to know what it was like to invest everything of yourself into something and see it come to fruition."

"All you had to do was ask."

She sniffed. "With Granny hogging your attention the whole trip?"

"I guess it's hard to get a word in edgeways with her."

Meggan nodded solemnly. "It wasn't just Granny hogging your attention that kept me quiet. I watched how she befriended everyone she met on the road. She knew she'd never see them again, so she felt free to say anything she wanted. The same way that she stole their money and watches and trust, she stole their stories. It was a lark to her. A way to take something without it costing anything. I didn't want to be like her. I didn't want to use you that way."

"I wouldn't have thought you were using me. I would've appreciated it. I wanted to get to know *you*."

Meggan watched the water lapping against the rocks at her feet. She wasn't sure she wanted him to. What if she only disappointed him?

"I'm sorry; I shouldn't speak ill of Gloria now that she's gone. She and Alice looked after me when I had no one. I believe they loved me in their own narcissistic way. I guess I loved them too. It's just hard loving someone while hating what they do and what they are."

Shane didn't answer. She didn't blame him. Most of the time she didn't understand her love-hate relationship with the two women either.

She leaned back over the water edge to refill her canteen. She splashed water on her hot face and smoothed her hair back with her wet hands. Though she had cleaned up at the hotel, the detestable smell of the mine still clogged her nose. She imagined it would take days to get the taste out of her mouth.

Shane moved to the tree to untie the horses. Meggan took the reins from the horse she had ridden and mounted up. They splashed through the stream and climbed a small incline. Shane's large house came into view.

"Oh," she exclaimed. "I didn't realize we were so close. I don't know if I'll ever get used to the lay of the land out here."

Her eyes widened at the realization of what she said. She didn't need to get used to it. She wasn't staying. No one had invited her to. Besides being kind and helpful and accommodating, Shane had given her no reason to make her think he was doing anything beyond keeping her alive until Detective Rollins came to town.

"What I meant was, I think it would be easy to get lost out here. The creeks and hillsides and meadows all look the same. In the city, any misstep can be remedied by a right turn. If you're lost, just turn right. Another few right turns and you're back where you started. Out here, I wouldn't know when to turn right."

Shane chuckled. "Not me. I can never find my way around a city street. The buildings, the people rushing around, the shops, the noise. It confounds the daylights out of me. Out here," he took off his hat and swept his arm through the air, "instead of the stamp of man, you see the stamp of God. Every bush, every tree, every gently rolling hillside speaks of His uniqueness. Even the stars in the sky are here to guide you if you know how to read them."

Meggan glanced toward the sky as if the stars were visible. "I guess I don't know how to read them."

"You can learn."

He smiled gently. Her heart rose in her throat. The warmth in his brown eyes suggested an invitation, but she couldn't dare hope he meant more in the simple comment.

How would she leave this place with Detective Rollins and forget she ever met Shane Casey? She may mean nothing to him beyond a woman in need, but he was beginning to mean much more to her.

They reached the road that led into the barnyard. Shane motioned toward the house. "I plan to put a second entrance on the right end of the house since it's closest to the big barn. There's a large room right inside that'd make a suitable office where I can confer with clients. The other half of the house will be my living quarters. I doubt I'll need as much space as the last family."

His gaze landed on her. Yesterday he told her the original owners built the sprawling house to accommodate twelve children. Is that what he wanted? A wife? A large family, along with a legacy to hand down to them?

Meggan's dream had always been a quaint cottage on the outskirts of a small town. A rose garden in front. A painted fence lined with fragrant white and pink peony bushes. A crackling fire opposite a secluded alcove lined with bookshelves and throw pillows.

No more picking up and moving the instant the authorities caught wind of a shill game involving a genteel old lady and her reclusive granddaughter.

The one thing Meggan never saw in her imaginings was people. Now she realized a life of solitude would never be enough. She didn't want her only companions to be flowers and books and long walks through the woods. She wanted everything this large farm could offer, beginning with Shane.

Hold her husband's hand. Rocking babies. Cooking large quantities of food and setting numerous plates around a long dinner table. Teaching children to read at the same table. Pinning up the hem of a dress for a dark-haired daughter on a stool in front of the window. Cutting her sons' hair on the porch. A tall, dark-headed husband coming in from the barn at the end of the day, a laughing child swinging off each arm.

A huge family. *Her* family.

A hard life. A good life. Full of love and laughter, of growing up and falling down.

"The house isn't my first priority," Shane went on.

Meggan snapped out of her reverie, glad he couldn't see the direction her thoughts had taken.

"The first few years I hope to be too busy serving patients to worry about the house. A room or two in the back will serve my needs until...things change."

He glanced at her from under the brim of his sweat-stained Stetson. What changes did he see? If only they could include someone like her.

"It doesn't look like anyone's been here but us," Shane said as they walked the horses through the barnyard. "Duggar probably doesn't even know about this place. I guess I didn't need to waste time coming this way. I just wanted to..."

His words drifted off. He glanced at her and then away. Meggan snagged her bottom lip and smiled to herself. She was pretty sure she knew what he was thinking. He wanted to show it off. To her. To impress her. She tried not to flatter herself. He surely wasn't thinking of a life with her. He was just proud of his accomplishments. Proud of what he built.

He looked in the direction of the setting sun. "I want to get to the quarry while we still have plenty of daylight. If the cabin's gone, we'll need to make alternative plans."

"Not another night in an abandoned mine, I hope."

He smiled. "There aren't any mines out that way."

She heaved an exaggerated sigh. "Thank the Lord!"

Shane chuckled. "It wasn't that bad, was it?"

"Worse! Worse than anything I've ever been through. I may never walk into a small room again."

Shane threw back his head and laughed. He moved his horse closer. Warmth flooded over Meggan at his nearness. The scent of pine from his morning shave filled her nose. He reached toward her. Her breath caught in her throat. He pulled at a twig snagged in her hair. The twig

169

resisted. He leaned closer and reached for the twig with both hands.

Meggan's skin tingled. He was so close. She stared in fascination at his smooth, strong jaw, straight nose, rich brown eyes, and his full lips, slightly parted.

His body drew her like a magnet. She leaned into his hands without realizing it. Shane freed the twig and flicked it away. He turned his attention to her face—her mouth.

Meggan leaned closer still. Shane slid his hands through her hair and behind her head. Her heart seemed to stand still as their lips touched. He had kissed her briefly in the mine to comfort her, and she had kissed him at the store to evade J.D. Nothing prepared her for this. A tiny sound escaped her lips. He pulled her closer in response. He moved his mouth under hers.

Meggan let go of the pommel and reached for him. The horse shifted under her. She needed to straighten in the saddle or risk falling, but she couldn't pull away. She didn't want to. She never wanted to.

She combed her fingers through the hair at the back of his neck and clung to him. His horse snorted and shifted. Their lips broke apart. Shane's eyes popped open, only inches from hers. Meggan stared into his eyes and smiled.

He pulled back first. "We...we should go," he murmured with regret.

She nodded. She didn't trust her voice to respond. She was beginning to think Shane Casey was more dangerous to her than J.D. Duggar would ever be.

Shane took hold of her chin with his finger and thumb. His lips parted. She needed to turn the horse around and run. She needed to get away from this man before her heart went and did something crazy like fall in love with him.

"Shane," her traitorous mouth whispered as she leaned into him. Before their lips could touch, hoofbeats of approaching horses pounded on the hard-packed ground.

Chapter Eighteen

Not again, Shane thought as he jerked away from Meggan's ruby red lips. How had Duggar escaped the root cellar and caught up with them so quickly?

He wanted to yell in frustration. He wanted to unholster his gun and take care of this situation once and for all. He was tired of running. Tired of cowering. Tired of waiting on a detective who may not have received Meggan's telegram.

He took a deep breath to rein in the mounting frustration. Beating Duggar required patience and shrewdness, not arrogance. Duggar was a fighter. He had escaped from prison. If Shane went face to face with him, there was a chance he wouldn't survive. Then where would Meggan be? Keeping her and the jewels around her neck safe until the detective got here must remain his first priority.

He jerked his chin toward the corner of the barn. They moved the horses quietly but quickly to the end of the building where a toolshed jutted off the backside of the sun-bleached walls.

Secluded in the corner, Meggan started to dismount. Shane put his hand on her forearm. She froze and looked at him, her emerald green eyes imploring. Part of Shane's heart crumbled. He had to get her out of this, no matter what it cost him.

He held up two fingers indicating two riders. If Duggar had taken a partner, they couldn't risk dismounting. They would either have to stay hidden and hope the men didn't see them, or make a run for it. Shane prayed it wouldn't come to that. The Trego horses were top quality, but he had never tested this pair. Meggan said she wasn't an experienced rider. She had evaded Duggar yesterday in the dogleg, but Shane couldn't test her skills in a mountain race against a man who had already killed for what he wanted.

She pulled her arm out from under his hand and tightened her fingers around the reins. Her green eyes flashed. "This is my fight," she whispered. "I can't keep putting you in danger."

Was she seriously thinking of going off on her own? Dread jammed like a punch into Shane's gut. He couldn't let anything happen to her. He wanted her. He needed her.

He loved her.

Impossible. He barely knew her. The heat and her kisses were playing tricks on him.

"You won't stand a chance out there alone." Urgency and irritation laced his voice.

He cast his eyes around the barnyard. They were partially secluded behind the walls of the barn and the shed, but if the riders came around the corner, they would see them and they'd be trapped. There'd be no escape.

It would be easier to find a hiding spot if they got off the horses, but they couldn't escape without them. Not to mention their food and water was in the saddlebags. Shane wracked his brain for a spot to hide that they could reach with two bandits on their heels. Before he could make a decision, he needed to assess the situation. The riders had reached the other side of the barn. They were moving slowly. Cautiously. He motioned for Meggan to sit tight, then dismounted. He palmed his gun and crept to the corner of the shed.

"Shane Casey?" a voice called out.

Shane's knees nearly buckled in relief. He slid his gun back in the holster and turned back to smile at Meggan. He motioned for her to follow and strode around the corner of the building.

Logan Kinski and his wife Harper sat atop two sorrel horses in the fading sunlight.

"Hello, neighbors."

Logan smiled down at him. "There you are. We're sure glad to see you. We saw signs of activity around the place yesterday and thought we'd investigate. Then we heard horses. We wanted to make sure you didn't have squatters hanging around."

Shane hooked his thumbs in his belt. "I appreciate you keeping an eye out for me. It was just us."

Harper Kinski's keen gaze slid past him to the corner of the barn. Shane knew without turning around Meggan had stepped into view, holding the horses' reins. Shane

174

took the reins from her and turned back to face the Kinskis. They were waiting expectantly from atop their mounts.

Harper was a pretty blonde with a lilting voice, who had moved to Willow Wood a few years back to live with her cousin Ellie Lundy. The Lundy mansion sat on the hill directly across the street from the Trego's. Shane had only met Harper a time or two and didn't know her well. But he believed women were more intuitive to intimate matters. He could see from the look on her face she had a whole lot more questions about the mysterious brunette than she would have if a houseful of squatters had taken up residence on his farm.

"Mrs. Kinski, Logan, this is Meggan Jones. Meggan, this is the Kinskis, my closest neighbors. They've been helping watch the farm while I was at school." He directed the next comment to Harper. "I met Meggan and her grandma on the stage Monday when I got back to town. They were—"

Meggan gently bumped into him as she stepped forward and dipped her head in greeting. Shane got the message. He shut his yap before he put his foot in it.

"Nice to meet you, Mr. and Mrs. Kinski," Meggan said. "My grandmother—she passed away yesterday. I didn't know anyone in town. Shane was kind enough to join me at the cemetery today for the service."

Shane marveled at how easily the half-truths slipped off her tongue. It wasn't exactly a lie. He had meant to join her at the cemetery—even though he planned to hide in a tree during the service and watch for the man bent on killing her—before he got cold-cocked by another neighbor who mistook him for a horse thief.

No need to bother the Kinskis with those details, though it still pricked at Shane's conscience. His mother taught him honesty was the only policy, and this didn't seem completely honest.

Harper wrapped the reins around her saddle horn and slid to the ground. She hurried to Meggan and pulled her into her arms. "You poor thing. I'm so sorry. What a terrible thing to happen all alone in a strange place."

The women embraced for a long moment. When they separated, Shane was surprised to see tears shining in Meggan's eyes. Gloria had mistreated and used her most of her life. Still, she obviously had feelings for the old woman. Maybe he had been too harsh in judging her for stretching the truth. Secrets and half-truths were the only means of survival she knew.

"Thank you, ma'am—Mrs. Kinski," Meggan said.

Harper kept hold of her hands. "Were you traveling to visit family? Do they know of your loss?"

"I—um—" Meggan glanced at Shane. "I don't have any other family."

Harper let out a whimper of sympathy. "Oh, dear. How terribly tragic. Where are you staying?"

She looked past Meggan to Shane. Questioning? Accusing? He couldn't tell.

Meggan must've seen the same misgiving. "I'm staying at the hotel in Willow Wood. Shane was kind enough to—offer to take me for a ride after Granny's burial. He's been nothing but a gentleman."

Shane saw true appreciation in her eyes. And something else he couldn't identify.

Harper gave her another quick embrace. "We wouldn't expect anything less from Shane."

She glanced at him as if to remind him every woman in Willow Wood would have her eyes on him from now on to make sure he continued to behave reputably toward the bereaved young woman.

Harper looked up at her husband, still astride his mount. "Logan, we must do something. I know; we'll have them to dinner. You must come."

Meggan shook her head, her eyes wide. "Oh, no, we can't impose."

"Nonsense, it's no imposition. Is it, Logan? I insist. Shane, Teddy would love to hear of your adventures at veterinary school. Whenever we bring him this way for a ride, we tell him all about your plans to build an animal hospital. He's anxious to meet you and your patients."

Shane was thankful for the diversion. "I'm anxious to meet them too," he quipped. "The last time I saw Teddy, he couldn't even sit up on his own. It's hard to believe he's old enough to care about what I'm doing here."

Logan chuckled. "Oh, he's old enough, and full of curiosity about everything. He'll be five next month. His little sister Suzanne is two. We left them at home with the housekeeper to ride over here to make sure all was secure."

Harper took Meggan's arm. "You can come home with us. The children would love to meet you. You look like you could use some rest too. And a homecooked meal."

Meggan looked desperately at Shane. "We would, but—I..."

Shane didn't know what to say. These were her secrets; he wasn't sure how much she wanted to tell. Not much from the looks of it. But they had to say something and say it fast unless she wanted the Kinskis to figure out there was a lot more going on here than Shane showing off his farm to a pretty girl.

Logan looked from one to the other. He glanced around the quiet barnyard as if he detected something afoul. He dismounted and stepped up next to Shane. "Is everything all right?" he said softly. "Nothing wrong inside the barn?"

Shane's eyes sought Meggan's. Her mouth was a thin line. He wouldn't betray her. "No—"

"He's helping me," Meggan burst out. She closed her eyes as if to summon courage. "I can't go back to the hotel right now. I need to stay out of sight. And Shane…"

Her words tapered off as if she couldn't manage more. Harper and Logan's expressions were mirror images. Confusion and doubt marred their features.

Harper spoke first. "What do you mean he's helping you? Helping you with what?"

Meggan hesitated barely a second. "Someone is following me. He followed me and my granny from Kansas City. I need to keep out of his sight for a couple more days. Then everything will be all right."

Logan's face darkened. "We can't just stand here. If someone is following or threatening you, we need to go for the sheriff."

Meggan reached for Shane and caught his shirtsleeve. "No! We can't do that. I can't put anyone else in danger."

Harper touched her elbow. "What do you mean? That's what the sheriff is for. He'll do whatever he can to help. So will we."

Logan stepped forward. "If you need to hide out you can stay at our place."

Harper turned hopeful eyes on Meggan. "Yes, that's the best idea. Logan can help Shane keep watch. We'll get more neighbors together. We'll send someone for the sheriff."

Meggan self-consciously toyed with the leather thong inside her neckline. "It's not that simple. You have children to think of. We can't let you get involved."

Logan's hand dropped instinctively to his holster. "How dangerous is this person?" He directed the question at Shane. All three of them looked to Meggan.

She glanced at Logan and Harper before settling her gaze on Shane. He nodded, hoping to make her see she could trust these people. He wanted to touch her hand, comfort her, protect her, but she had to realize it for herself.

She dropped her hand and squared her shoulders. "This man escaped from prison. He killed my granny. He'll kill me if he has to and anyone who tries to help me. He won't stop until he gets what he wants."

Harper gasped. Logan's eyes narrowed. "What exactly does he want?

Meggan looked at Shane again. "It's better if I don't say. The more you know, the worse danger you could be in."

She took hold of Harper's hands. "I appreciate your offer. But we have to do this ourselves. It'll all be over in a day or two."

"I have a plan," Shane assured them. "I know where I can keep her—and everyone else—safe."

Harper tightened her grip on Meggan's hands. "There's safety in numbers. We won't be intimidated in our own homes. You should—"

Logan cut her off. "I'm sure they've counted the cost, dear." He looked at Shane. "What can we do to help?"

"Stay here. Let us fix it. Don't get involved, and don't tell anyone you saw us. Especially my ma," he added with a smile.

"And pray," Meggan added. "We need the Lord's protection."

"And food," Harper said. "You need food."

Shane shook his head. "No, we're fine there. We brought plenty from town."

Harper glanced around the gathering darkness. "All right. If you're sure." She hugged Meggan one last time. "If you change your mind, if you think of anything else, don't hesitate to ride over."

Meggan hugged her back, seeming to draw strength from the other woman. "Thank you, Mrs. Kinski."

Harper and Logan mounted their horses. Logan touched the brim of his hat. Harper bit anxiously on her lip but managed a smile before they wheeled the horses and rode out of the barnyard.

Chapter Nineteen

D usk had fallen by the time Meggan and Shane reached a row of towering ponderosa pines on a craggy ridge. Meggan's muscles ached. She longed to get off the horse and stretch her back and legs. But she trusted the horses walking on the uneven ground more than she trusted herself.

Shane didn't talk much. He barely even looked at her. She knew his mind was focused on reaching their destination and leaving as little of a trail as possible. If they had trapped anyone else in the root cellar of an abandoned shack, Meggan wouldn't worry the person would escape for hours. But J.D. Duggar wasn't just anyone else. She was certain he had already escaped, stolen another horse and saddle—despite the men of Willow Wood's diligence to protect their property—and no doubt working to pick up their trail this very minute. She wouldn't breathe a full sigh of relief until the man was back behind bars. Even then, she wasn't sure she could.

What would happen to her then? The thought was never far away. Since the day Meggan moved in with the Hennessey sisters, Gloria and Alice tortured her with stories of jail. It was where they sent naughty little girls who didn't do as they were told or knew how to keep their mouths shut. Sometimes when she was licking an ice cream cone in the park, they'd snatch it away and tell her there was no ice cream in jail. There, she'd be lucky to get a mealy bowl of oats and a crust of bread.

Sometimes after buying her a new dress or giving her money for a fieldtrip at school she was really looking forward to, they'd remind her how good she had it with them and how terrible her life would be if they ever got tired of her and sent her away.

Meggan learned to keep her emotions inside. If she found pleasure or joy in anything, she kept it to herself, lest someone take it from her.

She wanted to tell Shane how much he meant to her. Not just for helping her evade J.D., but for everything he'd done. For his friendship, his patience, his understanding. She wanted to tell him she didn't know men like him existed, and she hoped someday he met a woman he could trust and love as much as she suspected she was beginning to love him.

How could a woman tell a man something like that? How could she tell him the things on her heart while protecting herself from pain or rejection?

Maybe some things were meant to be left unsaid.

Not for the first time, she wished she had a friend like Harper Kinski. She would love to have a woman to talk to about men and life and children and normal things everyone else took for granted but of which she had no knowledge or experience.

The halfmoon was the only light by the time Shane pulled his horse up and waited for her to come alongside him. "Down there."

Meggan looked in the direction of his pointing finger. All she could make out was a large pool of water illuminated by the moonlight. Her muscles groaned in anticipation of getting off the horse.

"Hallelujah," she said.

"Exactly." He looked at her for a moment. She couldn't see his expression, but she saw his white teeth. She smiled back, but it took some effort. What she wanted to do was cry. It had nothing to do with J.D. After Detective Rollins arrived, she would never see Shane again. The detective would take her back to Kansas City, either as a witness or a suspect.

Would Shane be sorry to see her go? Or relieved to be rid of her and happy to get back to his life?

As they descended the mountain, darkness crowded in. It didn't bother Meggan the way it had most of her life. She wasn't sure if it was the methodical rhythm of the creaking saddles or knowing Shane was in front leading the way.

The quarry property was cavernous and mysterious in the moonlight with a gaping hole of water in the center of it. It was nearly as unnerving as the inside of the mine, though she didn't fear the heavy ceiling of sky would fall in on her head. A small cabin and a shed leaning toward the water stood apart from the other sun-bleached work buildings. Two scraggly pine trees had sprouted nearby to keep the cabin from looking completely forlorn.

After feeding and watering the horses and securing them in a small shed, Shane handed Meggan the lantern they found in the barn. He shouldered the saddlebags and followed her to the cabin.

The cabin porch was three twisted planks that skirted the door. Meggan gingerly tested the wood with her weight before stepping onto it. The door hinges stuck with age and disuse. Meggan shoved against the door with her shoulder several times before it finally yielded and pushed open. Scurrying feet sounded in the corners. Meggan shuddered, but she wouldn't worry about other cabin inhabitants tonight. At least she was above ground where she could see the sky and the moon and breathe fresh air.

She stepped aside to give Shane room to go in with their supplies. Her heel banged hard against a heavy metal object. She toppled backward. Shane snagged her with one arm and yanked her against him before she fell. The saddlebags dropped to the ground with a thud. The light from the lantern sent swaying patterns against the cabin wall.

"What happened? Are you all right?" Shane asked, keeping his arm around her, as his eyes darted around the surrounding quarry.

The pain in Meggan's heel paled in comparison to the sensation of his arm crushing her against him. "I'm all right. I tripped—" She extricated herself from his arms and looked behind her. "—over a wheel?"

"It's from an old mining cart." Shane picked up the metal wheel and dropped it off the edge of the porch.

They gathered the saddlebags and went inside. He must've heard the same rodents in the corners of the room. "We'll leave the door open for a while and let whatever's in here find their way out. We'll sleep better with some fresh air to clean out the place anyway."

Sleep.

Meggan's stomach tightened at the thought. It was one thing spending the night with Shane last night when she feared suffocation or a mine cave-in. But tonight, she didn't know how she'd fall asleep with the memory of his kiss on her lips and him only a few feet away.

She pushed the thoughts aside and set the lantern on the dust-covered table. The one room cabin was completely utilitarian, which suited her just fine. Four beds lined one wall with barely a foot of space between each. The scarred table and four dilapidated chairs were the only other furniture. A stove covered with dust, cobwebs, and mouse droppings stood against the opposite wall. The oven door hung cockeyed with the remnants of an animal's nest hanging out. She put her hand on the back of one of the chairs and wiggled it. Sturdier than it looked. It might even hold her weight.

"I'll clean off a couple beds if you can get a fire going," she said.

He could figure out what to do with whatever was living inside the stove.

It took thirty minutes to strip the beds and remake them. While Shane hauled water from the well, she toted the blankets and thin mattresses outside, threw them on the porch floor, and beat them with a shovel handle until her arms couldn't manage another swing. She didn't want to think about what creepy-crawly critter might share her bed. While she worked, Shane cleaned out the inside of the stove and built a fire. He didn't mention the stove's inhabitants, and she didn't ask. She planned to only use the stove to heat water for cleaning and coffee.

"How long has this place been here?" she asked as she dusted off the last chair and pushed it under the now-clean table.

Shane stepped back from the stove and slapped his hands together. "Longer than Willow Wood. You'll find rocks from this quarry on buildings all the way down in Nevada and Utah. Not that anybody'd take the time to look."

He poured a bucket of water into a small pail to wash their hands. "I heard once the original cabin burned down. The owner had this one built good and proper. Then a year or so later, they abandoned the quarry and everyone forgot about this place."

"How far are we from Willow Wood?" What she wanted to know was how hard would it be for J.D. to track them here.

He seemed to recognize what she wasn't asking. "Five miles. A little more. It's pretty remote. I think that's why the quarry was abandoned. The only ones who bother to come out here now are kids looking for mischief."

"Like you and your friends?"

"Ah, you remember that, huh? Whatever you do, don't tell my mother."

For the briefest instant, Meggan warmed to the notion of meeting his mother. Of becoming part of Willow Wood, part of Shane Casey's life. But it was a fantasy. A warm memory that would serve her well as she lived out the rest of her life in isolation, either by her own doing or courtesy of the State of Missouri.

This wasn't her life. Setting up house and discussing the day's events with a man who loved and cherished her. It never would be. Her life was running from the likes of J.D. Duggar.

He wasn't the only outlaw the Hennessey sisters had turned in for their bounty. Once J.D. was captured and sent back to prison, another one could turn up, seeking justice for what Gloria and Alice did. Their hatred would not cool because both women were dead. The thirst for revenge would shift to Meggan, and she'd go through this all over again.

Shane stepped outside to check on the horses. Meggan quickly scrubbed her hands, arms, and face and then set out the food from the saddlebags.

When Shane came back inside, he blessed the food and they settled in for another cold meal. Meggan was ravenous. Her stomach had calmed down from the stress of escaping J.D.—again. Finding a hiding spot above ground was enough to restore her appetite for sustenance.

"I'm sure girls get into mischief growing up too," Shane said after a few minutes of focusing on the food. "Tell me about one of your adventures as a kid."

Meggan nearly choked on a bite of baked chicken. Her life had never been boring, but she wouldn't call it adventurous, either.

She studied her plate. She wanted to tell him everything. Every sordid detail. But she hadn't told a living soul about the crimes they'd committed or the punishment she received at home when she made a mistake. She'd had chances to tell, to ask for help, but she never could.

Even the time a burly cop caught her running out of a vendor's stall with a beaded reticule in her hand. He grabbed her by the collar and held her in place while the vendor stuck his heavy-jowled, red face nearly against hers. Meggan could do little more than hold her bladder as the vendor screamed in her face, calling her a dirty, rotten little thief. The policeman—despite his size and gruff exterior—held her gently while keeping the vendor at bay with his free hand.

On the other side of the officer, Meggan saw Alice charging up to them, her face as red as the vendor's and her jaw clenched tight.

Meggan began to shake. Her mouth went dry. She wanted to hide behind the officer's meaty arm. She wanted to tell him to take her to jail so she wouldn't have to go home with Alice. She didn't want to be a dirty, rotten little thief anymore. She wanted to go to school like other girls. She wanted to have friends and eat dinner around the table with a mama and a papa and brothers and sisters. Couldn't he do something to help her?

Alice arrived and grabbed the policeman's arm. She demanded to know what he thought he was doing manhandling her granddaughter. He tried to tell her the man who owned the stall had seen Meggan snag the purse and take off. Alice hollered right over him. She was a child, for crying out loud. Couldn't he see she was scared to death? She wasn't a thief. She must've lost her money that was meant to pay for the purse. When the stall owner yelled at her, she panicked—that was all. She was afraid she'd get in trouble for losing the money and for stealing the purse. Didn't the policeman have a compassionate bone in his body? How dare he accost scared little girls when there were real criminals roaming the streets and knocking old ladies in the head! What was the name of his supervisor? Why, Alice was going to march down to the precinct, and raise the roof until something was done about officers who couldn't see the difference between real criminals and children.

By the time she stopped talking, the officer was apologizing to Meggan, who still had the stolen bag in her hand. After the policeman walked back to the stall to return the reticule and smooth things over with the vendor, Alice turned to Meggan.

Even now, the flat rage in Alice's eyes behind the serene grandmotherly smile sent a chill down Meggan's spine. That night, she nearly passed out from the beating before Gloria finally stepped in and told Alice she'd had enough. But she learned. She wasn't careless enough to get caught again.

She hadn't told the policeman that day, and she wouldn't tell Shane. She didn't want him to think she was trying to excuse her actions. Instead, she'd tell him a story he would like to hear.

"I was about twelve when Alice and Gloria collected the bounty on a man named Harold Watkins. Gloria showed you his poster on the stage. He was the one who lived with his mother in Lawrence, Kansas. That's where I lived with Grandma Elsie when I met Alice and Gloria. Anyway, the neighbors figured out how Harold got caught, and that's bad for business. After that we had to move a lot. On Sundays, Alice and Gloria took me to the lake to escape the heat of the city. The park was lovely with paved trails and arched bridges. I loved it there. I could pretend..."

Meggan took a bite of applesauce, sweet with a tang of cinnamon just how she liked it. She nearly said she could pretend she was someone else, but she wouldn't spoil the light mood.

"Once they paid a street artist to sketch my picture with my favorite bridge over my shoulder. I still have it somewhere."

"I'd love to see it," Shane said. "I'd like to see what you looked like as a girl."

Warmth flooded Meggan's face. She took another bite of applesauce. He might have meant nothing by the compliment. Or like hers, his feelings had changed, and he had begun to see her as more than a charge to keep alive until the professional arrived to take over.

A breeze picked up and blew sand and grit in the open door. Meggan got up and kicked at the dirt since she didn't see a broom. "It looks like we might get a storm." She wrapped her arms around her middle and stared into the night.

Behind her, Shane got up from the table. "I'll check on the horses again before we turn in."

Meggan knew he was really scouting the area to make sure they were still alone. She didn't look at him as he passed. She couldn't speak if she wanted to. For the first time since Grandma Elsie died, she felt like someone truly cared for her.

Instead of bringing her comfort or peace, it settled on her heart like a weight. What good would love or compassion do when Detective Rollins got here, and Shane learned a fraction of the crimes she'd committed?

Once the whole truth was laid out by a man who spent his career bringing people like her to justice, Shane's compassion would scatter like dandelion seeds in a mountain gale.

Chapter Twenty

Early the next morning Meggan and Shane headed back to Willow Wood. Meggan's stomach tightened with each hoofbeat that drew them closer to town. She was anxious for news from Detective Rollins. She couldn't wait to hand the problem of J.D. Duggar and the Gochberg jewels over to someone more qualified to deal with them. At the same time, the detective's arrival meant her reprieve was over. She would be arrested or her property seized as retribution for past crimes.

And Shane would know everything.

She hadn't slept well despite her mental and physical exhaustion. She had tossed and turned on the narrow bed, her tortured mind recounting more and more episodes from her youth of lifting pocket watches and wallets from unsuspecting men or cheap trinkets from crowded shops.

For a time during the night, her mind settled on the buyers in Seattle. What would they think when she and Gloria didn't show up in a few days? She knew nothing about them except they were willing to fence stolen property. Like J.D., would they come looking for what they believed they were entitled to? When she told them Gloria was dead, they might not believe her and instead think she was trying to double-cross them.

She tightened the brown shawl around her shoulders against the early morning chill. She couldn't bear the thought of one more person intent on taking the cache from around her neck.

Maybe it had been a mistake to stay in Willow Wood so long. It might've been better if she'd taken her chances that first morning and headed back to Kansas City as soon as she realized Gloria had been murdered and J.D. had searched the trunk. She should've taken her chances on her own instead of dragging Shane into this. Her hasty decision could get an innocent man killed.

She prayed God would forgive her.

Shane drew his horse alongside hers. "You're awfully quiet this morning."

Meggan had to turn her head nearly ninety degrees to see him around the brim of the poke bonnet covering her hair. J.D. had seen her in the same get-up yesterday and wouldn't be fooled by it today, but she felt more protected wearing the disguise.

"I can't stop thinking about J.D. I wonder if he's still trapped in that hole in the ground."

"Not likely. He's a resourceful sot. When we get to town, I'll go past that way just to make sure while you're at the hotel."

The knot in Meggan's neck from sleeping on the narrow cot tightened. "What will you do if he's there?"

"Nothing. I'll just look from the clearing to see if the cellar door's open. If it isn't, we'll know we won't have to worry about him for a few more hours."

"Just don't put yourself in danger. More than you already have."

•••

Shane watched Meggan's slumped shoulders in the saddle as if she were carrying the weight of the world. He'd give anything if he could take some of it off her. Last night as she told him about growing up with the Hennessey sisters, he knew there was a lot more she wasn't telling. She probably never would. Not that it mattered. She was leaving soon. As soon as the detective slapped the shackles on Duggar, she would go back to her life in Kansas City, and Shane would never see her again.

It was for the best, he supposed. He had a life to get back to himself. He should be at his farm right now watching over the place so Logan and Harper Kinski wouldn't have to. He needed to get things ready for the horses he planned to buy off Lester. Strangely, though, he couldn't muster any enthusiasm for what should be the most exciting time of his life. All he could think about was Meggan Jones riding out of it.

What was the matter with him? How could he think of himself when a murderous thief was bent on killing Meggan for what she carried around her neck, and now him?

Shane needed to get his head on straight before he did something stupid like falling in love with this woman.

He led the horses a different route into town in case someone was paying attention to their comings and goings. When they reached the first outlying houses, he reined in his mount and faced Meggan. He stared into her green eyes looking out at him from under the brim of the bonnet. He wanted to assure her everything would be all right, but he wasn't sure it would. He wanted to tell her how much she meant to him, but he wasn't sure of that either.

He wanted to kiss her.

"I'll wait for you behind the church at the bottom of the hill below the Trego mansion," he said simply.

Meggan nodded. She looked like she was having as much trouble deciphering her thoughts and feelings as he was. After a long look, she wheeled the horse and rode down the street. Shane watched her slim shoulders swaying in the saddle until a small house blocked his view. A squeezing in his chest made it near impossible to draw a full breath. What if Duggar was waiting on the opposite corner? Shane cursed his carelessness. He shouldn't have let her out of his sight. If something happened to her, he'd never forgive himself. If he never saw her again, he'd never...

Never what?

He wasn't going to see her again in another day or two. He needed to accept that fact right now. Meggan Jones didn't belong in Willow Wood. Besides allowing him a few kisses, she'd never given him a reason to think she'd want to stay in this rough little town with a simple animal doctor who spent more time dreaming of horses than women.

Until now.

He took off his hat and ran his hand over his face. As much as he hated having her out of his sight for the next few hours, they both had things that needed done. Best get to them.

Shane turned and rode to the next street before taking a circuitous route through town. He didn't ride past the leather works factory. He didn't want someone to recognize him and tell his mother he was in town. The less she knew about where he was and what he was doing, the better.

He was worried enough about keeping Meggan safe. He didn't want to worry about Ma as well.

He rode around the backside of the hill that led to the cemetery. It took a few passes to find the neglected path through the trees to the abandoned house. It only took a few moments to determine Duggar had indeed freed himself from the cellar. Shane hadn't expected to find the man, but knowing he was out there searching for Meggan again made his heart sink like a stone.

Gooseflesh rose on the back of Shane's neck. He grabbed his gun and whirled around. Had he heard something in the brush? He cocked his ear and listened but heard nothing over the usual early morning sounds. Keeping the gun cocked and ready, he walked the horse back to the road.

Sweat trickled down his back, though it was cool under the trees. Duggar was out there somewhere. He almost wished the man would charge out of the trees at him while they were alone and far from town. They could get this over with without the danger of hurting someone else.

He reached the road and the intersection that led into Willow Wood without hearing anything else. But he couldn't shake the sensation of someone's eyes on his back.

They needed fresh supplies for another night at the quarry house if the detective didn't show up today. First, Shane would circle around the hotel to see if he spotted Duggar staked out, waiting for Meggan.

After getting mistaken for a horse thief and whacked on the head yesterday, he knew Duggar's preferred hiding spot. He smirked at the image of Duggar arriving back at the woodshed to find his stolen horse reclaimed by the owner.

Sticking to backstreets, Shane rode slowly toward the center of town. Apprehension settled on the back of his neck again. He lifted his hat as if to dry the sweat from his brow and glanced over his shoulder. A big man with wide shoulders on a black horse with a white blaze down its face followed about fifty yards back. Shane picked up his pace. When he looked back, the big man was still there.

He urged his horse into an easy trot and turned sharply down a side street. A few moments later he heard the big man turn onto the same street. The man slowed the black under a leafy tree and looked around as if lost. Shane wasn't fooled. His first instinct was to ride back and ask the man what he wanted. Maybe he was the detective Meggan was waiting for. But how would the detective know who Shane was, and why would he follow him?

197

More than likely this man was a partner of Duggar's.

While Shane would love to neutralize the added threat right here and now, his priority was Meggan. He couldn't risk getting shot in the street and leaving her on her own. He wheeled his horse to the left and ducked into a narrow alley. Immediately, he heard the rider spur the black into action.

He sniffed in derision. Good luck keeping up on these streets with me, pal, he thought.

Before the other man rounded the alley, Shane cut through a yard and came out on the adjacent street. He stopped and listened. The other rider hadn't slowed down. Shane cut through another yard and ducked behind a chicken house, setting off a cacophony of squawking.

Smiling to himself, he wheeled the horse and turned in the opposite direction. Zigzagging between sheds and around a backyard garden, he crossed another street and doubled back until he was adjacent to the original street.

Sure enough, the other rider had gone in the direction of the squawking chickens. He had slowed and was now looking from side to side between houses. Shane made sure to stay out of sight. He couldn't get a clear view of the man, but he knew it wasn't Duggar, the detective, or a local who had mistaken him for a horse thief.

When a house momentarily obscured his view, Shane ducked over the saddle and urged his horse as fast but as quietly as possible halfway down the next street. He slid out of the saddle and tied the horse to a clothesline post. He ran to the street and climbed into the branches of a large leafy elm. He positioned himself on a thick branch hanging over the street. He put his hand on his pistol grip to remind himself it was still there, should he need it. He didn't plan to need it yet.

When the big man rode under him, Shane propelled off the branch, making sure his momentum was enough to carry both of them out of the way of the black's hooves. He sure didn't want to go to all this trouble only to be beaten by a kick in the head from a horse.

He hit the man at the shoulders and wrapped his arms around him as they fell. They rolled once with Shane coming out on top. He pinned his legs around the man's middle, blocking access to his gun belt. He wrapped his hands around the man's throat, driving his chin up and back so the man could barely draw a breath.

"Okay, mister, you better tell me quick who you are and why you're following me before I snap your neck."

The older man chuckled as best he could with his head at the unnatural angle. "Easy there, cowboy." He twisted his head to gasp out the words around Shane's grip. "If you raise up a mite, you'll see who I am. Your elbow's jamming my badge into my chest."

Badge?

Without lessening his grip on the man's throat, Shane shifted to get a look at his chest. No badge. The man freed his arm and reached toward Shane. Shane stiffened again and applied more pressure to his throat.

"Just trying to show you." He flipped the corner of the vest over, revealing a tarnished badge pinned to the other side.

Shane relaxed his grip on the man's throat.

"Now, I think it'd be a good idea for you to let me up, kid, before you find yourself in a heap more trouble than you are already for assaulting a lawman."

Chapter Twenty-One

S hane stared in disbelief at the badge. After a stunned moment, his joints loosened, and he jumped to his feet. He scooped the peace officer's hat off the ground and slapped it against his leg to remove the dust. With his free hand he caught hold of the black's reins, though the horse didn't look like it was going anywhere. He reached out to help the man to his feet, but the lawman got to his feet with no help from Shane.

The man was only an inch or so taller than Shane, but his broad shoulders and square head made Shane feel puny in comparison. He brushed the dust off his vest and the seat of his trousers before taking his hat. Shane figured the relaxed smile was meant to put him at ease, but it didn't match the suspicion in the lawman's blue eyes.

"I'm sorry, sir," Shane said, as his brain tried to catch up with what had just happened. "I didn't realize..." The words trailed off. He didn't have much to apologize for. The lawman *had* been following him. In some frontier towns, the man would've gotten himself shot before anyone took the time to ask questions.

The man's easy smile widened, though Shane still didn't trust it. "I'm Officer Preston Walker of the fifteenth precinct in Kansas City." He adjusted the big hat over his curly blond hair. "I've been tracking two ladies who left there last week. Don't suppose you know anything about them?"

Irritation rose up in Shane. He didn't have time for games. "I figure you already know I do, else you wouldn't be trailing me. I'm sorry for knocking you off your horse, but you gotta expect it when you go following a man for no reason."

The man sucked air through a gap in his mouth from a missing incisor. "No, boy, er, Mr. Casey, I reckon you're right about that. But I'm in the middle of an investigation here. I can't go introducing myself to ever'body who's done got my attention."

Shane bristled at the condescension in the man's voice. "How do you know my name?"

"I'm an investigator, Mr. Casey. I saw you with Miss Jones yesterday. I made it my business to find out who you are."

Shane liked that even less than the man knowing his name. Willow Wood was a close-knit community. Everyone knew him and his mother, and they had long memories. What would people think of a lawman from Kansas City asking questions around town about him? It

201

could ruin his reputation before he had a chance to build one. Not to mention how it would worry Ma if she caught wind of the inquiries. Was she safe? Had the lawman's questions made her a target of Duggar's?

"If something happens to my mother because of you sniffing after me…"

The lawman raised a hand in the air. "Now, I assure you, Mr. Casey, I didn't say nothing that'd cause your dear mother grief or worry. I've just been waiting for an opportunity to have a word with you without Miss Jones around."

Shane figured this was the man he'd heard following him through the woods and not Duggar. It hadn't been his imagination. So, where was Duggar?

"If all you wanted to do was talk, you could've called out to me instead of slinking through the woods like a polecat. The whole thing makes me think you suspect me of something. Or you can't be trusted."

The flat stare was back in Walker's eyes. "Sometimes you learn by hanging back and watching than by barging in and demanding answers."

Shane couldn't argue with that. The original adrenaline that made him climb the tree had evaporated, but he asked, "What'd you mean earlier when you said I'd be in more trouble that I am already. I haven't done anything."

Had Walker followed Meggan and Gloria from Kansas City to arrest them? Was Meggan guilty of more than Shane believed?

Walker sucked air through his teeth again. "Well, now, I don't know yet if you've knowingly broke any laws. I mean, you are aiding and abetting Meggan Jones, a known jewel thief."

"She's not the thief."

What did he really know about her? Only what she'd told him, and that was darn little.

Smug satisfaction shone in the lawman's eyes. "I didn't come here to take nobody into custody but Miss Jones. And her granny if she hadn't…well…" He dipped his head, though Shane figured there was no actual respect there. "She's gone now, so she's no one's concern but the Good Lord's. The only reason I'm still in town is Miss Jones. And you if'n you got a notion of obstructing justice."

He leveled a hard stare at Shane. His earlier easy-going manner was gone. "Mr. Casey, I need to know what you know about the jewel heist in Kansas City, and how long you've known it. We got an escaped fugitive reportedly headed this way and some missing jewels that got an upstanding businessman from our community murdered. Now, the way I see it, there's two explanations for you and me having this conversation."

He hitched up his gun belt and arched one eyebrow. "You're either another unwitting dupe who got hisself hoodwinked by Miss Jones's pretty face. Or, you're her accomplice."

Shane respected the law, but he was about two seconds from knocking the man's enormous head off his shoulders.

He struggled to rein in his temper. He couldn't believe what Walker was suggesting about Meggan. And him. He wasn't an unwitting dupe. But didn't all unwitting dupes think that?

"Meg—Miss Jones had nothing to do with stealing those jewels. She's trying to return them."

For the first time, genuine humor lit up Walker's face. Now, Shane wanted to knock his own head off.

Walker smoothed his vest down over the badge. "She's a purdy little thing, I'll give you that. A man sometimes has a hard time keeping his head straight when she directs those big green eyes at him."

Shane swallowed hard, struggling to keep his mounting fury from showing. Meggan had never used her womanly wiles to seduce him. But maybe the innocent, damsel-in-distress act was part of her game. Either way, he wondered if he had been played the fool. His only question was who was playing him. The lawman? Or Meggan?

"Now, Mr. Casey," the lawman said, once again placating, "I'd hate to think you'd stand in the way of justice in this matter. We have an escaped convict to capture and stolen property to return to Missouri."

Shane wondered who was *we*.

He only saw one man standing in front of him, and he didn't think much of what he saw.

"Has Miss Jones shown you the stolen jewels? Where is she keeping them?"

Shane thought about pretending he had no idea what the lawman was talking about. Everything Meggan told him about the theft implicated Gloria and Duggar. Shane only had her word for sending a telegram to Detective Rollins. What if, instead of sending it to the detective, it had gone to an accomplice who was now headed to Willow Wood to help her escape to Seattle and cash in the jewels?

Or the telegram may have gone to the buyers in Seattle. The only reason she needed an accomplice at this point was to evade Duggar. She had Shane for that. An unwitting dupe. Was that what was happening here?

He knew absolutely nothing for sure except there was a fortune's worth of jewels around her neck and a man chasing her who was willing to kill anyone to get them.

Meggan was crafty; Shane had seen that for himself when she escaped Duggar in the canyon and somehow managed to single-handedly trap him in a collapsed root cellar. Shane didn't know many other people who could think on their feet the way she did. What could it mean if she wasn't a criminal mastermind herself?

"Mr. Casey? The jewels."

Walker was staring at him. Shane couldn't tell if the lawman thought he was hiding something or was plain dull-witted.

"I don't know anything about any jewels," he answered honestly enough. He hadn't even seen them. For all he knew, Meggan had a fistful of gravel in that pouch.

Walker sucked air again, never taking his eyes off Shane. Shane didn't look away. He didn't like the man and respected him even less. A tin star pinned to his vest wasn't enough to earn Shane's trust.

Walker rocked back on his heels as if he and Shane were having a friendly conversation. "The good people of Kansas City just want justice, Mr. Casey. I'm sure you understand that what Miss Jones and her grandmother did was reprehensible. A widow is waiting in Kansas City for her property. She can't have her husband back, but she should be allowed her dignity. I would think you'd care about that."

"I do care. That's why I helped Meg—Miss Jones stay out of sight."

"If you're being honest with me, it was the only option you had. You wouldn't want Miss Jones, or anyone else, to fall prey to the man I believe is tracking her. I don't think even she realizes how dangerous he is. Before he broke out of prison, he killed another inmate. Gutted him like a fish over some petty disagreement. You're not protecting Miss Jones by hiding her from this animal. You're only making yourself look like an accessory to grand larceny. If your only goal was to protect her from that killer, you would've turned her over to the local sheriff the minute you met her. It's his job to protect citizens in his town, not yours."

Shane had been second-guessing that decision himself. But something about what the man was saying didn't ring true. He hadn't believed Meggan because she was beautiful and soft spoken. He didn't believe her because she needed him, and he wanted her story to be true. He believed her because of the hurt little girl he saw inside her. He knew that little girl was real. Meggan hadn't made it all up to fool him into helping her until her partner arrived.

"There has been a man following us," he admitted.

His skin crawled at how dangerous Duggar really was. "Miss Jones believes he killed her grandmother. That's why I wanted to help her."

Walker sucked air through the gap in his teeth and narrowed his eyes thoughtfully. "You can see why I came all this way to take care of this matter. But I have to know what Miss Jones has done with the jewels. Does she still have them? Has she mentioned anyone else who may be involved in the theft?"

Shane knew the man wasn't telling him the whole story. He seemed more interested in the jewels than capturing an escaped murderer.

"I don't know anything about jewels or a robbery or a murder," he said crisply. "I met Miss Jones and her grandmother on the stage to Willow Wood. The doc assumed Miss Hennessey had a heart attack. Meggan was scared and alone and needed someone to stay with her until..." He shut his mouth just before he mentioned the detective. "...Until she could get word to a friend in Kansas City."

The sheriff's eyes narrowed further. "A friend? Is that so?"

"I don't know. I guess. I had no reason to doubt her."

The lawman angled his large head. "Let me tell you a little about Miss Hennessey and Miss Jones. If you're involved, you already know those two women are bounty hunters. They turned in a ruthless killer for the bounty on his head and then stole the jewels he'd stolen in Kansas City. I like you, Mr. Casey. You seem like a nice enough fella. I believe you came back to town to open your animal husbandry practice, but then you met that purdy little gal and she got your head all twisted around. If I was you, I'd stick to my original plan and forget I ever met Meggan Jones and her conniving grandmother."

"You're not me," Shane bit out.

"Nope, you're right, I'm not. I just hate to see a young man throw his life away over a gal who's no good. I've known about Meggan Jones and her grandmother for a long time now. They know just what to say to get a man to lower his guard. Then they go in for the kill. You're obviously a smart man. I trust you'll make the right decision."

Walker removed his hat, knocked the last of the dust off it, and set it back on his square head. He threw a leg over his horse and looked down at Shane. "You have a nice day there, Mr. Casey, and for your own good, think long and hard about what I said."

Shane didn't respond. He didn't break eye contact either until the lawman wheeled his horse and rode away. Shane stared after him. He kept staring, even after the black disappeared from view.

Everything Walker said lined up with what he already knew. Meggan told him from the beginning how she and Gloria came to possess the jewels. But had she simply been using him?

He thought back to the first time he saw her in Smithfield before they boarded the stage. She had seemed to barely glance in his direction. But maybe she was drawing him into her web even then. Had he fallen for a pack of lies because they were hidden behind a pretty face?

He hoped he wasn't that gullible. If so, it was too late. He was already in love with her.

Shane felt his face go white under the rising sun. Was it possible? Had he fallen in love with a jewel thief? If so, he knew why. She was vulnerable and alluring, but beautiful and smart. Something about her had drawn him in the first moment he saw her. Was it love? Or was he a chump?

Chapter Twenty-Two

At the telegraph office, Meggan learned she had not yet received a telegram. It didn't mean Detective Rollins wasn't coming, only that he hadn't bothered to write to give her an arrival time. She knew he wouldn't let anything short of a train derailment keep him from coming to Willow Wood, even if he had to hike across the mountains to get to her. He wasn't in town yet, which meant another day and night avoiding getting killed, and another trip to town tomorrow morning.

Meggan wanted to cry right in front of the telegraph agent. She didn't know how much more she could take of keeping out of J.D. Duggar's clutches. Yesterday had been too close. She could still feel his hand on her arm and his hot breath on her face.

She tightened the brown shawl around her shoulders as she stepped out of the telegram office into the bright July sunshine. It was hot for nine o'clock in the morning. She hurried across the street and down the alley that led to the back of the hotel. A burly man with sweat-soaked hair and a soiled apron stepped outside with a bucket of breakfast remains just as she reached for the door. He barely acknowledged her as he dumped the bucket into a barrel. Meggan jumped aside to avoid any scraps from splashing on her and dashed through the open door.

She wished she had time to go upstairs, take a proper bath, and change her clothes. But she didn't want to get cornered by J.D. She untied her steamy bonnet and yanked it off her head. She immediately felt ten degrees cooler.

The kitchen inside the hotel was bustling. Servers and cooks scurried back and forth, shouting orders and banging dishes and clanging pots. The noise and chaos were comforting. With so many witnesses, she was confident she was safe from J.D. for at least a few moments.

She glanced around the crowded kitchen for the maid she had spoken to yesterday, though the woman wasn't a kitchen maid. She was probably upstairs stripping beds and cleaning rooms. Meggan went to the back staircase and looked up, half expecting to see J.D. at the top, glaring down at her. She started up when she heard movement coming toward her. She nearly ducked behind a serving cart, then chastised herself for being so jumpy. Of course, she would hear people coming and going in a busy hotel.

She sighed with relief at the sight of the maid she was looking for coming downstairs with an armload of bed linens rolled into a ball.

Meggan stepped into the doorway of the laundry room to wait for her. "Good morning, ma'am," the woman said as she entered. "Can I get you something?" she asked after Meggan's rushed greeting.

"Has there been anyone here asking about me?"

The maid glanced over Meggan's shoulder as if hoping someone else would appear to answer the question. "Um, we saw someone early this morning coming out of your room. Well, I didn't. It was Greta. I was just getting to work when she came rushing downstairs. She was very shocked to see a man come out of your room. He had black hair and the darkest eyes Greta had ever seen. I told her you were expecting your uncle, so it was probably all right."

Meggan's mind whirled. She tried not to let her terror show. Thank the Lord she hadn't been here when J.D. was in her room. "Did he say anything to anyone? Do you know if he took anything?"

The maid's pale brows slid together. "I don't think so, miss. I'm sure he'll be back soon, though. If I see him, I'll be sure to tell him you're upstairs waiting."

Meggan had no intention of waiting for J.D. to come back. "Thank you," she told the woman anyway. "Has anyone else been here asking about me? A tall man with gray hair, probably dressed in a smart dark suit."

"No, ma'am, I haven't seen anyone like that."

"If he comes, could you get word to me without my uncle finding out?" Meggan didn't care if the maid thought she was embroiled in a tryst with an older man

211

her uncle didn't approve of. She needed to avoid the hotel as much as possible, especially now that J.D. was becoming more brazen every day.

"My uncle and I don't get along. He always thought my grandmother was too lenient with me. I fear he believes I'm too young to handle my own affairs and he'll try to control them for me."

The maid's eyes gleamed. She seemed to like the idea of helping Meggan escape the confines of a meddling uncle. "I could do that."

Meggan wanted to go upstairs and get a fresh change of clothes, especially a lighter hat. But if J.D. could return any time, she was afraid to risk it. The brown dress and poke bonnet would have to do for another day. She thanked the maid and hurried out the back door.

An American flag hung limp against the pole over a sign that read: *Endicott's General Store.* Meggan circled the block and tied the horse behind the store to keep it out of sight. She didn't want anyone to recognize the horse from the Trego stables and start asking questions about who she was and her business in Willow Wood. Shane had taken care of food and provisions the last two days. Most of her life, other people had taken care of her. Made decisions for her—good or bad. She was alone now, wholly responsible for herself. It was time she learned how to do it.

The general store was as quiet as the morning streets when Meggan stepped inside. A woman, somewhere in her fifties—Mrs. Endicott, she presumed—with faded auburn hair liberally streaked with gray, looked up from behind the postal counter where she was sorting mail.

"I'll be right with you, dear," she called out. She had open, welcoming features reminiscent of the countless shopkeepers and clerks Meggan had encountered all her life.

"No hurry," Meggan replied. "I'll find what I need and call when I'm ready."

As she moved down the narrow aisles, putting a few items into a shopping bag, she thought of the shopkeepers and small business owners she had lied to and cheated over the years. None suspected when she stepped into their shops that she would leave them a little poorer when she walked out. Even now, it would be so easy to lift a few items from the crowded shelves and Mrs. Endicott would never know. No other customers were inside the store. The shelves sufficiently blocked her from Mrs. Endicott, who wasn't paying attention anyway. Meggan's fingers stretched toward a display of dried beef jerky. She could easily slide a few of the tangy sticks up her sleeve. Beef jerky was cheap. Mrs. Endicott wouldn't even miss it. She'd done it hundreds of times before with items more valuable than beef jerky. She, Alice, and Gloria even added extra depth and strength to their skirt pockets so no one would suspect how many pounds of stolen property were hidden among the folds of their skirts when they walked out the door.

She closed her hand into a fist and dropped it to her side. Shame colored her cheeks. What was she thinking? She wasn't a thief. Not anymore. But she couldn't even trust herself. Maybe it was impossible to change.

A few moments ago, she had lied to the maid at the hotel by making up a fictitious uncle to explain J.D.

Duggar. Anytime it behooved her, she lied without thinking twice to get the results she wanted.

Could she change? She wasn't sure she knew how. She just knew she didn't like the person she was; a liar and a thief. Undeserving of the things she wanted most.

Friends. A family. Love.

She grabbed what she needed and went to the counter. She considered paying extra as restitution for her evil thoughts of stealing the beef jerky. But overpayment wouldn't change who she was. She needed a change from the inside; one that only came from God. The problem was He knew everything she had ever done. She couldn't fool Him.

Knowing Shane had probably finished his errands and was waiting for her, she hurried down the street to the butcher shop. Before they left the cabin this morning, Shane had set traps for meat, but a little bacon would flavor the beans tonight and fry up nicely for breakfast tomorrow morning.

No one else was inside the shop. The old man with a bald pate and a bloody apron tied around his girth was anxious to talk. Meggan said as little as possible so she wouldn't have to lie about who she was and why she was in town. A few questions of her own, and he was off and running on every topic from the heat to his lumbago to the local government to his regret over the quality of the pork.

If Meggan was good at one thing, it was making men think she was interested in whatever they were saying while divulging very little about herself. The vanity of men had always served her well.

She finally broke away from the shopkeeper and stepped outside.

Straight into the arms of a large man with shoulders broad enough to block the sun.

She jerked back. Her heels cracked hard against the doorframe. The man grabbed her elbow as if to steady her. She knew it meant more.

"Miss Jones, I been looking ever'where for you. You sure are a hard woman to track down. I suppose it's by design."

Sandy-blond curls stuck out from beneath the man's sweat-stained Stetson. Icy blue eyes bored into hers as if they could see right inside her, the way they had from the first time she saw him. He was the last person she expected to see in Willow Wood.

"H…hello, Officer Walker. I…I didn't see you there."

His customary easy laugh rumbled in his throat. "I 'spect not. If you had, you'd've asked the butcher to let you out the back."

"No, I…" She swallowed to moisten her throat. Why was he here? It couldn't be to find J.D. Duggar. No one knew to look for him in the streets of this sleepy frontier town.

The lawman hadn't tracked J.D. here. He was tracking her.

Her eyes scanned his muscular chest. She didn't see his badge. He sometimes wore it concealed when he visited their Kansas City apartment in an "unofficial capacity" to talk to Gloria. Gloria had always obliged. She couldn't resist an audience who wanted details on how she outsmarted a cunning criminal like J.D. Duggar.

Meggan knew talking too much to anyone was dangerous, especially a lawman. She just couldn't convince Gloria.

Today, Officer Walker's shirt was open at the collar. Meggan stared at the sweat glistening in the hollow of his throat and fought down the rising panic.

He had come to arrest her; why else would he be here? He had figured out the whole story. She was almost relieved. This terrible experience was over.

Or had it just begun?

If Officer Walker knew she, Gloria, and Alice had stolen the jewels from where J.D. hid them, he wouldn't believe she sent a telegram to Detective Rollins in an attempt to return them. Didn't all criminals claim to be returning the loot as soon as it was found in their possession?

It was over. She was going to jail where she would be tormented and starved the rest of her life. Still, it was almost better than running from J.D. another minute.

She needed to talk to Shane. She needed to explain why she was being arrested. She didn't want him to wonder if everything she ever told him was a lie. Much of it was but not everything. She couldn't leave until he knew how much better she was for having met him.

She couldn't leave until she told him she loved him.

It was crazy and unfair, but she did love him. The knot in her stomach rose to her throat, choking her with unshed tears.

"I wasn't trying to hide from you," she told the lawman.

She hadn't known she needed to.

"I...my granny..."

He sucked air through the gap in his teeth. "I know all about her. Gloria Hennessey was buried on that hill yesterday." He wagged his chin in the direction of the cemetery without taking his eyes off her.

Meggan didn't look away either. She couldn't. He was a snake charmer, and she was hypnotized by his gaze.

He put his hand on the wall behind her, pinning her in with his closeness. "I suppose you know why I'm here."

Meggan resisted the urge to step away. "I assume it has something to do with J.D. Duggar breaking out of prison."

One side of his mouth twitched. "Now, how would you know about that?"

She fixed her gaze on his Adam's apple. "You know Granny. She kept abreast of any news about convicts and a possible payday. An escaped prisoner would bring a good price."

"I 'spect she paid particular attention to that prisoner, especially since she knew he'd come after her soon as he got the chance."

He lowered his arm and looped his thumbs in his gun belt as if he had all morning to stand and shoot the breeze with her. "I'll never forget all that hollering he did about you ladies in court."

Even though Meggan was sure he had the evidence he needed to arrest her, she couldn't keep from defending herself. "He has no reason to chase after us."

Walker chuckled a mirthless laugh. Dampness rose under Meggan's arms. She hoped the lawman couldn't smell her fear.

"I reckon he thought he did since he claimed all along you ladies were the ones who had the Gochberg jewels." He took a toothpick from his shirt pocket and poked at a spot between his teeth.

"I don't know what he meant by—"

"Yup," Walker went on. "We all thought he was shooting a load of bull to get us off his trail. Most of the flat feet in Kansas City still do."

He sucked air around the toothpick.

"Not me, though. Duggar is a lot of things, but he wouldn't give credit where it wasn't due. I figured all the fuss he kicked up deserved a little investigating."

He rocked back on his boot heels. "Your granny was a very interesting lady. That's why I came by your place so often. I loved to sit and listen to her talk. With her, a man had to listen real close. You know, for the things she didn't say. Those were the interesting parts. I figure if Duggar went to all this bother to trail you, I'd tag along and see what he was after."

Meggan wanted to step out of the lawman's intrusive shadow, but she couldn't move. She wished Shane were here. But she had to stop relying on others and face the consequences for what she'd done herself.

She struggled to get her thoughts in order. "I—I don't know—"

"You ain't seen him hanging around, have you?" Walker asked as if she hadn't spoken.

The pouch inside Meggan's blouse prickled against her skin. "I've been busy taking care of Granny's effects. I haven't…" She stopped talking. Even she heard the lies in her voice.

Walker sucked air between the gap in his teeth and glanced around. "This here sure is a nice little town. Not a bad place to hang around a day or two to see if Duggar shows hisself." He nodded at the brown wrapped package from the butcher shop. "Looks like you're making yourself comfortable."

Meggan had nearly forgotten the bacon she just bought. "I—no—yes—"

"Does that cowboy's been following you around know you and your granny made some serious enemies?"

Her eyes widened. *Shane.* What did he know about Shane?

"I—he's only been a friend to me. I can't leave town and he—"

She stopped talking. She didn't owe this man an explanation. Until he arrested her and took her in front of a judge, she needn't say another word to him. She was going to make everything right but only with Detective Rollins.

Walker laughed with real humor this time. "Miss Jones, don't you know a fella don't never want to be a *friend* to a gal that looks like you." He laughed again as his piercing blue eyes raked over her face and down the front of her blouse. "No, Miss Jones, that ain't why he's hanging around."

When he brought his gaze back up to hers, all traces of humor were gone. "If I was you, I'd stick close to town. Safer that way. I'd hate to see the same thing happen to you that happened to your granny, I mean, Miss Hennessey."

Fear squeezed Meggan's middle, making it hard to breathe. What did he know about what happened to

219

Gloria? Everyone in town believed she had a heart attack. And why had he called her Miss Hennessey? No living soul but Shane knew she wasn't Meggan's real granny.

Her gaze drifted back to his shirt collar. Suddenly, it became clear. She bit back a scream. With a shaky breath, she looked into his eyes. "Don't worry, Officer Walker. I'm not going anywhere," she managed levelly.

He smiled again, an oily, knowing smile that set her teeth on edge. "I'm counting on that, Miss Jones. I'll be seeing you around. And your friend too." He tipped his hat and walked away.

Meggan spun in the opposite direction and ran. The package of bacon slipped to the ground, but she didn't stop to pick it up. Gloria had been murdered, and not by J.D. Duggar. She had the evidence in her satchel. She only hoped she lived long enough to prove it.

Chapter Twenty-Three

Shane jerked around at the sound of the horse galloping into the churchyard. He had stopped at the Trego house to check on Ma before coming here to wait for Meggan. She spent the short visit talking and smiling and bustling around the kitchen, thus easing his worries that she had heard he was doing anything besides getting his ranch ready for his first purchase of horses. When she halved a biscuit and stuffed it with egg and a couple slices of bacon, Shane managed to choke it down around his dry throat. He didn't like keeping things from her. He didn't want to worry her either. He had everything under control. He hoped.

He pocketed another biscuit and egg, kissed her goodbye, and hurried out the back door. The brief conversation temporarily took his mind off Walker and his allegations about Meggan and her granny. But as soon as he rode off the Trego property, it all came rushing back. Had Meggan sent a telegram to a detective in Kansas City the way she said? Or to someone else?

Was there an accomplice somewhere, and Shane had simply been her safety net until the man she really wanted arrived.

Then he remembered her touch, her lips on his, the way she looked at him, and he was confused all over again.

At the appearance of the horse thundering into the churchyard, he knew something was wrong. Raw fear etched Meggan's flushed face. Had she seen Walker? Was Duggar following her? Or was it all an act to keep Shane on the hook?

She brought the horse to a stop but didn't dismount. "I bought a few supplies for the night." She indicated the bulging saddlebag. "Are you ready? Can we go?" She glanced over her shoulder.

Shane caught hold of the horse's bridle. "What's the matter? What's wrong?"

"Nothing. I—" Another glance toward the street.

Shane made up his mind he wasn't taking one step further until she told him the truth of what was going on.

"Meggan, tell me what happened. Did you see Duggar? Is someone after you?"

He watched her face under the shade of the oversized bonnet. Her green eyes sparkled.

"Tell me," he demanded through clenched teeth.

She fidgeted. She looked at the horse's mane, the churchyard, the steeple. Finally, she brought her gaze back to him. "I never should've brought you into this. I'm so sorry. I wouldn't blame you if you went back to your farm and left me to face the consequences of this myself."

Shane slid his hand up the horse's neck until he reached her hand. He grasped it. "What consequences, Meggan? I won't leave you, but I need to know the truth. The whole truth."

Was he wrong to trust her? Was she playing him for a fool? Looking into her eyes, he didn't believe so.

She pulled her hand out from under his and swiped it across her flushed cheeks. "Please. We need to leave right away. I'll tell you everything as soon as we get to the cabin. I just have to get out of town. We both do."

Shane knew she was right. Whatever the situation, he was in it now. He'd do whatever it took to protect them both until the detective arrived.

If there was a detective.

He swung into his saddle. On the way out of town, they kept to back streets and alleys to avoid as many people as possible. Shane kept his ear tuned for sounds of someone following them. He saw no one or nothing besides what was expected on the streets this time of day. He remembered the days when no greater worries hounded him than leaving hoofprints in someone's yard or getting close enough to sneak a handful of succulent fruit from Blanche Balty's strawberry bushes. He wished someday he could share those memories with Meggan.

If they ever had a someday. If she wasn't a jewel thief on her way back to Kansas City for prosecution.

At the edge of the town, they urged the horses into a gallop. Shane headed west away from the direction of his farm and away from the quarry. If someone was keeping an eye on them—and he was sure someone was—he didn't want the pursuer to know where they were headed.

He breathed a little easier when they reached a fir-lined ridge about a mile from Willow Wood. In the deep shade, they reined the horses to a stop. Shane turned in a full circle, his eyes scanning the countryside below.

"Where are we going?" Meggan's voice was tight.

"The quarry. I just want to make it hard if someone's following us."

She pressed her full lips together. Shane spotted a barely discernible trail and began to follow its meandering course through the woods.

They rode in single file until they reached a clearing. Shane cut east, and they galloped across a wide meadow. On the other side, the terrain became steeper and rockier. It was harder travel and slower going but provided cover if someone was watching. Shane focused on the horses' footing, thankful for the respite of thinking about anything else.

It had only been four days since he met Meggan Jones. It felt like a lifetime. He barely remembered what he'd done before her. He sure didn't want to think about what he'd do after.

After an hour of picking their way up the mountainside, they reached another ridge. Shane heard the welcome sound of rushing water below them. The horses heard it, too, and headed that way on their own.

The way to the creek was steep, but Shane knew of a level spot where a small waterfall emptied into a shallow pool. He and his friends had dipped there many times over the years.

At the creek he and Meggan slid out of their saddles and led the horses to the water's edge. The temperature was cooler near the water, but Shane was still hot and sweating. He removed his hat and set it on the rocks beside him. He cupped his hands and poured water over the top of his head, then ran his wet hands through his hair.

Meggan moved away from him and the horses and knelt close to where the waterfall crashed into the pool to sate her thirst. He watched out of the corner of his eye as he scrubbed his hands and face with the cool water. He should be mad at her. She had lied, or at least not told him everything. But he wasn't. She'd had a rough life; she never knew who she could trust. He didn't want to be one more person who let her down.

He got up and walked over to her. She straightened beside him but kept her gaze on the tumbling water. She had taken the brown bonnet off and let it hang down her back. Her bare forearms and face glistened from the spray of the waterfall.

Shane turned toward it. It was nice standing here, saying nothing, thinking nothing, contemplating nothing. The last four years had been so busy. He seldom got a decent night's sleep. Most meals were swallowed nearly whole as an instructor or mentor called for him to hurry so they could answer another call. His only priority was absorbing everything they had to teach. He knew soon he'd be on his own, and the notion was daunting.

To some degree, Meggan faced the same thing. Her granny was gone. Even if she didn't have two men chasing her, Shane knew firsthand how scary and overwhelming it was to be alone for the first time. He wanted to make things easier on her, not worse.

He closed his eyes and prayed silently, "Lord, help me see the truth."

225

When he opened his eyes, Meggan was watching him intently. Crystal droplets of water dotted her face. The sun shone on them and made them look like beads of emeralds and sapphires, reflecting the trees and water back at him. Shane's heart stood still. Tall and willowy she reminded him of a fragile china doll he wanted to protect.

Tears pooled in her eyes, making them sparkle in the dappled sunshine. "I was standing here thinking how nice it would be if Gloria was here." She glanced toward the waterfall. "She would've loved this. She loved seeing new things. You should've heard her during our trip west on the train. She was like a child squealing at each new experience. She had never been farther west than Kansas City."

She blinked and a tear slid down her cheek. "The other morning when I found her, it felt like a hundred-pound weight had lifted from my shoulders. Isn't that terrible? I thought; I'm free. Gloria was dead, and all I could think about was myself."

The tears began to flow faster. Meggan sniffed to hold them in check, but it was no use. Shane stepped closer. Meggan moved into his arms, buried her face on his shoulder, and sobbed.

Shane rested his cheek on the top of her head and held her gently until the tears subsided. He fumbled one-handed for his handkerchief in his pocket.

He handed her the handkerchief as she stepped out of his arms. They immediately felt empty without her.

"You went through a lot with Gloria and her sister," he said gently.

She shook her head as she dried her face and blew her nose. "Maybe, but she and Alice saved me. If they hadn't taken me in after Grandma Elsie died, who knows what kind of life I would've had. I know what happens to children in foundlings' homes. They're often worked to death or brutalized in ways…"

She knelt in front of the water and washed out the handkerchief, then washed her face. She folded the handkerchief into a neat square and handed it back to him.

"Gloria and Alice used me to help them take advantage of other people's kindness, but they also kept me safe and fed. Sometimes we can't expect more than that."

Shane grasped her hand. "You should expect more from someone who loves you."

Meggan's eyes widened. He could tell she wondered if he was talking about himself. Was he? He wanted to tell she was a beautiful, kind, loving person who had the right to true, unconditional love. He wanted to say he thought he was the person to show it to her.

She looked back toward the waterfall as if confession was too difficult while facing him.

"Over the last few days, I realized I actually miss Gloria. Sometimes I even miss Alice. They did terrible things. They stole and lied and hoodwinked people for their own benefit. I fear they were unrepentant, even to the end. But they could also be kind and generous and funny, and they loved each other. Oh, how Gloria grieved when Alice died. I think they loved me, too, in their narcissistic way. I guess I love them too. It's strange loving someone and empathizing with them when you know everything about them is wrong."

He squeezed her hand and then let it go. "You have a good heart, Meggan. They used you and hurt you, but you still saw the good in them."

"I just wish I'd done more. Especially after Alice died. I had a better chance reasoning with Gloria without her sister's influence. If I had tried harder, I might've convinced her to turn herself in to Detective Rollins. We could've paid restitution or something. But I didn't do or say anything. I went along down the path we'd started. Now I fear it's too late."

Her eyes took on a faraway expression. Whether sad or resigned, Shane couldn't tell.

"After J.D. was arrested, the neighbors sat around on their stoops discussing his case. Everyone was shocked to learn he was a killer and a jewel thief. They were especially interested in what became of the jewels. Alice and Gloria speculated along with the rest. That's what they did—they made every person think they were just like them. No one knew who tipped off the authorities. J.D. figured it out by the time his case went to court, but by then, it was too late. We knew where he had hidden the jewels. That's what mattered. We knew all his secrets."

Light reflected off the drops of water in her jet black hair. Her green eyes sparkled like rocks in the bottom of the river. Shane indicated a fallen log a few feet back from the water protected by trees from the waterfall spray. Once she was settled, he sat next to her. His knees angled toward the sky, and he rested his elbows on them.

"How did you three get your hands on the jewels from Duggar in the first place when the police couldn't find them."

Meggan exhaled wearily. "We had been surveilling J.D. for nearly a year. He lived one street over from us. Gloria and Alice believed everyone was hiding something, I guess because they always were. But they thought everyone has a secret they'd do anything to protect. They loved to say you never knew which person you met that day who would become your next goldmine.

"They first noticed J.D. at the market. He went out of his way to ignore their overtures of friendship. To their way of thinking, that meant he was hiding something really big. In this case, they were right.

"They watched him and learned his habits the way they did everyone else in our neighborhood. Once they discovered you were an upstanding citizen who worked hard every day, they lost interest in you. Those people were too tired at the end of the day to participate in activities that could benefit Gloria and Alice. They didn't waste their time at the window with their looking glasses watching mothers pushing prams or shopkeepers sweeping their walks.

"But J.D.—he fascinated them from the first moment they saw him at the market. They realized he was someone worth watching. I took my turn at the window too. It was a round-the-clock operation. You never knew when something interesting would happen. We surveilled about five people in the neighborhood at that time, but J.D. quickly became the main focus. He was the kind of man who blends into the background that witnesses can't identify later. Alice and Gloria were convinced that meant he was a criminal. A dog always recognizes its kind."

She shifted on the fallen log. Her elbow bumped into Shane's side. She smiled in apology. "Others came in and out of our periphery. Small potatoes. But they knew J.D. Duggar was gold. When a person works that hard *not* to be noticed, they're hiding the most."

Color rose in her cheeks. "That's where I came in. I conveniently ran into him at the market one day. Literally. I knocked his parcel out of his hands. He glared at me and tried to get past me, but I knew my part. I insisted I make it up to him by purchasing the things I had ruined and bringing him a homemade cake. He kept telling me to forget it, but I wouldn't take no for an answer. The three of us showed up at his apartment that night with a pound cake. Even J.D. Duggar couldn't shake Gloria and Alice once they were on the hunt. They actually made a friend of him, or as much of a friend as you can with a man like that."

Shane swallowed his impatience. As interesting as the story was, when would she get to the jewels.

"They had cleared the first hurdle. They got into his apartment. As soon as we got home that night, Alice drew a map of it. After that, they followed him everywhere. They learned everything there was to know about him by being two sweet little old ladies who wanted to feed him cake.

"When they found the news article about the jewelry heist and read the thief's description, they knew their hunches were right. J.D. had a five-hundred-dollar price on his head. Nice but not enough. They wanted the jewels too. I'd never seen them so giddy. They sat around and daydreamed about never lifting a finger to work the rest of their lives—not that they ever did much. Over the months of watching him, they noticed he kept walking along a rock wall behind a livery stable as if making sure it was still there. The night he was arrested, while the police searched his apartment, we went straight to the rock wall. We brought chisels and ice picks. It only took about fifteen minutes to find the spot where J.D. spent so much time. After we found the pouch, we cleaned up after ourselves so no one knew where to look but J.D."

She shivered. "I was scared to death they'd release him or he'd talk his way out and realize what we'd done. Then Alice passed away. I wanted Gloria to turn the jewels over to Detective Rollins. She wouldn't hear of it. She said we needed the money more than ever. We followed the case. J.D. refused to tell what happened with the jewels. I'm sure he planned to go back for them as soon as he broke out. Other neighbors must've noticed the same thing we did because the investigators began searching behind the livery. They didn't find anything, not even the hole we made. Once J.D. learned the police hadn't found the jewels, he knew we had. He spent the next two months hollering to anyone who would listen that the old ladies had robbed him. No one believed him. Naturally. They figured he was just trying to throw off the scent.

"I couldn't sleep at night. I kept imagining J.D. bursting in and killing us in our beds. The police came to the apartment a few times. Detective Rollins was in charge of the case. He's the only one I trusted. Some of the others—" Meggan tightened her arms around herself though the air was warm. "There were others who seemed interested in finding the jewels for themselves. I should've talked to Detective Rollins back then. If I had, maybe all this could've been avoided."

Tears glistened in her eyes. "Had I told the truth, Mrs. Gochberg would already have justice for her husband and Granny—Gloria—would still be alive. Of course, she never would've forgiven me."

She sighed sadly and looked at Shane through lowered lashes. "But if we hadn't come here, I never would've..." Her gaze drifted to his mouth. She stared at him, frozen in place.

Shane couldn't move. He couldn't think about anything but kissing her again.

Meggan blinked as if snapping out of a daze and scrambled to her feet. "We should go," she mumbled.

Shane jumped up. His foot shifted on the loose rocks and he stumbled. "Meggan, wait," he said as he caught his balance. She stopped and looked hopefully at him. Her eyes were dark with intensity.

Walker couldn't be right about her. If she planned to keep the jewels for herself, she would've left the first day without arranging a proper burial for Gloria. She wouldn't wait in Willow Wood for Gloria's killer to catch up with her.

Shane put his hand on her elbow. "This isn't your fault. Gloria and Alice would've done what they wanted to do, with or without you."

"I just wish I could've made a difference."

He tightened his hold on her elbow. "You have made a difference."

To me, he nearly added out loud.

"Justice will be served.," he said. "The jeweler's wife will have her property back because of you."

Tension slid out of her shoulders. She laid her trembling hand against his cheek. She scratched gently through the stubble on his cheek and down his chin. Shane could barely draw a breath. Meggan's warm hand left a scalding path as she encircled his neck and held it there. Shane put his hands in the gentle curve of her waist and drew her to him.

Damp, dewy tendrils of hair trailed across her face. She drew back a fraction of an inch to brush the hair out of the way. Her face was suspended only inches from his. Shane tightened his arms around her and pulled her against him.

Her lips were as soft and sweet as he remembered, but so much more. Her arms encircled his neck, drawing him closer as her mouth explored his. She fit perfectly into his arms. He held her close as the kiss deepened. He had never felt like this. Nothing he'd heard this morning mattered anymore. He just wanted this kiss to last forever.

A breeze kicked up through the trees, rattling the leaves together. A gust of spray from the waterfall sprinkled over them. They pulled back, laughing. Water droplets shone on Meggan's cheeks. Regrettably, Shane pulled back and dried them with his thumb. He felt her warm breath on his face. Her eyes smoldered. With all the resolve he could muster, he dropped his arms.

Meggan swallowed hard and stepped away. She walked around him to where the horses waited.

Chapter Twenty-Four

From the moment Meggan sent the telegram to Detective Rollins, she knew she couldn't stay in Willow Wood. One way or another, she would have to go back to Kansas City to pay for her crimes. She just hadn't known how difficult leaving would be, especially after meeting Shane Casey.

Why had she let him kiss her? Why had she kissed *him*? Facing justice was one thing. Leaving him here while she rotted in jail was another altogether.

Her arrest would make life easier for Shane, to be sure. After she quietly disappeared, he could go back to building his practice. He would find a sweet local girl from his ma's church, and they could fill that gigantic house with dozens of babies.

Meggan's heart ached. She didn't want to go. She didn't want any other woman doing anything in *her* house. With Shane.

She never should've stayed in this town. She should've headed east the moment she realized Gloria was dead. She may not have made it to Kansas City alive, but her heart wouldn't have gotten involved. It was bad enough looking at a future where the only time she saw the sun was in a prison yard. But now she had to face that prison without the man she loved.

She kept her gaze fixed on the back of Shane's head as they rode through the trees. "God, I don't have the right to ask you for anything," she prayed under her breath. "But give me the strength to face what's coming. I don't want to leave Willow Wood. I want to stay here. With Shane. I'm thankful to You for what he did for me, but I almost wish I never met him."

With Shane changing direction at every rock formation in the road, it took an extra hour to reach the quarry. At the cabin, Meggan barely looked at him as she dismounted and took her supplies inside to start their meal. He seemed to realize she didn't want to talk. Or maybe he didn't want to talk to her. After securing the horses in the shed, he headed to the creek to check the traps he'd set that morning.

Meggan hauled water from the well and lit the fire. She couldn't bear the thought of another cold meal. She also couldn't bear thinking of the generations of critters who had lived inside the stove. She set a pan of hot water on the floor, leaned into the oven, and began to scrub.

Focusing on the stove helped her forget the warmth of Shane's kisses. Every time she thought of him, her hands began to shake. Was this what love felt like? She wasn't sure. She'd never loved anyone wholly and completely except for Grandma Elsie. That was so long

235

ago. Sometimes she barely remembered the warm, comforting presence that had been her grandmother. The grandmother who sang her songs at night and told her stories of Jesus and could make a feast out of greens and a skinny fried chicken.

The firewood had been stacked beside the cabin for years and was aged and dry. By the time the stove was clean enough for Meggan to risk eating any food cooked on it, the temperature inside the cabin was like a furnace. She wrestled the window open in its warped casing and went out on the porch to wait for Shane. She should've started a fire outside to cook whatever meat the traps held, but she had never cooked over an open fire and wasn't sure she could. They would just have to brave the heat.

She dried the sweat off her face with a handkerchief and fanned herself. Wisps of hair had come loose and stuck to her forehead and neck. What she wouldn't give to strip down to her chemise and dive headfirst into the quarry pool. Boys had all the fun. The closest she'd come to swimming when she was a girl was shedding her shoes and stockings and wading in the park fountains.

A wisp of a breeze drifted past the cabin and lifted the tendrils of black hair off her neck. She dropped her head in her hands. For the last few hours she had managed to push the encounter with Officer Walker to the back of her mind. Now it was back in force.

She wasn't sure how to tell Shane about seeing Walker in town. What if he didn't believe her when she told him what she figured out? He could think she was trying to cast doubt on the lawman in order to diminish her own blame. She wasn't. She knew what she knew, and it was worse than anything she could've imagined.

Fast moving feet sounded across the hard-packed earth. Shane called out. Meggan jumped up in alarm, tangling her feet in her skirt. She slipped her hand inside her pocket and closed it around the derringer. The little gun was always loaded. It had been since she was fourteen when Alice showed her how to fire it. She'd only brandished it twice to men who made the mistake of thinking she wouldn't protect herself. The sight of it in her firm grasp had been enough to defuse both situations. It would, however, have no impact on J.D. Duggar. Or Officer Walker.

Shane rounded the corner of an outbuilding at a run. He carried his rifle in one hand and a rabbit by the ears in the other. He bounded onto the porch and looked past her through the open cabin door.

"Are you all right? Are you alone?"

"Yes, I'm alone. What's wrong? What happened?"

He ushered her into the cabin. He dropped the rabbit on the table. "Someone's been here. They know where we are."

The blood drained from her face. How was it possible? Would they ever have just one night of peace?

"How do you know? Did you see somebody?"

He went to the small window and ducked his head to see past the pane. "I set two traps this morning. They were both set off. Whatever was caught in the other one is gone."

"That doesn't mean anything. An animal—"

He turned away from the window and shook his head. "Too clean. Had to have been a man. The grass was trampled some too. Could've been a trapper or hunter, but that's unlikely. They don't usually mess with another

237

man's traps. Maybe a kid or someone who found himself in a bind. Or…"

Meggan's stomach tightened at the words left hanging. Kids would've emptied both traps.

Shane took his knife out of his boot and picked up the rabbit. "Regardless, we need to eat. I'm going to step outside to clean this. Put the bar over the door."

"No! If something happens, I need to be able to help." She pulled the derringer from her pocket.

"You a good shot with that thing?"

"I could shoot us another rabbit from the porch step."

He smiled appreciatively. "Let's hope it doesn't come to that." He checked his sidearm to ensure it was still loaded before going outside. Meggan stood a few feet from him, listening and watching while he made quick work of skinning and cleaning the rabbit.

He scrubbed his hands and tossed the bloody water off the side of the porch. "Looks like we're eating light tonight," he said as Meggan placed the two halves of the rabbit in the hot skillet.

"We have some provisions from town." Meggan thought of the packet of bacon she had dropped as she ran away from Walker. They wouldn't have much of a breakfast either—if they made it through the night.

"I passed a full to bursting blackberry thicket on my way from the creek," Shane said. "Too bad only the birds are going to enjoy them."

Meggan smiled in spite of the danger around them. She couldn't think of a more pleasurable way to spend the evening than berry picking with Shane. Instead, they were stuck in the sweltering cabin like trapped rats. It was the same way she felt trapped in the cave. But she was with Shane. That took out some of the sting.

She put the potatoes and carrots she had cleaned and diced earlier in the skillet with the rabbit. While the food cooked, Shane paced from the window to the door.

Finally, Meggan couldn't take it anymore. "Will you please sit down? You're making me a nervous wreck. Have some coffee while supper cooks."

Shane took one last look out the window. He still had his gun in his hand. He set it on the table and sat down warily.

Meggan filled two cups she had found in the cupboard and set them on the table. "I'm sure Detective Rollins will get to Willow Wood tomorrow."

He nodded and blew steam away from the cup.

Meggan picked at her broken fingernails. Her hands were usually well groomed, but the last few days had been rough on them. Her fingernails were caked with dirt. Several had broken down to the quick. Blisters and red patches stung from hanging onto the horses' reins. The condition of her hands was the least of her worries. She felt Shane's eyes on her, but she didn't look up. Looking at him would remind her of his kiss, and she needed to put that out of her head. She couldn't torture herself with memories of it the rest of her life.

"I'll be relieved when Mrs. Gochberg gets her jewels back," she said, still picking at her nails. "I hope it will help put her life back together."

Her voice cracked. Shane's hand slid into view and covered hers. Meggan blinked away tears as she stared at his tanned, calloused fingers covering hers. She'd never paid much attention to a man's hands before. Maybe because she had very little contact with them. Once a butcher had yelled at her for standing too close to the strings of sausages hanging in his booth. Meggan started to cry. An officer appeared out of the crowd and took her hand in his and led her through the crowded market to where Alice and Gloria waited. She couldn't remember the particulars of the day except the officer's hand had been huge and warm and comforting, and she hadn't wanted to let go of it. Especially after Alice realized she failed in her quest to snag a string of sausages.

"As anxious as I am to get the jewels out of my hands, I'm also afraid. The jewels were stolen and I have possession of them. That makes me guilty of crimes I'm not even aware of. I…I don't know what's going to happen to me."

Shane's hand tightened around hers. "That detective is going to see how much danger you put yourself in to make sure he gets them. That will have to stand for something in your defense."

Meggan stared at his hands. "I don't know. I hope so. I just want to do the right thing like you would."

"What makes you think I'd do the right thing?"

"You would, Shane. I know you would. You worry about old horses when other people would just drive them over a cliff. I want to be like you. I want forgiveness. For that to happen, I need to make sure Mrs. Gochberg gets her property back and then face the consequences of what I did."

"That's not how forgiveness works, Meggan. Have you asked God to forgive you?"

She looked back at her hands. "I ask Him every day."

"Then stop asking. You are forgiven. God doesn't hand out forgiveness based on the number of times you ask or the depth of your remorse. He forgives the first time a contrite heart asks for it."

Was it that easy? She was afraid to hope.

"I'm not saying you won't have to pay for what you may have done. It just isn't a condition of forgiveness."

She tightened her fingers around his. "Thank you, Shane. For everything. For being kind to Granny on the stagecoach and listening to her stories. For staying with me after she— For not turning me over to the sheriff or the doctor and walking away. For being my friend."

Her voice cracked again. She smelled the meat and sizzling vegetables. She quickly unthreaded her fingers from around his and went to the stove. She was thankful for something to do with her hands. Shane seemed to sense she was finished talking for a while. He picked up his gun and went back to the window.

Meggan stirred the contents of the skillet and then served up two bowls. The carrots were a little undercooked, but everything smelled delicious. She set the bowls on the table and sat across from him. They looked at each other over the steaming bowls as the food cooled enough to eat.

"I'll sit up tonight and keep watch while you sleep," Shane said. "in case Duggar is the one who emptied the trap."

Meggan handed him a fork. "Duggar isn't the only one who may have followed us here."

His brows slid together in question.

"I saw someone in town today. Someone else who knows about the jewels."

Shane clenched the fork. "Who?"

"One of the officers who came to arrest J.D. after Gloria and Alice turned him in. His name is Preston Walker. We had no reason to see him after J.D. was taken into custody, but he kept coming to our apartment. He acted interested in Gloria, and you know how she loves attention. They would talk and talk about the case and speculate about the jewels. Every time he came, I was sick to my stomach, afraid she'd say too much or the wrong thing. J.D. told everyone in the jail he didn't have the jewels. They'd been stolen. No one gave his claims any credence, but I think Officer Walker did. That's why he's here. He knows I have them and he's come to get them."

Shane's eyes grew narrower and narrower as she talked. "If he's a man of the law, why don't you hand them over? Wouldn't that solve your problems?"

She shuddered and shook her head. "I'll never turn them over to him."

"But he's—"

"No," she cried. She wrapped her arms around herself and began to shake, the food on her plate cooling in front of her.

Shane's eyes darkened in concern. "Meggan? What is it?"

"He isn't interested in justice. He followed Granny and me here to steal the jewels for himself. I have no doubt he'll kill me as soon as he gets his hands on them. I don't know why he didn't drag me into an alley and do it today."

Shane pushed his plate aside and reached for her. "If you're that worried about him, we'll go to the sheriff in Willow Wood. He's a good man. He'll protect you."

"Walker has probably already talked to the sheriff and told him I'm a jewel thief." She gulped down the lump in her throat. "I thought J.D. was the one who killed Granny, but now I know I was wrong. Officer Walker murdered her."

Shane's face went white. "Meggan, accusing a lawman in a serious matter."

She slammed her hand on the table. "It's true and I can prove it." She kept her gaze locked on Shane's as she reached into her pocket. She opened her fist to reveal a silver tie slide.

"This belongs to Officer Walker. When I first saw it, I thought it was J.D.'s, but then I saw Walker today and realized it was his. He always wore it. Today, he didn't because I had it."

"Where did you get it?"

"From Granny. That's how I knew she hadn't died from a heart attack in her sleep. It was in her hand the morning I found her dead in the hotel bed."

Chapter Twenty-Five

Shane stared at the slide in her hand. "Are you sure it belongs to the lawman?"

Meggan dropped it on the table as if it burned her hand. "He had it on every time he came to the house."

Shane shook his head to clear it. Was it possible? "He killed that little old lady?" He said it more to himself than to Meggan.

"Yes," she exclaimed. "I never trusted him, but I couldn't get Granny to stop talking to him every chance she had. She was so proud of what she and Alice had done. They hadn't only outwitted an outlaw to earn a bounty; this time they outwitted the entire legal system. She always assured me she knew what she was doing. She wouldn't implicate herself, but obviously she said enough to prove J.D. was telling the truth for the first time in his life."

Shane didn't speak. He couldn't wrap his head around a lawman killing someone. He remembered the story Gloria had told him on the train about the lawman who murdered his girlfriend and her mother. That couldn't be the case here. Lawmen protected people. They didn't murder old ladies in their sleep for their own gain.

Meggan took a deep breath. "After Alice died, I redoubled my efforts to convince Gloria to leave town. I wanted to get a job. Doing what, I don't know. I've never worked an honest day in my life. But I hated everything about what we were doing. I was tired of moving and tired of worrying about someone coming after us. I hated lying to every person I met. I hated who I was. I wanted a family A husband." She glanced at him and quickly looked down at her plate.

Shane stared at her. She must've felt his eyes on her because she didn't look up. She took tiny bites of her meal. Shane tried to eat too. He was hungry, and he knew he needed the sustenance if he was going to sit up all night to keep watch. But he couldn't stop thinking of how her words stirred something in him. He hadn't thought much about a family over the last few years. Since meeting Meggan, he could think of little else.

She managed a few more bites before pushing the plate away. "I thought about leaving her. Just taking off. But I couldn't bring myself to do it. Her health was failing. She was grief-stricken over losing Alice, I didn't know if she could handle losing me too. I wanted to be free, but I—I didn't know who I was on my own. Now I'm even less sure."

She took a sip of coffee cup and grimaced at the bitterness. "I've ruined everything, Shane. The Gochbergs will never get their jewels back. Granny's dead and it's my fault."

Shane reached for her hand, but she pulled away. "How can it be your fault?" he asked gently.

"Because I prayed for God to do something to free me from the life we were living. That's why He can't forgive me. The night before Gloria died, I knew she was ailing. She had been for months, but it had gotten worse recently. I told her that after we sold the jewels, we'd have enough money to quit the business. We could buy a little house and she could relax and enjoy her old age. She laughed and said, 'Honey, I *am* enjoying my old age. I'll never stop until they put me in the ground.'

"I knew she meant it. As long as she had breath in her body, she'd keep dragging me all over the country, hunting down outlaws, and I'd always be responsible for her. The only way I'd have ever been free was for her to die. I prayed to God that if she was going to go anyway…" She blinked away tears. "…He take her quickly."

•••

Shane jerked awake against the wall that faced the door. His hands instinctively reached for the rifle in the darkness. He hadn't meant to fall asleep. Meggan had prepared a bed for him farthest from hers, but he refused it. He needed to stay awake to guard against whoever had cleaned out the other rabbit trap. He was sure they'd come in the night when his defenses were lowest.

He pulled in his legs and stood, trying to be quiet. The temperature had gone down a bit, but the cabin was still stuffy. He crept across the floor to open the front door. He'd step out for a spell to see if anyone was moving around. He looked down at Meggan, curled up in sleep. Last night he had tried to console her about Gloria's death. He told her whoever had killed Gloria—more than likely, the lawman he met yesterday—was responsible, not the weary prayers of a young woman who wanted a life of her own. A life that might have room for Shane.

He couldn't imagine an outcome where she wouldn't have to go back to Kansas City with the detective. Even if the jewels were returned to the rightful owner, Shane figured Meggan was right; the detective would take her into custody and back to Kansas City. She may not have taken the jewels herself, but she had them now. That would account for a lot in the eyes of law enforcement who were probably embarrassed that two old ladies and a young woman had done something they couldn't.

The jewels were stolen. A man lost his life. Someone should pay. In all likelihood that someone would be Meggan.

Shane eased the door open. Fresh cool air bearing a hint of rain soothed his skin. He opened the door wider.

Meggan stirred behind him. "Is everything all right?"

He turned to see her pushing herself upright. Her hair had come loose during the night and fell like a sable curtain over her shoulders. He tried to answer, but his mouth seemed to have forgotten how to form words. He couldn't help wondering what it would feel like to wrap his hands in that hair.

She combed her fingers through her hair and continued to watch him.

"I didn't mean to wake you," he mumbled.

"It's all right. Did you hear something?"

"No, I just wanted to have a look. Let a little cool air in."

He turned back to the door. His gaze swept the barnyard. Nothing moved in the gray light of dawn. The only sound was the whisper of a breeze across the grass. Even the animals were still asleep.

He holstered his gun and put the rifle in the crook of his arm. "I'm going to take a look around and we'll get ready for the day."

An hour later, Meggan refilled Shane's tin cup with coffee. The only thing they had in the cabin to eat for breakfast was bread. Meggan told him she dropped the bacon in front of the butcher shop when she realized it was Walker's tie slide she had found in Gloria's hand. She didn't seem to have much of an appetite anyway and only swallowed a few bites of bread.

"I'm sorry I forgot to buy butter or honey," she apologized.

He took a large bite of dry bread. "No problem. If you remember, I forgot butter last time."

She smiled appreciatively, but he could see she was worried. "I pray Detective Rollins gets to Willow Wood today," she said. "I don't think I can handle another day of waiting around, especially with Officer Walker in town too."

Shane wasn't looking forward to another day either, but he'd wait with her for a month if that's what it took.

He watched her over the rim of his tin cup. Dark smudges outlined her green eyes. They were red-rimmed from worry and lack of sleep.

"Where will you go after this is all sorted out?"

Her face fell. She looked like she didn't want to think about it, though he knew she'd been doing little else. Neither had he.

"I'm sure Detective Rollins will take me back to Kansas City with him. Gloria and Alice stole the jewels with the intent of selling them. I was as complicit in the crime as they were."

"You didn't steal them."

She sighed wearily. "That's for the courts to decide, not him. The jewelry heist got a lot of attention, especially since Mr. Gochberg was killed. People were fascinated since the jewels weren't recovered. Local authorities will want me back no matter what. They'll want to make an example of me"

It seemed pointless to Shane for authorities to waste time and money arresting a woman who had endangered her own life to return stolen property. But he could see why they would want to wrap up every loose end to prove to the community they took prosecution seriously. "I pray you're wrong."

"I do too."

His jaw worked. He was tired of this. He wasn't going to hide in this cabin another day. He had let Meggan talk him into not confronting Duggar the first day so the killer wouldn't know she saw him in town. But Shane was through cowering like a whipped dog.

If the detective was indeed coming, he should arrive today. Both Duggar and Walker were no longer keeping their presence in Willow Wood a secret. So far, Shane had done things Meggan's way. No more. If he saw either man trailing them today, he was going to take care of them himself. No more waiting for a Kansas City detective who could turn out to be as corrupt as Officer Walker.

Shane didn't look forward to killing anyone, but he would do whatever it took to protect Meggan, even if she hated him for it.

"You're not alone in this, Meggan. It ends today."

Determination shone in her green eyes. "I appreciate it, Shane. I really do. I've been afraid most of my life. I was afraid when I lost Grandma Elsie. Then I was afraid of Alice and the things she made me do. Now, I'm a grown woman and I'm still a scared, lost little girl. One way or another, it *is* going to end today. I'm tired of hiding. I'm tired of being afraid. I don't want this to be my life."

Though it was exactly what Shane wanted to hear, part of him dreaded her resolve. Did she need him as much as he needed her?

He stood and strapped on his gun belt. Time to head to Willow Wood and take care of business, whatever that was.

A foot shifted on the soft earth outside.

Chapter Twenty-Six

S hane grabbed the sidearm from his holster and insured it was loaded. He barely glanced at Meggan before rushing to the door.

Blood pounded in Meggan's ears. She nearly called Shane back. He was rushing headlong into danger again. For her. Something no one else had ever done before him.

Outside, Shane called for someone to come out of hiding. Further away she heard a man's voice, but she couldn't make out any words or tell who it was. Then she heard running feet. A body collided with Shane right outside the door. Whether J.D. or Walker, Meggan had no intention of staying inside and letting Shane fight her battles for her.

She felt for the derringer in her pocket. It contained one shot, and it wasn't that accurate at a distance. Unless she hit her target dead center, it would only serve to make J.D. or Walker mad.

Her gaze swiveled to the rifle leaning against the wall. Last night as Shane loaded it, he asked if she knew how to use it. "Sort of," she hedged. She had actually never fired a rifle and barely know how they operated. But how different could it be from the derringer?

"Well, it's big," he had warned. "A big gun leaves a big hole if you fire at close range. All you have to do is fire and let the rifle do the work."

She could do that. She hurried to the door.

"Please, God, don't let anything happen to him," she whispered. "He deserves a good life. With a good woman who'll make him happy."

She choked back a sob that she'd never be that woman.

Less than two strides off the narrow porch, Shane and J.D. rolled on the ground, punching and kicking. Meggan gasped at the sight. She raised the rifle and looked down the sights. The men rolled back and forth on the dusty hard-packed earth. They were too close together for her to take a shot. She tried to follow their movements with the barrel of the gun. She quickly gave up afraid she'd pull the trigger by mistake and kill both of them with one shot.

Keeping the gun between her and the grappling men, she stepped off the porch and circled them. Her sweating hands barely kept hold of the gun. They continued to roll back and forth, exchanging punches, bites, and kicks. When J.D. caught Shane on the side of the head with his elbow, Meggan cried out. They rolled again and J.D. came out on top. He punched Shane in the face several times. Blood flew and splashed onto Meggan's dress. She raised the rifle. Was this it? Could she pull the trigger before they shifted again? She nearly pulled the trigger when Shane rolled and knocked J.D. off balance. It was barely a moment before J.D was back on top. He wrapped his big hands around Shane's throat.

Shane clawed at J.D.'s hands but had no luck dislodging his grip. Meggan bit back a scream. She stepped closer with the rifle. Shane kicked the ground to gain purchase. He bucked hard, but J.D. managed to keep his hands tight around Shane's throat.

Meggan's hands shook around the rifle. She couldn't hold it steady enough to set it against her shoulder. She had to do something. She wouldn't stand here and watch J.D. kill Shane.

The man she loved.

She shifted her hands on the rifle and swept it through the air. The heavy gun caught J.D. on the side of the head jarring Meggan all the way up to her shoulders. J.D. dropped off Shane like a sack of wheat. Meggan crouched at Shane's side. She grabbed his arm and helped him sit up. He scrambled to his feet and took the rifle from her. Breathing hard, he held it over J.D.

"You should've shot him," Shane said, gasping. His hands were shaking nearly as hard as hers.

"I couldn't. I was afraid I'd shoot you instead."

"I wouldn't have liked that."

"Are you all right?"

"I'll live."

"Thank God," she breathed.

At their feet, J.D. began to stir. He groaned and clutched the side of his head. He was bleeding but not enough to indicate a serious wound. Meggan wished she had swung harder.

Shane grabbed his sidearm from where it had fallen in the dirt during the fight. He handed the rifle to Meggan and leveled his sidearm at J.D. J.D.'s own holster was empty. Meggan glanced around but didn't see his gun.

"Don't move, Duggar," Shane growled. "I don't want to blow your head off, but I will."

J.D. put a hand to the side of his head and opened his eyes. He blinked up at Meggan. "I wish he'd'a killed you instead of the old lady."

She gasped, knowing right away he was referring to Walker. "How did you find Granny and me?"

"You're joshing, right? All I had to do was ask people about the beautiful girl and the gabby old lady who never stopped talking." He smirked around his pain. "You may as well have drawn me a red line across the map to follow."

Shane kicked the outlaw's boot. "Enough yapping. We're taking you to town and will let the sheriff figure out what to do with you. You're telling him Meggan had nothing to do with the theft of those jewels."

The man snorted. "I'm not telling him nothing."

"There's a detective coming from Kansas City. As soon as he sees you, he'll know Meggan is innocent, even if you don't say a word. You wouldn't be here if you weren't looking for what she had."

J.D. shifted his gaze from Meggan to Shane. "It's not too late for you to take me up on my offer. We can get rid of her right now and ride out of here rich men. Nobody'll ever know."

Shane stepped heavily on J.D.'s wrist. "Not gonna happen. You just lay right there."

J.D. groaned and glared up at him.

Meggan suddenly realized their problems weren't over. Officer Walker was still out there. She wasn't sure why, but he scared her more than J.D. Maybe because he was a wolf in sheep's clothing.

The sun had just begun its ascent over the mountain peaks. A light rain had fallen during the night, but it promised to be another hot day. She didn't want to spend one more night in this cabin, hiding.

"How did you know we were out here?"

"Same way I found you at the cave and at the cemetery. I'm a patient man. While your cowboy here was skulking around the hotel looking for me, I filed a mark on his horse's hoof. Eventually I picked up enough of a trail to follow."

Meggan glanced at Shane and tried to quell the rising fear. It would be just as easy for Officer Walker to track them here too. They needed to get moving fast.

Shane must've been thinking the same thing. He grabbed the wheel to the old mining cart Meggan had tripped over in the dark the first night. He stuck J.D.'s hands through two of the spokes and tied them together. J.D. would have enough movement to hang onto a saddle but not enough to reach for his gun or try to escape.

Shane whistled for J.D.'s horse. It appeared from the other side of the shed where it had been grazing in the shade. He caught the horse's reins and handed them to Meggan.

"I'll tie one of his feet to the stirrups," he told her. He jerked the outlaw to his feet. "I don't want you getting hurt on the way to town should your horse stumble or get snakebit. We need you to live long enough to tell the detective Meggan wasn't in on this with you."

J.D. snorted. "I guess she told you she's as pure as the driven snow. Cowboy, you've got it bad. Not that I blame you. I'd take her for myself if I didn't want those jewels more. I got no time for beautiful women no how. Stick with the homely girls. Nobody remembers you that way." He laughed.

Shane shoved the man toward the horse. "Shut up." He jabbed him with the barrel of his gun. "Get up there or I'll have her slam you on the other side of your head with that rifle butt. Meggan, fill the canteens from the water in the cabin and we'll head out."

Still clinging to the rifle, though she hoped she wouldn't have to shoot it or swing it or do anything else with it, Meggan backed up toward the cabin.

Shane leaned over to secure J.D.'s right foot to the stirrup. A gun blast shattered the morning stillness. The world stood still for a terrifying moment as J.D. Duggar's head exploded.

Chapter Twenty-Seven

Shane dropped to the ground. Meggan spun around and dove toward the porch. She landed hard on her stomach a few feet in front of the bleached boards, blinking through the dust. J.D.'s gun lay within arm's reach, partially concealed under the cabin. She held her breath and listened. No other shots came. The only sound was her blood pounding in her ears and J.D.'s horse galloping away.

"Shane," she whispered. Had he been hit? She couldn't see.

"Meggan."

She gasped, inhaling a mouthful of dirt. He was alive! She coughed and spit. She rolled over and looked toward the sound of Shane's voice. He was on his hands and knees. The horse had given him cover from whoever had fired at them, but now the horse was gone, and he was crouched in the wide open.

J.D. lay sprawled in the dust next to him. The top of his head and most of his face has been blown away. No matter how much Meggan feared the man, she hadn't wanted his life to end like that.

Before she could process what had happened, a man stepped out from behind the pumphouse. Her stomach plummeted. Walker.

In two quick strides he was at Shane's side. He kicked Shane to the ground and stepped on his forearm, pinning him to the ground. "Easy there, cowboy. You don't need to go no further."

Shane swiveled his head to see the owner of the boot. He winced in pain as the pressure increased.

Officer Walker looked over Shane's head to Meggan. "Get up off the ground, little girl, so I can take a look at'cha."

Meggan kept her gaze fixed on his as she got to her feet. Walker removed his boot from Shane's arm and stuck the barrel of his gun against his head. "Now it's your turn, cowboy. On your feet. Nice and slow like."

As Shane got to his feet, Walker stepped back a foot so he could cover them both with the gun. He shoved Shane toward Meggan. Shane stopped about ten feet from her. He looked into her eyes as if to tell her it would be all right, then turned to face the lawman.

Walker chuckled. "You didn't think I was going to let you three ride into town and hand over what I came all this way for, did you?"

He kept the gun leveled at Shane but looked at Meggan as he spoke. "Now, you both know what I want. Might as well hand it over. I might feel charitable and let you live."

Meggan looked at Shane. His expression was unreadable. If she gave the lawman the jewels, maybe he would ride away. She hated to lose the jewels after everything she'd gone through, but she didn't want to die over them. Or lose Shane. She wanted this to end.

Walker must've read something in Shane's face. He tensed. "Don't try any funny business, cowboy. There's nothing you can do before another bullet slices off the top of her head just like it did your friend over there. I can take what I want from the two of you, dead or alive. Don't make no never mind to me."

He opened his vest. The morning sun glinted off the badge pinned there. "This here gets me a lot of cooperation wherever I go, especially once I tell that local yokel sheriff he's got a jewel thief in his town. I can either tell him you both got away. Or…" He jabbed at the air with the gun. "…I can tell him you resisted arrest and I shot you. He won't care as long as I cleaned up his trouble for him. Things would end there if you hadn't sent for backup from Kansas City."

Meggan's eyes widened. How did he know that?

Walker chuckled. "Didn't your knight in shining armor here mention he told me what you done? I appreciate the head's up, by the way, cowboy," he told Shane. "I guess nobody'll believe you ran off with the jewels since you went to the trouble of telling Rollins where to find you."

"It can still end here," Shane said. "Nobody knows about you. All we have to do is get rid of Duggar and tell the authorities he jumped us in the night and stole the jewels."

Walker nodded thoughtfully as if actually considering the plan. He burst out laughing. "That'd work if I could trust you as far as I can throw you." He gestured at Meggan with the gun. "Now, I know she's a liar and a fraudster, through and through. But you, you're the one I don't trust. You're well regarded in this town. I don't see you lying to your kin. You'd blab the truth before I got over the first ridge."

Meggan looked at the back of Shane's head. He was still several feet in front of her and hadn't taken his eyes off Walker. He was going to die, and his body dumped into the quarry hole because of her. She had to do something. She felt the weight of the derringer in her pocket, but she'd never untangle it from the folds of her skirt before Walker put holes into them both.

Walker wasn't finished taunting Shane. "Bet you don't think she's as sweet and innocent now, do you? That pretty face is her money-maker. It's how those three women lived so high on the hog. Distract some poor sucker with this one while the two old ladies robbed him blind. A pretty good gig, I reckon. Worked every time until they met up with poor ole Duggar there. Turned him in for the bounty and then double-crossed him by stealing his loot."

He laughed and looked back at Meggan. "I don't fault you none. I respect ambition. But I don't have a pretty face and those huge green eyes. I gotta work for a living."

His gaze traveled appraisingly up and down Meggan's form. "Now that I think about it, I might just take you with me. You'd come in handy in more ways than one."

Meggan tried not to react, but bile rose in her throat. Shane stiffened as if preparing to rush the corrupt lawman.

"Don't try it, cowboy," Walker snapped, reading his mind. "You can't beat a bullet. You're about to find yourself among the rocks out here for the buzzards to pick your bones clean. But if you don't cause me grief, I'll let the girl live. We'll make a pretty good team, don't you think, Miss Jones?"

Shane had edged a few inches away from Meggan. She realized he was lengthening the distance between them to draw fire away from her. She took a sliding step in the opposite direction.

"Stop!" Walker bellowed. "You insult me, little girl." He looked at Shane. "Hand over that pea-shooter in your belt."

Shane reached for his holster.

"Not like that. Put your right hand in the air and keep it there. Nice and slow with your left hand, get the gun and drop it on the ground. Kick it this way."

Shane did as instructed. Keeping his eyes on Shane, Walker squatted down and scooped the gun off the ground. He stuck it in his gun belt behind his back. "All right now, nice and easy, come over this way. I'm going to tie you up nice and tight and put you in the shed. Then me and your gal are going to have a conversation about what she did with my jewels. I'm sure I can think of a few ways to get her to talk."

Gooseflesh rose all over Meggan. She resisted the urge to scream. Or run. Or lunge at the man and take her chances with the derringer. She had to keep her head. She wasn't about to let Walker incapacitate Shane and do whatever he wanted with her. She had to do something; she just didn't know what.

The sun had inched into the sky. Out of the corner of her eye, Meggan noticed light reflecting off the barrel of J.D.'s gun under the porch step. Any moment Walker would see it too. She edged back, hoping her skirt blocked it from view. She remembered the knife in Shane's boot. It wasn't much to protect them against a trained lawman with everything to lose, but it could be the only chance they had.

Walker put a massive hand on Shane's shoulder and shoved him toward J.D.'s prostrate body. Meggan stepped back and pretended to stumble. She sat down hard on the porch step, fanning her skirt as she went down. She cried out as if injured. Walker glanced in her direction. Shane seized the diversion and dove at the big man's midsection. As Walker stumbled off balance and managed to sidestep the brunt of the attack, Meggan reached under the porch and grabbed J.D.'s gun.

Walker spun away from Shane and cracked him on the head with the butt of his revolver. Shane grunted and landed hard on his stomach. He reached for his boot as he rolled to avoid the next blow.

Walker sucked air through his teeth and raised the gun. He aimed at Shane's head. Meggan jumped to her feet and fired.

Chapter Twenty-Eight

All the strength seeped out of Meggan's limbs. She collapsed to the ground in a heap. Shane ran to her and gathered her in his arms. She sank against him, her entire body shaking. "He was going to kill you."

Shane tightened his arms around her. "I know."

It felt like his hands were shaking, too. She nestled closer. Over his shoulder, she saw the two outlaws on the ground. "What do we do now?"

"We go for the sheriff and tell him everything."

Neither moved. Shane buried his nose in Meggan's hair. She clung to him. They sat on the ground in each other's arms as the sun scattered the shadows around them.

•••

After stowing both men's bodies in the shed and securing the door against scavengers, Meggan and Shane saddled their horses. They stuck to the main road and arrived in Willow Wood faster than Meggan thought possible. She folded back the brim of the poke bonnet to catch a breeze. It no longer mattered if anyone recognized her or not.

She felt depleted, as if she'd been holding her breath for the last week and could finally exhale. The burden of the last two years when the Hennessey sisters put J.D. Duggar in their sights was gone. Now all she felt was exhaustion. It was over. She would hand the Gochberg jewels over to the detective, admit her role in their theft, and accept her fate, whatever it was. She was as guilty as Gloria. She had lied to investigators and obstructed justice in a major crime. Gloria had paid with her life. Meggan got off much easier. She supposed it was only fair her freedom was required of her.

She and Shane didn't say much on their way to town. Meggan could scarcely find the nerve to look at him. How would he ever trust her now that he almost died for having gotten mixed up with her? He knew that to know her meant trouble.

It was just as well that she was leaving Willow Wood. She prayed he wasn't around when Detective Rollins put the handcuffs around her wrists and led her away. She didn't want that to be his last image of her.

As they rode up to the jail, Sheriff Deavers stepped outside. Meggan's heart lurched in her chest. Detective Rollins stepped out behind him and stood side by side with the sheriff. Both men crossed their muscular arms over their chests. Meggan hadn't seen Detective Rollins since the last time she and Gloria sat in the back of the courtroom observing the proceedings. As always, he wasn't wearing a hat, and his graying hair was combed over with not a hair out of place. He must've been in his fifties, but he was still a handsome man with a square, lean jaw, and shrewd blue eyes. Meggan had always seen patience and caring in those eyes, even when he must've known she wasn't being completely forthright with him.

"Morning, Miss Jones. Shane," Sheriff Deavers greeted them. His words were benign enough, but his eyes narrowed with suspicion.

Meggan wondered how much Detective Rollins had told him about her. She and Shane exchanged glances and dismounted. Shane's face was shielded by his hat and his expression unreadable. She wished she had asked him what he was thinking on their way to town. What he thought of her. But she had been afraid to ask. Now, it was too late.

They secured the horses to the hitching rail and stepped onto the sidewalk.

"We're glad to see you two come to town on your own," the sheriff said. "According to Detective Rollins, you have a lot of explaining to do, Miss Jones."

Shane set his hands on his hips. "First off, Sheriff, I need to tell you there are two dead men out at the quarry cabin."

Sheriff Deavers stiffened. "Dead men?"

Detective Rollins' piercing gaze never left Meggan's face. She didn't look away.

"They're both from Kansas City," Shane explained. "The detective here was probably looking for one of them. When he hears what happened out there this

265

morning, he'll be interested in the other fellow too. I can ride out with you and a deputy or two to retrieve them. I'll explain everything on the way."

The sheriff looked from Meggan to the detective, clearly blindsided. "I reckon that's the best course of action for the time being. Detective, feel free to use my office as long as you need to. I can keep one of my deputies on the premises in case you need assistance."

He looked Meggan up and down as if determining how much of a threat she presented.

"That won't be necessary, Sheriff," Detective Rollins said. "Miss Jones and I are just going to have a little chat."

He and Meggan stood on the sidewalk as the sheriff and Shane walked around the side of the building to the livery to collect another man, horses, and a buckboard.

Detective Rollins opened the door and stepped aside for Meggan to go in first. The tiny building was just what Meggan expected of a small-town jail. A one-room space with a scarred desk and battered chair along one wall. A spittoon sat next to the desk. Years of stains on the floor and wall indicated the sheriff's aim wasn't always true.

On the other side of the room stood a table flanked by a couple of straight-back chairs. On a shelf on the wall was a bucket of water and a dipper hanging above it on a nail. Through an open doorway, two cells faced them. She swallowed hard as she imagined the door of one clanging shut behind her. At least the cells were empty. She wouldn't have to worry about Walker and Duggar in the other cell, hurling insults at her and trying to reach through the bars to throttle her.

Instead of ushering her that way, Detective Rollins motioned her toward the table. He took a glass she hadn't noticed before off the table and filled it with water from the bucket. He set it on the table in front of her.

"Sheriff claims this is the coldest, purest water in town."

Meggan took a long drink, grateful she didn't have to drink from the dipper after the sheriff, deputies, and any number of townspeople who made their way inside. She wasn't sure if the water was the coldest or purest, but it sure washed away the trail dust and fatigue clogging her throat.

"Thank you," she said as she set down the glass. She stared at the pattern on the table made by the water droplets inside the glass. *Help me through this, Lord,* she prayed. *Let me accept whatever happens. Even if it means I never see Shane again.*

A sob lodged in her throat. She hoped she would get a chance to tell him goodbye. To tell him she loved him, but she wouldn't pray for it. She didn't deserve more grace than she'd already been given.

The detective hooked a chair leg with his foot and pulled it away from the table for himself. "I trust one of the dead men the cowboy was talking about is J.D. Duggar?"

Meggan nodded. "He followed Granny and me here."

"Did he have anything to do with your granny's death?"

Meggan clasped her hands atop the table. "I thought so, but, no, it was Officer Walker."

Detective Rollins' response was a puzzled frown.

267

Meggan took the tie slide out of her pocket and set it on the table. "Preston Walker. He was one of the local officers who arrested Mr. Duggar. He was the only one on the force who believed J.D.'s claims that Granny and I had the jewels."

She pulled the leather thong from around her neck and set it on the table. "You'll be needing these too."

Her neck immediately felt a hundred pounds lighter. After telling him the rest of her story, she asked for another glass of water.

Detective Rollins obliged and poured one for himself. "That telegram of yours saved me a world of trouble and the State of Missouri a heap of money hunting down Duggar. You easily could've absconded with the jewels after your granny died and both of those louts were out of the picture. No one would've been the wiser and you would've been able to afford a decent life for yourself."

"I couldn't do that to Mrs. Gochberg. Her husband died because of these jewels. The least I could do is make sure she gets her property back."

He took a drink of water and set the glass down with a hardy clink. "Well, then, Miss Jones, it looks like my job here is done. I'm going across the street to the hotel and ordering the biggest steak they've got in the kitchen. Tomorrow morning I'm taking the train back to Kansas City. I'd be proud to have you ride with me. I'll pay for your ticket. I'm sure the Gochberg family will be happy to shake your hand and thank you in person."

Meggan blinked, confused. Wasn't he going to arrest her? She had been complicit to the breaking of so many laws. "I don't deserve gratitude. I could've spared them so much grief by coming forward sooner."

"Maybe so, but there's no point costing the people of Missouri a fortune by prosecuting you. We never would've recovered the Gochbergs' property if not for you. Considering the Hennessey sisters' histories, it's obvious they were the ones behind the theft. Duggar is dead. No one within the penal system is going to lose a wink of sleep over that one.

"My hands will be tied for some time investigating this officer's—what'd you say his name was, Walker?—involvement in the death of your grandmother and conspiracy to steal the jewels. You're a free woman, Miss Jones. You can go back to your life in Kansas City and hopefully put all this business behind you."

It took a moment for the detective's words to sink in. Free.

Meggan was free for the first time in her life.

Somehow, the word didn't have the impact she expected. She didn't feel free. She certainly had no life to go back to in Kansas City. No friends. No family. Absolutely no one to notice or care if she went back or didn't. She figured even J.D. and Officer Walker would be missed more than her.

The detective was staring at her, expectant. "I'm sorry," she said.

He smiled kindly. He must've understood she was trying to process everything he had said.

"I asked if you'd be at the hotel this evening. After the sheriff brings back the two deceased men, I'll need to go through Officer Walker's things. I may have more questions for you about him."

"Yes, I'll be there." She couldn't imagine having anywhere else to be.

They both stood, and he walked her to the door. He thanked her once more, and Meggan stepped out of the jailhouse a free woman.

Chapter Twenty-Nine

For the first time, Meggan thought of Grandma Elsie without a sense of guilt or shame. Not only had God forgiven her for her sins like Shane said, she was deemed innocent of any crimes against the State of Missouri. She could live all the things Grandma Elsie taught her without hiding or shame. She was free of danger from the pouch around her neck. She was finally free of Alice and Gloria. No longer would anyone guilt her or force her into doing what she didn't want to do or knew was wrong.

Most of all, she was free to begin a new life.

With the money in her reticule and what she'd get when she traded in Gloria's train ticket, she could afford to go wherever she wanted. She would have to find employment right away, but as long as she was frugal, she could live simply until she decided what she really wanted to do.

The realization didn't liberate her. It only reaffirmed the fact that she didn't belong anywhere.

As she crossed the street toward the hotel, she looked at the businesses lining Willow Wood's town square. The frontier town had captured her imagination the moment she and Granny stepped off the stage. If things were different, she could see herself building a life here. But she couldn't stay in this town with Shane. Even if she found a good job, she couldn't bear seeing him every day and knowing he would never be hers.

As she stepped onto the sidewalk in front of the hotel, she spotted a familiar figure about to go inside with another woman.

Harper Kinski noticed her at nearly the same moment. "Meggan Jones!" she exclaimed. "Oh my, how good to see you. I've been worried sick. How are you? Where's Shane?"

Meggan's heart warmed at the compassion in the woman's voice. No one had worried about her since Grandma Elsie. "I'm fine. Everything's fine. Shane is with the sheriff. The danger is over."

Harper grabbed her arm and pulled her inside the hotel and out of the way of other patrons. "Are you sure? The other night Logan and I were so scared to leave the two of you. Then we didn't hear a thing about what had happened. We knew we couldn't ask Shane's mother and get her to worrying."

She motioned to her companion and made introductions. "Meggan, this is Jessa Hammersmith. Her husband Rodney is an engineer at the Lundy List corporation, my cousin Ellie Walsh's railroad and mining company. Jessa and I have become good friends over the last few years. Jessa, this is Meggan Jones. I didn't tell you about meeting her because, well frankly, I couldn't."

She clapped her hand to her bodice. "Thank the Lord you're safe. Jessa and I are about to have lunch. You must join us and tell us everything that's happened since Logan and I left you at the cabin the other night."

Meggan's stomach growled at the thought of food. She had only eaten a few bites of dry bread for breakfast and not much at all last night. "I couldn't. I'm tired and need to freshen up."

She hadn't had a proper bath since the night she and Gloria arrived in Willow Wood.

"I should go upstairs—"

"There's plenty of time for that," Jessa said. "You look like you could use a good meal. Please join us. We so seldom meet new women in Willow Wood. And Harper has piqued my interest. It's not fair to leave us without telling me what's going on. I hate it when Harper knows something that I don't."

The two friends laughed at each other and eyed Meggan expectantly. Meggan thought it must be so nice to have a friend with whom to tease and share secrets. She had never been in that situation. It was another reason she didn't want to leave Willow Wood. It was the kind of place where she envisioned befriending women like this with whom she could be herself.

"If you're sure I'm not intruding."

The women beamed with delight. Each took hold of one of her arms and led her to the dining room between them.

After ordering three lunch specials, Harper and Jessa peppered her with questions about how she came to be in

Willow Wood. Meggan was tired of secrets. She was tired of pretending she lived a similar life to other women. If she was going to stay here—or stay anywhere—she needed to learn honesty, a foreign concept to her. People could accept her or push her aside—it was up to them. She was through with pretending.

She told the women about learning of the jewelry heist and turning in their neighbor for the bounty on his head. She told them how she, Alice, and Gloria had dug the jewels out of the hole in the wall after J.D. Duggar's arrest. She told them Granny planned to sell them in Seattle.

She left out much of the particulars of her life of crime. Details weren't important at this point. She would rather look forward than back.

Harper and Jessa were more interested in how she and Shane evaded their pursuers for the last four days. When she told them about trapping J.D. in the root cellar, they hooted with laughter and applauded her bravery and ingenuity. She shuddered as she told them about the night in the abandoned mine. She hadn't been brave then, she admitted, as she described the scurrying rats and smoke and very real possibility of being buried alive.

Finally, she told them about this morning. She glossed over much of it. She didn't want to remember J.D. Duggar getting shot right in front of her or how she shot Officer Walker to keep him from killing Shane. Harper and Jessa seemed to understand and didn't press for details.

"Shane saved my life and I guess I saved his," she finished.

Jessa sat back in her chair and wiped away a tear. Harper reached across the table and patted Meggan's hand. "I'm so thankful you had each other. If you hadn't met Shane on the stage, I don't know how you would've survived the last few days with those evil men after you."

"I've thought the same thing a hundred times this week," Meggan confessed. Grandma Elsie used to tell me God could use any situation for His good purpose. I guess that's what she meant. Shane was here in this very hotel the morning I discovered Granny was dead. He had come to meet someone about buying horses. A delay prevented the man from keeping their appointment. If that hadn't happened, Shane probably wouldn't have been here, and I would've had to deal with it all alone."

Jessa shook her head at the incredulity of it all. "It was a miracle. Think of it; the whole thing orchestrated by the Maker of the universe."

Harper nodded in agreement. "We must buy your lunch. It's the least we can do after the harrowing ordeal you've been through."

"No, I can't do that."

"We insist," Jessa said. "You're a guest in our town. What kind of hosts would we be if we didn't try to make up for a little of your troubles?"

"None of this was your fault."

Harper signaled for the waitress as if Meggan hadn't spoken. "We must have pie," she told the women as the waitress wove her way between the tables. "Cherry and rhubarb are in season, but I'm partial to the blackberry."

When Meggan started to protest again, Jessa cut her off. "You aren't getting up from this table until you have pie. It's divine. Besides, you aren't finished. You told us what led up to the moment we met you outside, but you haven't told us what you plan to do now."

Before Meggan could say she hadn't made plans beyond a long hot bath upstairs, the waitress arrived. After they ordered pie and fresh coffee, Harper and Jessa looked expectantly at her.

"Are you going back to Kansas City?" Harper asked. "Please don't. You said you have no other family. Consider staying in Willow Wood. I'm sure Shane would be devastated if you left."

"I don't know about that."

Harper arched her dark blond eyebrows. "I saw the look on that man's face the other night. He may not have said it yet, but I know he wants you to stay."

Meggan didn't tell her that she had also seen the look on his face as he headed to the quarry to retrieve J.D. and Officer Walker. He had almost been killed because of her. He would probably be happy to see her get on the stage and ride off in any direction.

"You haven't told me anything about you," she reminded them after the waitress delivered their dessert. "Harper, didn't you say the other night you have a son and a daughter?"

The women immediately brightened to the new topic. "Yes, Tommy turned five two weeks ago. Suzanne is two and a half."

"I have three boys myself," Jessa put in, "all under the age of six. Edward, Peter, and little Frank, named for my father." She leaned across the table and lowered her voice. "Maybe they'll have a little sister around the first of next year."

Harper gasped and playfully smacked her friend's hand. "Jessa, you didn't tell me."

Jessa lifted her shoulders. "I'm telling you now."

Meggan lifted a forkful of pie. "To little sisters."

"To little sisters," the others echoed and began to eat.

It was nice spending time with the women. Meggan had always imagined this was what friendship was like. It was also bittersweet. Once she left town, she'd never see these women again. Every moment she spent in Willow Wood made it harder to leave.

"How are your numbers, Meggan?" Jessa asked after they finished their pie and exhausted the conversation on babies. "Have you ever done bookkeeping? Rodney was saying the other day Lundy/List needs another clerk in the accounting office."

Meggan didn't want to admit she'd never done bookkeeping or any kind of actual work. Nothing that led to a position anyway.

Jessa seemed to read her hesitation. "Even if you have no experience, it's something you can learn. Ellie Walsh, Harper's cousin, is always on the lookout for bright women to advance inside Lundy/List. The Trego sisters like to do the same thing at Trego Leatherworks if you don't want to work for the railroad."

"What is it with all the women in Willow Wood running everything?" Meggan exclaimed with a smile. "I've never seen a more progressive town. Even the doctor's a woman."

Harper and Jessa laughed.

"I suppose it is unique," Harper said. "We're so used to it we seldom give it a second thought."

"So, what do you think?" Jessa asked. "Should I tell Rodney to put in a good word for you at the company?"

"No. I don't know. I'm not sure. I haven't had a chance to think past the next hour."

Harper and Jessa reined in their enthusiasm. "Of course not. How thoughtless of us. Thinking only of ourselves when you haven't even caught your breath. You poor thing. Please forgive us."

"No, it's all right."

The morning had been a blur, even the last hour sharing lunch with these lively women. Meggan could almost imagine what a regular life would be like in Willow Wood. Is this what God wanted for her? Had He placed this opportunity in her lap the same way He orchestrated her meeting with Shane after Gloria's death?

With a full stomach, fatigue washed over her. She was ready for a nap. But first, a bath. A long hot soak in a tub without fear of someone bursting in on her.

After Jessa and Harper paid for lunch, the women left the dining room and crossed the lobby's polished floor. They stopped near the potted plants at the front door and exchanged kisses and goodbyes. Meggan spotted Shane crossing the street toward them. Her heart rose into her throat. Had he talked to the detective? What would she say to him?

Jessa and Harper turned to follow her gaze. Harper nudged her. "Go talk to him and tell him you're well. I'm sure he's worried about what happened with that detective. Put his mind to rest and then you can go upstairs and freshen up. You can even tell him you have a position in town, should you decide to stay."

Jessa put her hand on Meggan's elbow. "Come to my house this evening for dinner. You and Shane. You can meet my husband Rodney and our boys, if you dare," she added with a smile. "I hope they don't scare you off. Rodney can tell you everything you need to know about Lundy/List. Even if you don't decide to stay, the information may help you make plans"

Meggan could barely keep her eyes off Shane drawing closer. "I don't know."

She didn't want to tell them she wasn't sure Shane wanted her to stay in Willow Wood.

"Well, please consider it. Shane knows just where we are. We'll expect you at six if that's agreeable. Harper, why don't you and Logan and the children join us?"

Harper pulled a face. "We already have plans."

"All right. Maybe next time." She looked back at Meggan, smiling broadly.

Meggan nearly laughed out loud at the way Jessa let Harper off the hook but wouldn't take no for an answer from her.

"It's settled then," Jessa said. "Dinner at six. Or at least I hope you can make it." She winked at Harper, and the two women flitted out the door in a flurry of skirts. Meggan watched through the door as they paused and spoke to Shane.

They glanced back at the hotel a few times while talking to him before linking arms and moving down the street. Meggan considered telling the desk clerk she was going upstairs to rest and didn't wish to be disturbed. She needed time to think. Time to process everything that had happened since Monday when she first laid eyes on Shane Casey.

He had nearly reached the door. Meggan squared her shoulders. She wouldn't hide. Her whole life she had let other people decide where she'd go, what she'd do, who she'd be. It was time she made her own choices. She would start with Shane.

Chapter Thirty

S hane tipped his hat at Jessa and Harper and bid them good day. As soon as they told him they'd had lunch with Meggan he hadn't been able to focus on much else they said.

Meggan. Was she leaving tomorrow with the detective? Would he ever see her again? He had to know.

He strode purposefully to the broad hotel entrance. He'd either wish her well and tell her goodbye or he'd tell her he loved her. He figured he'd know as soon as he saw her.

He hadn't seen his ma since their brief visit yesterday. So far, she had been patient and understanding with his dropping in and out of her kitchen every other day. But once she heard how he spent the last few days: chased by a killer, trapped in a mine, mistaken for a horse thief, and nearly strangled and shot, among other things, he'd have a lot of explaining to do.

He hadn't been in touch with Lester Cheney either. There was probably a message waiting for him at the house to reschedule their meeting. Shane really needed to get on that. His first priority, though, before anything else, was Meggan.

What would she think if he grabbed her by the hand and begged her not to leave? Or, better yet, pulled her into the alley and kissed her like she'd done him when she first realized Duggar was following her.

He wasn't sure how Meggan would react, but the idea sure appealed to him.

When he, Sheriff Deavers, and the deputy had delivered the dead men to the undertaker, Detective Rollins was waiting outside the small storefront. He told them Meggan would not be charged for theft or any other crime. She was free to leave Willow Wood at her earliest convenience. He had invited her to take the train with him back to Kansas City in the morning.

Though relieved she'd been exonerated of all charges and thankful her pursuers had been stopped permanently, Shane's heart sank at each of the detective's words. He wouldn't blame Meggan if she left. She was probably anxious to put this town and everything about the past week—including him—behind her as fast as she knew how.

After repeating his account of how Duggar and Walker met their ends to Detective Rollins, Shane headed across the street to the hotel. He had to see Meggan, even if he found her in the middle of packing. He didn't want her to go, and he had no right to ask her to stay. But he would tell her goodbye. He might even tell her he loved her. If he didn't, he'd always wonder if he missed his chance at true love.

He entered the hotel lobby, a lump in his throat. Meggan stood in the middle of the large room as if she wanted to see him as much as he needed to see her. Her black hair was disheveled and covered with dust. But it still looked as glossy and soft as a raven's wing. Concern and worry darkened her smoky green eyes.

She took a tentative step toward him. Shane wanted to rush to her and pull her into his arms. He wanted to kiss her in front of the whole town.

"You're all right," she said, her throat tight. She glanced around the lobby to see if anyone was watching. The lunch crowd had dispersed. A few people moved around, but it was mostly quiet.

Shane closed the gap between them. "Sure, I'm all right. At some point I'll have to talk to my mother. That's when I might find real trouble. I don't suppose I'll tell her everything, but she's going to wonder about these claw marks on my neck."

"And that shiner on your eye."

Meggan gingerly touched the swollen flesh under his eye. Shane winced, though the butterfly pressure of her touch couldn't begin to add to his pain.

He hadn't yet looked in a mirror. He could only guess at the sight he made. He was sure handprints and bruising had begun to show under his tan. His lip was busted, and his left eyelid had swollen and drooped down into his line of vision. The spot behind his ear where Wes Harrison cold-cocked him yesterday still throbbed. Not to mention a wrenched shoulder, a pulled muscle on the back of his leg, and about half a dozen ribs that clenched every time he tried to breathe too deep. By tonight he'd be covered with more bruises and sore places.

None of it would compare to the sore place in his heart if Meggan told him she was leaving.

She dropped her hand and glanced around as if remembering they weren't alone. "Could we go somewhere to talk?" Her voice was barely a whisper. "Someplace private."

Shane took it as a good sign. If she were on her way upstairs to pack, she could just as easily tell him now.

He took her hand and wagged his head toward the door. "I know just the place."

She looked dog-tired and nearly as bad as he felt, but she fell into step beside him. They didn't exchange a word as they walked down the street and turned the corner.

Shane didn't let go of her hand, and Meggan didn't pull away. They reached the brick church at the bottom of the hill below the Trego mansion. Shane had practically grown up in this church, attending with his Ma and Felicity Trego.

Belinda, the elder sister, hadn't attended church much in those days. All that changed after she rekindled her love affair with Carl Rayburn. Now she and Carl were major benefactors of the church among other charitable organizations around town. The Trego sisters and their husbands had built a new foundlings' home on the edge of town and were instrumental in finding placements for the orphans as well as fair employment for the older ones. They had arranged Wes and Flo Harrison's adoption of the Pollard boys, as well as helping other families at various levels of need.

Shane pushed open the large, heavy door. He stepped aside to allow Meggan to enter the darkened, hushed interior ahead of him. The sanctuary was empty, as expected, and the interior provided a welcome respite from the rising temperatures outside.

They slid into a pew near the back. Meggan looked around quietly for a moment as if reverent of the place.

She folded her hands in her lap. "I can't remember the last time I've been inside a church." She looked embarrassed by the admission.

"I've missed quite a few services myself these last few years," Shane said. "Seemed like every Saturday night a farmer would stop to ask for help with a horse that had gotten into a scrape or a cow having trouble birthing."

She pursed her lips. "I don't have a good reason for missing church. Gloria and Alice always had plans for Sundays. We'd go early to a park or festival to get a good spot. Weekends, when the weather was nice and the crowds were large, were our busiest workdays."

Shane set his arm on the back of the pew behind her. His shoulder popped in protest of the movement. Didn't matter. He had to get closer to her. Touch her.

His heart ached at the pain in her voice. "Meggan, you were a little girl. None of that was your doing."

She sighed as if she wanted to believe him but wasn't sure she could. Her gaze drifted to the front of the sanctuary where a huge wooden cross was nailed to the wall behind the lectern.

"I know I'm forgiven for everything I did. But I still wish I could make up for it."

He brushed her shoulder. "I hate to tell you, but there's no undoing the past. You can't find those people

285

and pay back everything you and Gloria and Alice took from them. The only thing that any of us can control is our actions from this moment on."

He touched the swollen flesh under his eye. "I wish I'd'a ducked quicker."

Meggan laughed appreciatively and nudged him with her shoulder. Shane bit back a gasp of pain. She jerked away and covered her mouth with her hand. "I'm so sorry. Are you all right?"

Shane nodded and pulled her back against him, but gently. "I'm fine. Now."

She sank into the back of the pew and his arm encircling her. The silence stretched out before them. Shane wondered what she was thinking. If she was gathering her nerve to tell him she was leaving tomorrow. Or, if like him, she wanted to enjoy the moment and pray it lasted forever.

After a few minutes, she turned to look at him. "I suppose the sheriff wanted to know exactly what happened this morning with J.D. and Officer Walker."

Shane nodded. "He was mighty curious about how two dead men came to be at the quarry camp. He could tell from the damage on my face I was telling the truth."

He touched the swollen place under his eye. "When we got there, he examined both men to see if the way the bullets hit them confirmed my account. Yesterday, he got word that Duggar had escaped from a prison in Missouri. Now he can let authorities know they have one less escapee to fret over. A feather in his cap that such a notorious criminal was taken in his jurisdiction, even if he wasn't the one who did the taking."

Meggan shivered in the cool shadows of the church. "I'm thankful it's all over. I'm thankful I can go back to the hotel and change this dress." She laughed.

She brushed her fingertips over the marks on his neck. "I'm especially thankful you're all right."

Shane reveled in the touch of her cool fingertips on his skin. He forced himself to focus on her words. "I am until Ma gets a look at my face."

She smiled. "She'll think it's as handsome as I do." Color crept into her cheeks at the realization of her words.

Shane's chest swelled. She thought he was handsome. What else did she think? Did she think she could stay here forever? If he asked, would she laugh out loud? They'd only known each other for five days. What kind of man fell in love with a woman in five days?

She dipped her head. "I'll never forget everything you did for me, Shane. I wouldn't have survived the last few days without you."

Shane shifted a few inches away to get a better look at her face. Was this the beginning of goodbye?

"You're pretty resourceful," he said carefully. "I think you'd've done all right."

She looked up at him from under a heavy fringe of eyelashes. "Thankfully, we'll never know."

She took a deep breath. "Despite everything that's happened, I miss Gloria. I never thought I would. I even miss Alice. I've never been alone. I've never made my own choices. I just waited for them to tell me what to do next. Now there's no one to tell me. It's scary. But it's also...exhilarating. I just don't know if—if I'm up to it. Maybe I don't know how to be strong when it counts."

"Are you kidding me?" Shane exulted, his voice ringing off the rafters of the church.

Meggan's eyes widened. He chuckled at the surprise on her face but quieted his voice.

"Meggan Jones, you are one of the strongest people I know. You stood up to Duggar and Walker. You could've left Gloria's satchel on the bed at the hotel any time you wanted and walked away from it. One of those crooks would've scooped it up and walked out of that room and out of your life. You made the jewels your problem and both those men your problem because it was the right thing to do, even though you knew they were willing to kill for it."

Her lips quirked in appreciation. "I'm beginning to think God had a reason for bringing me to Willow Wood. For putting the two of us on the stage together. In fact, I know He did. He knew I needed you to help me keep the jewels safe. Even more, He needed you to show me I can have a second chance."

Shane shifted toward her. Was Willow Wood her second chance? Was he?

Or was she ready for a fresh start without Gloria and Alice pulling her strings?

"The detective said you might go back to Kansas City with him in the morning."

She stared at her hands for a long time. Shane held his breath. He wanted to beg her to stay, but it had to be her choice. If he talked her into staying, she would always wonder if someone else had made the decision for her.

"I don't know," she said. "My head is still spinning."

She looked at him again. Was it hopefulness he saw in her eyes?

"I had lunch with Jessa Hammersmith and Harper Kinski at the hotel. Jessa invited us to dinner at her house tonight, by the way. She said her husband Rodney could find a position for me at the railroad company, if that's what I want."

"Is that what you want?"

"I don't know. Maybe. I've never worked in an office before. I've never worked anywhere. I suppose it would be interesting to learn something new."

"How about you work with me at my practice instead?"

Her brows rose in question. "I know even less about treating animals than I do working in an office."

"Well, I always hoped my wife would help me keep the books for my practice and treat some of the animals once she learned the basics of animal husbandry. After that, she'd learn by experience."

"Wife?"

"I love you, Meggan. I don't want you to go back to Kansas City."

She reached for his hand but pulled back. Her eyes filled with tears. "I—I don't want to go back either. But I don't know if I can stay. Especially with you. You deserve a wife who'll bring you honor, not shame. What if everyone in town finds out who I am, what I've done? What will they think?"

"I would never be ashamed of you. And I don't care what people think, except for my ma, and she's going to love you. She'll think the same as I do. That no one's past should dictate who they are today."

He reached for her hand, and she let him take it. "This is what Ma always wanted. Me at home in Willow Wood with a wife I love—and hopefully a houseful of grandchildren."

Color rose in her cheeks again. "Oh, Shane. Are you sure you can love me after everything you know about me?"

He put his hand on her chin and tipped her face up to his. "Of course, I love you. All I ever cared about was helping horses and their owners. Until I met you. Now, I know my life will be empty without you in it."

Meggan blinked. Her green eyes sparkled. She nestled carefully against him, mindful of his injuries. "I love you too."

Shane settled his sore arm on her shoulders and drew her closer. She gazed up at him. Her gaze moved from his eyes to his bruised mouth. Her lips parted slightly as he moved toward her. After a tender kiss, she drew back. "Do you think it's a sin to kiss in church?"

He grinned. "I expect the preacher will have us do it at our wedding."

She snagged her bottom lip with her teeth. "A wedding. I never thought one would happen for me."

"You will marry me, won't you?

Her answer was another long kiss. When she finally pulled away, Shane let out a whoop and threw his battered Stetson into the air.

"Oh, Shane," she said as he caught it. "In church?"

"The Lord don't mind. He knows I'm thanking Him for answering my prayers."

"And mine, too," she said. She put her hands on either side of his face and pulled him to her.

The End

Before you Go

As I wrap up the Willow Wood Brides series, it is a bittersweet experience for me. This was my first historical western series, but hopefully not my last. I learned a lot in the process—about cowboys and horses and how difficult life was on the frontier—especially for women, who often got stuck with the worst jobs. I also had a lot of fun. I hope you did too.

If you enjoyed *A Cowboy for Meggan*, or any of the books in the Willow Wood Brides series, please take a moment to leave a review on Amazon, Goodreads, your blog, or any other site that allows reader reviews.

Don't forget to sign up for my newsletter to stay up to date on new releases, promotions and contests. When you do, you'll get a free download of *A Promise for Josie: A Willow Wood Brides Prequel*. See how it all began.

After a broken promise and a broken heart, is love worth
the risk?

Chapter One

What is now Present Day Montana
June, 1854

JOSIE SEGAL SPUN AROUND ON THE SOFT HAY toward the noise at the side door of the barn. She put her hand over her heart when she recognized the familiar shape. The golden light of a rising sun shone behind her fiancé in the barn door, concealing his face.

"What are you doing here?" she whispered across the large space. "Pa will skin you alive if sees you."

She glanced around the barn, though she knew they were alone except for the cows and a few cats waiting for a pan of cream. The rest of the family was either still abed or tending their own chores. Milking was Josie's. A solitary chore in the early morning hours that she relished. Today was bittersweet. It was the last morning she'd milk in this barn. The last morning she'd do any chore as part of the Segal family. While anxious to begin her life with

Elisha, she nearly cried every time she thought of leaving Pa and Ma and her younger sisters.

Elisha Sweeney stepped out of the doorway and shuffled toward her. He was nearly beside her before she could clearly read his expression in the barn's dim interior. Dread rose inside her. She stood and set a steadying hand on the cow's side. Three more cows waited their turn, munching hay in the manger. Josie didn't have time for dawdling. Milking six cows didn't take long for someone who'd been doing it since she was ten, but there were always other things that needed doing. Especially today.

Today she needed to hurry with the milking for a completely different reason.

The look on Elisha's face sent shivers of trepidation down her spine that had nothing to do with the morning chill.

"Josie."

Tears pricked her eyes. Her heart sank to her worn shoes. She mustn't let him finish whatever he was about to say. "You shouldn't have come," she said. "It's bad luck to see the bride on your wedding day."

Elisha came closer. He removed his hat and began twisting the brim in his hands. He kept his gaze fixed on the hard-packed earth of the barn floor. He wouldn't look at her.

"Elisha," she said warily. No other words worked past her closed throat.

After what seemed like an eternity, he brought his gaze up to hers. "I'm sorry, Josie. I should've told you weeks ago."

Don't say it.

She wanted to cover her ears. Once he spoke the words out loud, they couldn't be taken back. Couldn't be unsaid. Josie looked toward the house through the open barn door. The wide, never-ending sky stretched toward the horizon, pinking with the rising sun. A horizon she had never seen beyond.

"Pa will be out here any minute," she repeated, though she knew he wasn't coming. He was already in the other field, getting an early start on chores before the parson came. And all their family and friends.

Her stomach cramped. "You need to go before he sees you." Each word came smaller and smaller until the last came out as barely a squeak.

"Josie, listen to me." Elisha's voice echoed off the rafters, startling the cows.

Josie inhaled. Elisha never raised his voice to anyone, least of all, her. She had loved him since they were kids in school together. He was twenty, two years older than her. The handsomest boy in school. Not the smartest, but surely the most fun. He always made her laugh. That's what she loved about him most. Elisha was never serious. Not like Pa. Sometimes she'd laugh so hard at one of his stories, she thought her sides would split wide open. He never worried about anything either. Everything about Elisha was easy and fun. When they were together, he made her forget work was hard and money was scarce. She was going to spend the rest of her life listening to his stories and enjoying every carefree moment with him.

The easy, happy-go-lucky expression wasn't on his face today.

"I can't go through with it."

Josie stared. His words didn't make sense. He squared his shoulders and stopped spinning the hat. She wanted to snatch it from him and throw it on the ground.

She thought of the pale blue dress hanging upstairs in her room. Last year her sister Anna had married a successful attorney and moved to the city, leaving the whole room to Josie. She, Mama, and her two younger sisters had spent the last month working on the dress and the rest of her trousseau.

"Go through with what?"

Elisha looked uncertain. Ashamed. His gaze moved to the barn door. She knew he was looking at that endless sky and imagining what was on the other side of it. She knew because they'd dreamed about it together many times before. He swiveled back to her in his broke down boots. "I'm going west. A man can make his mark out there. There's nothing for me in this nothing town."

He didn't say *we*. He wasn't taking her. He wasn't even asking if she wanted to go.

Her throat wouldn't work. She couldn't loosen her tongue. She wanted to scream. Cry. Throw the pitchfork at him. Instead she stood there and thought of her pretty blue dress she wouldn't be wearing today.

Elisha looked her in the eye for the first time since entering the barn. "I'm not going to work myself into an early grave the way my pa did. I don't want to die staring at the backend of a pair of mules. I want adventure. I want to see the ocean. I want to do something with my life."

"Without a nothing wife like you holding me back."

He didn't say the rest, but he may as well have.

Josie couldn't breathe. The sounds of the barn, the smells, the heat from the cow she'd partially milked—all

of it faded into nothing. If only she could draw a full breath, she'd tell him she wanted the same thing. She'd spent her life dreaming about what was over the hills fencing them in. What the sky looked like anywhere but the spot where she'd been born eighteen years and eight months ago.

If she left with Elisha to chase adventure—whatever that meant—she'd miss Ma. And her sisters. And her friends. It would be hard not being here to see her sisters fall in love and marry and have babies. She might not be here when Ma and Pa's time on earth was over. It was too sad to think on, but that's how it worked when a woman married a man. Like turning the last page of a beloved book. Sad, but exciting at the same time to pick up a new book, full of possibility and unknown adventure.

Today she would marry Elisha. They could head west by late afternoon. Whatever he wanted. Her heart swelled with excitement. She drew in a breath to tell him she was ready for whatever mysteries life held for them.

"I know you'll forgive me, Josie. You wouldn't want me to stay here and do something I never wanted to do."

Never wanted?

He never wanted to marry her? She thought…he loved her.

Elisha's eyes shone bright. Brighter than the sun cresting the trees on the ridge at the thought of the adventure awaiting him in the West. Adventure that apparently didn't include her.

It wasn't just this dusty little town he wanted to leave. He wanted to leave her too.

"But, Elisha, you promised." She knew she sounded like a petulant child, but she couldn't help herself. "You promised you'd die making me happy."

Elisha ducked his head the way he did the time he got caught putting a frog in the teacher's desk. Any punishment was worth the thrill of the prank and the laugh he got from the other kids.

Josie's chest surged like she was trying to lift a new calf. Tears pushed forward, but she fought them back. She wouldn't cry in front of him. There'd be plenty of time for that later. She would not let his last image of her be of her crying and begging him to stay.

Elisha watched her intently, hopeful she wouldn't cry and make this harder than it needed to be. He was leaving. She could imagine him waking up tomorrow someplace new with his eyes sparkling, telling a joke to whoever was around to listen, with no thoughts or worries about her at all.

He had already left. His body just hadn't caught up yet.

"You've always been my special girl, Josie. You always will be." His smile widened, totally oblivious to her feelings. He came forward and kissed her cheek. If she could move, she would've pushed him away. Slapped him. Cursed him. Anything but stood there and took his kiss as though she wished him well.

"This is for the best, Josie. I promise it is."

How dare he promise anything. Didn't he realize his promises were worthless now?

He plunked his hat on his head and strode out of the barn, the spring in his step springier than ever. Josie didn't want to watch him go, but she couldn't turn away.

She followed as far as the barn door and watched him stride to where he had left his horse at the edge of the meadow so Ma and Pa wouldn't hear. She watched him swing into the saddle and turn the horse toward the road.

He didn't look back. Josie was glad. She didn't want him to catch her watching. She didn't want him to know her heart was breaking while his was apparently alive with a newfound freedom she would never know.

A breeze rustled the grass in the barnyard. It caressed her cheek and scattered his broken promises all the way to the horizon.

Sign up for my newsletter and receive a link to download **A Promise for Josie—A Willow Wood Brides Prequel.** Stay up to date on upcoming releases in the exciting Willow Wood Brides series, among other books and series in the works. You'll also be among the first to learn of promos, giveaways, and contests.

I love hearing from readers. Email me at teresa@teresaslack.com anytime with your thoughts or questions about the Willow Wood Brides or any of my books.

About the Author

Teresa Slack loves reading, writing, and falling in love. Creating clean and wholesome western romances where rugged cowboys still sweep independent women off their feet was an easy choice for her.

She writes from her home in the beautiful southern Ohio hills, which she shares with her husband and rescue dog and rescue cat.
Any errors and typos she blames on the cat randomly running across her keyboard.